Praise for
DO

"Loaded with subtle emotions, sizzling chemistry, and
som... ...n the real choices [Grant's]
char... ...as they choose their loves
for e... —*RT Book Reviews* (4 stars)

"Viv... ...and enchanting characters
grab... ...on't let go."
—*Night Owl Reviews* (Top Pick)

Praise for the Dark Warrior novels

MIDNIGHT'S KISS

5 Stars TOP PICK! "[Grant] blends ancient gods, love,
desire, and evil-doers into a world you will want to
revisit over and over again."   —*Night Owl Reviews*

5 Blue Ribbons! "This story is one you will remember
long after the last page is read. A definite keeper!"
—*Romance Junkies*

4 Stars! "The world of the Immortal Warriors is a thoroughly engaging one, blending powerful ancient gods,
fiery desire, and touchingly human love, which readers
will surely want to revisit."   —*RT Book Reviews*

4 Feathers! "*Midnight's Kiss* is a game changer—one
that will set the rest of the series in motion."
—*Under the Covers*

5 Stars! "Ms. Grant mixes adventure, magic and sweet love to create the perfect romance story."

—*Single Title Reviews*

MIDNIGHT'S LOVER

"Paranormal elements and scorching romance are cleverly intertwined in this tale of a damaged hero and resilient heroine." —*Publishers Weekly*

5 Blue Ribbons! "An exciting, adventure-packed tale, *Midnight's Lover* is a story that captivates you from the very first page." —*Romance Junkies*

5 Stars! "Ms. Grant weaves a sweet love story into a story filled with action, adventure and the exploration of personal pain." —*Single Title Reviews*

4 Stars! "It's good vs. evil Druid in the next installment of Grant's Dark Warrior series. The stakes get higher as discerning one's true loyalties becomes harder. Grant's compelling characters and the continued presence of previous protagonists are key reasons why these books are so gripping. Another exciting and thrilling chapter!"

—*RT Book Reviews*

4.5 Stars Top Pick! "This is one series you'll want to make sure to read from the start . . . they just keep getting better . . . mmmm! A must read for sure!"

—*Night Owl Reviews*

4.5 Feathers! "If you're looking for an author who brings heat and heart in one tightly-written package, then Donna Grant will be a gift that makes your jaw drop. You don't want to miss *Midnight's Lover*."

—*Under the Covers Book Blog*

BURNING DESIRE

DONNA GRANT

St. Martin's Paperbacks

This is a work of fiction. All of the characters, organizations, and events portrayed in this novel are either products of the author's imagination or are used fictitiously.

BURNING DESIRE

Copyright © 2014 by Donna Grant.
Excerpt from *Hot Blooded* copyright © 2014 by Donna Grant.

For information address St. Martin's Press, 175 Fifth Avenue, New York, NY 10010.

ISBN: 978-1-250-06070-9

Printed in the United States of America

St. Martin's Paperbacks edition / October 2014

St. Martin's Paperbacks are published by St. Martin's Press, 175 Fifth Avenue, New York, NY 10010.

10 9 8 7 6 5 4 3 2

To Steve—
For the laughter, the love, and everything in between!

ACKNOWLEDGMENTS

So much goes into getting a book ready, and I couldn't do it without my fabulous editor, Monique Patterson. Thanks to Alexandra Sehulster for being so wonderful, and everyone else at St. Martin's Press who was involved. Y'all rock!

Hats off to my street team—Donna's Dolls. Words can't say how much I adore y'all.

A special thanks to my family for the never-ending support.

And to my husband, Steve. For . . . well, everything! I love you, Sexy!

CHAPTER ONE

Pretending. Misleading. Mimicking.

Kiril and the rest of his brethren had been perfecting those acts since they sent their dragons away and set about blending in with the humans. They had honed their skills to a degree that only a handful of people in the entire world knew who they really were—Dragon Kings.

It had been difficult for the first millennia to pretend they weren't once rulers of the realm. After that, it became a habit, a way of life. What else was a Dragon King to do when the dragons were gone?

Kiril spent many centuries deep in his cave, asleep, hidden from the world and the shockingly easy way their reign had passed from legend to myth. Even then he wasn't free from his memories or the longing to be the dragon he was born to be.

No, in the dragon sleep, he relived the glorious time when the dragons ruled the Earth, when roars filled the air, and dragons were free to roam the skies, the ground, and even the waters as they wanted.

And then the humans came.

Kiril clenched his teeth together as he drove down the winding, narrow road toward Cork. He wasn't sure if he would ever be rid of his repugnance for them. He didn't blame all humans. After all, five of his fellow Kings had recently bound themselves to human females.

However, eons ago, it had been a human female who had made a vow to one of them, only to betray him and set in motion a war that could have destroyed them all. It was only the Kings banding together, and Constantine, the King of Kings, who came up with a solution—sending the dragons to another realm.

Kiril sped his sleek Sepang brown Mercedes SLS AMG Roadster along the winding roads with the top down and the wind whipping around him. It was the closest thing to flying that he could allow himself while remaining in Ireland amid the foulest enemies of the Dragon Kings—the Dark Fae.

The Dark were set on capturing a Dragon King. Recently, they had managed to hold two—Kellan and Tristan—for a short period before both escaped. Though it had been a close call, especially with Kellan.

Each time it had been narrow escapes. The Dragon Kings and their friends hadn't escaped unscathed. There were injuries, but the worst was that Rhi had been taken by the Dark.

Rhi. Kiril couldn't help but grin as he thought of the Light Fae. Though the Kings had waged war on both sides of the Fae, Rhi was different. For a time, she had been the lover of a Dragon King.

And no King would ever forget that.

None of them really understood what tore Rhi and her lover apart, and they likely never would. He never spoke of her, never mentioned her name. And Rhi . . . had returned to the Light to take up her duties. Oddly enough, it was her interference in telling a Warrior that he was half-Fae and her prince that brought her back into the fold of the Kings.

She hadn't been thrilled about it, and had, in fact, told them all where to go. Yet, when trouble came, it was Rhi who rushed in to save Kellan and his mate, Denae. Then she did it again with Tristan and Sammi—to Rhi's peril.

Kiril was determined to locate where the Dark were holding Rhi. It was one of the many things he was going to ascertain while spying. Every minute of every day brought him closer to danger. Returning time and again to the Dark's pub, *an Doras,* only quickened the inevitable.

Not that a Dragon King ever shied from danger.

It was all worth it if he could rescue Rhi and learn who was out to reveal them to the world. The fact their faceless enemy aligned themselves with the Dark Fae as well as MI5 meant that they were prepared to do anything.

And so was Kiril. He would give himself up to the Dark before he allowed anything to happen to his brothers. It just might come to that too.

The Dark knew who he was, had known for days. It was a game they played with each other. He pretended not to know they watched the home he bought, and they were never far from wherever he was while they pretended that they had no idea he was a Dragon King.

He had to guard his every word, mind his every move. It was exhausting. And exhilarating. It had been ages since he'd had such an opponent. In the end, however, he had to remember it wasn't a game. Their competition would decide who got to remain on the realm—the Dark or the Kings.

Not once since he came to Ireland had Kiril dared to take to the skies—even in a rainstorm. The urge to shift into a dragon and have the air rush over his scales and along his wings was irresistible, crushing.

He gripped the steering wheel and gradually took control of himself. He slowed the car as he drew closer to Cork. Cork, like Venice, was built on the water with the city center situated on an island in the River Lee, upstream from Cork Harbor. With the River Lee separating into two branches and surrounding the city center, there were numerous bridges giving Cork a distinctive look and feel.

The city was pretty, but it wasn't home. Kiril longed for Scotland and Dreagan. He came to a stop at an intersection and waited for the light to turn green. The Shandon Bells of the eighteenth-century Church of St. Anne suddenly filled the air. The old-world style of Cork only made him miss Scotland all the more, but most especially Dreagan and the mountains that were home.

The sixty thousand acres of Dreagan were a haven for the Dragon Kings. With restricted airspace over their land, they could shift and fly whenever they wanted. The fact Dreagan whisky was the finest in the world kept them in luxury. Every restaurant and pub sought to sell Dreagan, but they were selective in who they allowed to sell their whisky. The Irish whisky he sampled while in Ireland was passable, but what he wouldn't do for a bottle of Dreagan.

Kiril found a parking space and quickly pulled the Mercedes in before he cut the engine. He didn't plan on being in the city long, but the dark clouds hinted at rain. Kiril closed the roof with a simple press of a button and stepped out of the car.

He fastened the first button of his suit jacket and glanced around to see how many were watching. Three Dark were visible and doing a poor job of trying to blend in. Kiril imagined there were at least four more watching him as they did on previous nights.

"Here we go again," he mumbled to himself and locked the car before he strode to the sidewalk.

Every time he came to Cork it was for show. He ate at expensive restaurants—sometimes alone, sometimes with different women. He visited different pubs, but always he returned to *an Doras* before heading home.

Occasionally alone, and at times with women.

Kiril had one hand in the pocket of his slacks when his gaze snagged on a pair of legs that seemed to go on for miles. Her black skirt skimmed high up on her thighs, and her platform heels only made those shapely limbs appear longer.

He paused and let his gaze wander up her legs to the curve of her hips. A silver shirt sparkled with sequins at the hem banded around her, accentuating her trim waist. The shirt was loose, flowing while the back crisscrossed in a large X showing a wealth of creamy skin. Her black hair was pulled to the side in a messy braid that fell over her left shoulder. She kept her back to him as she peered in the window of a shop.

Her eyes lifted and locked with his through the window. He was thoroughly mesmerized. Awestruck.

Entranced.

Her beauty left him speechless, dumbstruck. His gaze was riveted on her. Kiril took a step toward her when she turned to face him.

His lungs locked, the air trapped as he gazed upon loveliness unlike any he had ever encountered. Her oval face was utter perfection. Thin black brows arched over large silver eyes. Her cheekbones were impossibly high and tinted with a hint of blush. Her lips, full and wide, made his balls tighten and his cock ache.

She was Fae, but not even that made him turn away. Kiril had encountered many beautiful Fae, yet there was something entirely different about this one. He blinked, and that's when he saw her glamour shift. If he hadn't been so enamored, he would have spotted it sooner.

Disappointment filled him when he noticed the thick strip of silver hair against her cheek and her red eyes signaling she was Dark Fae.

It didn't take much for him to deduce that the Dark wanted to use her against him. It was a good thing he could see through glamour, or he might really have found himself in a pickle.

He should walk away, but he couldn't. Nor did he want to. He wanted to know the female, and by getting close to her she might let something slip that could help him in his quest.

His game just became infinitely more dangerous, and yet, there was a small thrill that made his stomach tighten at the idea of learning more about the Dark. She was thoroughly intoxicating to look at, and if the intelligence he spotted shining through her eyes was any indication, she was going to completely fascinate him.

His mind made up, Kiril walked to her wearing his most charming smile. "Find anything you fancy?" he asked as he nodded to the window of sparkling jewelry.

She laughed, the sound making his blood heat. "I love the glitter of the gems. It's a weakness." Her head tilted slightly as her red eyes regarded him. "It's not every day that a Scot visits Ireland. What brings you to our green isle?"

"Business. And pleasure."

She let her gaze slowly wander over him. Kiril wished he knew what she was thinking, and if she liked what she saw. When her gaze returned to him, her smile of approval said it all.

It was all he could do not to press her against the window and devour her lips in a kiss that would leave them both breathless.

She shifted her small silver clutch from one hand to another. "I've lived in Cork all my life. It's a beautiful city, isn't it?"

Kiril nodded and belatedly noticed the Dark who had been watching him were gone. He had taken the bait, after all. It also made him aware of just how completely he was enamored of the female. He was going to have to watch himself for sure, lest he find himself bound in chains. "Are you waiting on someone?"

"I was. They're late, and I'm tired of waiting," she said, her eyes posing an invitation her words hadn't.

The offer was on the table. All Kiril had to do was take it. It was tempting, or rather she was. It would be a treacherous obstacle of quicksand if he accepted it.

The lies would grow, the deceptions would spread. But if he succeeded, the rewards for the Dragon Kings could be numerous.

Kiril held out his arm. "Would you like to join me for dinner?"

Her gaze lowered to the ground as she smiled coyly and took his arm. "I would like that very much."

They strolled arm in arm down the sidewalk toward the Italian restaurant that was his favorite.

"Glad to have you back," the maître d' said with a wide grin and motioned them to follow.

Kiril guided the woman ahead of him with his hand on her lower back. He felt her shiver when his fingers grazed her bare skin. He couldn't hold back his satisfied smile. She had been sent to seduce him, but she wasn't immune to his touch. That could work to his advantage. It gave him the thought to try to flip her to their side. It would be nearly impossible since the Dark Fae were notoriously devoted to their families.

A Dark's family was everything from their rank in their society to their authority. The more powerful a family, the more influence and control was to be had. It was archaic almost the way they bartered their daughters and sisters to gain rank within their antiquated and disgusting social system.

It was a challenge though, and Kiril loved challenges. Besides, with as beautiful as the Dark was, he didn't think he was going to mind the effort. To know the feel of her skin, to sample the essence of her sex.

Desire, dark and profound, smoldered through him. It wasn't the passion that alarmed him, but the raw, visceral need to know her, the yearning to taste her.

The hunger to fill her.

That desire swelled and intensified, spread and multiplied with every second they were together. It consumed him, devoured him. He was being incinerated from the inside out with a need that burned as hot as dragon fire.

Kiril slid into the half-moon-shaped booth beside her and promptly ordered a bottle of wine.

He opened the menu and decided to push her. It was either that or kiss her, and he was afraid if he started kissing her, he wouldn't be able to stop. Kiril didn't think anyone in the restaurant would want to see him have sex. "Why did you accept my invitation?"

Surprise flickered in her deep red eyes. "I was hungry, and you offered."

"Do you often go off with strange men?"

She laughed, the sound going straight to his cock. "You're the first. I'm Shara, by the way."

"Kiril."

"Kiril. A strong, unusual name."

He set aside the menu and regarded her. It was strange. He normally hated looking into the eyes of a Dark Fae. Something about red eyes seemed wrong, but he didn't seem to mind it with Shara.

Shara. What a beautiful name to match such an intriguing, captivating woman.

She cleared her throat and set her napkin in her lap. Her lips parted to speak, but before she could, the waiter brought the wine. Kiril continued to watch her even as he sampled the wine and nodded his approval to the server. Once their glasses were filled and their order given, the attendant walked away.

"You were saying?" he prompted her.

"I was going to ask, what kind of business are you in?"

Kiril thought about spinning another lie, and then realized there was no need. She knew he was a Dragon King, knew that he was from Dreagan. One less lie could only help him.

"I work for a distillery. I sample other whisky around the world for comparison."

Her red eyes held his as she lifted the wineglass to her lips and sampled the cabernet sauvignon. "Wouldn't it be easier to taste these whiskies at your distillery?"

"It might, but it adds to the taste of the whisky to try it at the place it's distilled. It's also helpful to sit in a pub and watch what the bartenders pour for their patrons."

"I see." She set down her glass and licked her lips.

Kiril swirled the red wine in his glass thinking how much he wanted to kiss her, to wrap her long hair around his hand and hold her hostage as he ravaged her lips. "What do you do?"

"I work in my family's business."

So she didn't lie either. Interesting. "And what is it your family does?"

"Import/export."

Another truth. Dark Faē were notorious for luring humans into their world, but it wasn't pleasure the humans received. The women were taken by the males, and though they might experience brief pleasure, unbeknownst to them their souls were being drained.

As for the human males, the female Dark used them for sex. Sex with a Dark was like a drug, and the humans could become addicted fast. The females rarely lived long enough to know what was happening, but the female Darks made sure to keep the human males alive for decades while having their fun.

"A lucrative business, I assume," Kiril said.

Shara glanced away. "It is."

Kiril let the questions drop as their food was delivered. The rest of the meal was spent talking of anything that neither of them had to lie about. It was . . . refreshing. For the first time in days, Kiril almost felt like himself. He was still on guard, but he was more relaxed. Perhaps it was because he knew what he was about.

Or maybe it was because he wanted to shove aside the food, yank her to her feet, and toss her atop the table to have his way with her.

CHAPTER TWO

It was lucky that Shara had gotten a look at Kiril the day after she was informed of her mission. She found Kiril attractive from a distance, but up close he robbed her of breath and thought.

He was tall and potent, overwhelming and dynamic. Compelling and persuasive.

He was—simply put—extraordinary.

Her fingers itched to sink into his wheat-colored hair that was thick and kept in longish waves. His eyes were the color of shamrocks—a bright, vivid green—and saw everything.

He wore the black suit with ease. The cut of it showing off his wide shoulders and narrow hips. The simple white shirt beneath was left unbuttoned at the top with no tie in sight.

The flash of onyx and pearl at his wrists drew her eye to his cuff links. It was the only jewelry he wore except for his watch.

He was all male—hard, vigorous, and intense.

His face appeared to be cut from granite. The hard line of his jaw only amplified his square chin and the little indent in the middle. Though he appeared relaxed and at ease, she knew he was anything but. His gaze swept the restaurant, taking in everything in that one glance. And when his green gaze focused on her, her heart skidded and her stomach fluttered.

While at one time she might have found some excitement at the thought of bedding a human, no male—Fae or human—stirred her as Kiril did. He faced the world as if daring it to challenge him.

He was the embodiment of excitement, intrigue . . . fascination.

Farrell had warned her that Kiril was an experienced flirt who had no problem getting any woman he wanted. With charm that could seduce an angel into Hell itself, she understood why. It wasn't just his charm either. It was the way he looked at her when she talked, as if she were the only person in the entire world that he wanted to be with, to listen to.

He made her feel special and unique.

Remarkable.

How amazing her time with him would be, but a glimpse of one of her brother's lackeys reminded her that she was proving herself and her loyalty to her family. She wasn't with Kiril for fun. She had a job to do. Her very life depended upon it. Her family was one of the most powerful in the Dark Fae world.

She had already shamed them. This was her last chance—in all ways.

Her brother, Farrell, waited in the wings for her to screw up so he could kill her. He was watching her every move, ensuring she carried through with things exactly as instructed and deliver a Dragon King to their father.

For a short time during their meal, Shara allowed herself to believe it was all real. Daydreaming. It's what had sustained her for six hundred years while being kept prisoner in her own room for her last transgression. Six hundred years of thinking how she was forgotten as her parents doted on her elder siblings and their accomplishments while she was left to do as she pleased.

Six hundred years yearning to make her own decisions and come and go as she wished. Six hundred years of no one but herself for company. She had been shunned by her family during the entire imprisonment.

Shara blinked and focused on her plate of pasta. She couldn't let anything ruin her mission, regardless of how handsome Kiril was or how interested he pretended to be.

"Family, Shara. It's all you have. This is your last chance to prove yourself. Don't muck this up. You won't like the consequences."

Farrell's warning sounded through her mind again. She couldn't screw up again. Farrell was expecting her to fail. He wanted her to so he could remove her as an embarrassment from the family.

No matter how appealing and attractive she found Kiril, he was a Dragon King, and the Dark needed him. And she would be the one to deliver him.

There were no excuses, no exemptions.

"Thank you for dinner," she said. She watched his throat move as he swallowed the last of his wine.

His skin was deeply tanned and appeared to have a golden tone in the dim lights of the restaurant. Farrell had gone into detail about the type of women Kiril was seen with. None of them had been Fae. It was one of a long list of reasons that Shara used glamour. Kiril wouldn't lower himself to associate with the Dark. No Dragon King would associate with any Fae, for that matter.

Oh, he might talk to her brother at the pub, but he would never take one to dinner. Or to his bed. She might wish he could see the real her, because he was the first in six centuries. But in the end it didn't matter what he saw. The end justified the means.

"It was my pleasure."

His voice, deep and seductive, made bumps rise over her skin. His accent, thick and stirring, made her legs weak. Damn him for affecting her this way, but then what did she expect after finally being free of her prison? Anyone would probably make her feel like this. Kiril was no one special.

The plan had been for her to tease him and walk away, but when he had asked her to dinner, she hadn't been able to refuse. To share a nice dinner with a man like Kiril. Besides, it was time alone with him. Now it was time for her to walk away.

He threw down a wad of money on the table and stood. Shara looked at the hand he held out for her. She recalled his touch on her skin all too clearly. Holding his arm as he walked her to the restaurant was one thing, but did she dare take his hand? The warmth, the strength. It made her feel like her insides had turned to jelly.

If he could do that with a simple touch of his hand, what would it be like in his arms, his lips on hers? His skin gliding against hers? His cock filling her?

Shara slid her palm against his and felt a shock zing through her. She jerked her gaze to him, but he was looking away.

Her legs wobbled a bit as she stood. She was going to have to do something about her needs before she saw him again. Being so near his magnetism, the sheer masculine confidence that he exuded was heady. Yet it was his sex appeal, the virile enticement that stole her breath and made desire pool low in her belly.

His long, tapered fingers wrapped around her hand. He pulled her to him until their bodies were a hairsbreadth from touching. His gaze slid to her, sucking her in until she was drowning in his shamrock green eyes. The world gradually faded away.

It was just the two of them.

He wasn't a Dragon King.

And she wasn't a Dark Fae.

They were a man and a woman, desire thick between them.

Then she blinked and reality crashed around her. If she didn't put some space between herself and Mr. Sexy she was going to do something really stupid. Again. All because her body was out of control.

Thankfully, he walked them to the door of the restaurant. When they stepped outside, she was grateful for the breeze off the water that cooled her heated skin and cleared her muddled head.

"It was nice to meet you, Kiril."

He didn't release her hand as she expected. Instead, he tightened his grip a fraction. "So you'll walk away? Just like that?"

He had no idea how she wanted to melt against him and ask him to do as he pleased with her. For six centuries no one had touched her. He had no idea how desperately she wanted to feel more of him. Walk away? She couldn't do it.

But she had to. Shara grasped the last shred of her control and held tight. "It's been an amazing evening."

"It has." He seemed as surprised as she at her words. "It wouldna be very gallant of me no' to walk you to where you want to go."

This made her smile. Leave it to a Dragon King to think she needed his assistance. "I know these streets, but I appreciate the offer."

"It appears I've no other recourse," he said and lifted her hand to his mouth. "Good evening, Shara."

Her stomach quivered when his warm lips touched the back of her hand. He lingered for just a moment, his eyes locked with hers, before he straightened and released his hold on her hand.

The hold he had on her mind and body, however, would remain for a long, long time.

Shara had to swallow before she could find her voice. "Good evening, Kiril."

Somehow she turned and walked away, blending in with the crowds. Her heart pounded in her chest with each step, and every fiber of her being urged her to go back to him. That was just her loneliness talking, however.

Shara walked four blocks, zigzagging around buildings as she did. When she was positive Kiril hadn't followed her, she sagged against a building in an alley and gulped in air. How foolish she was to think she could handle a man like Kiril. He was as old as time. He had seen everything human and Fae could do to each other and the Dragon Kings, and he expected every one.

Shara lifted one of her hands before her to see it shaking. She'd thought he might demand she reveal who she really was after dinner when he had looked so intently at her. Her ruse had worked, and because of that, Farrell would expect her to play it again.

There wasn't anything she wouldn't do for her family. Family was life in the Fae world. They had asked her to play a part in bringing down a Dragon King, and she wouldn't fail them.

Shara walked to the end of the alley and turned right only to come face-to-face with Farrell's livid face. She knew his hatred, knew how he sought to have all the glory so their father would favor him. At one time she had looked up to him, but that was a long time ago. Now, she could barely stand to be around him.

He shoved his forearm under her chin and slammed

her against the brick wall viciously. "We had a plan. All you had to do was stick to it."

"It was the plan," she said as she pushed against his arm. Farrell had always loved to try to hurt her. It was his way, a way no one in her family thought twice about. But she had never been the meek female expected of a Dark. "I moved things along a little sooner. The idea is to capture a Dragon King. I don't think Father cares how we go about it."

Farrell peeled back his lips, his red eyes flashing in fury. "That wasn't my plan. You need to learn to follow my orders."

"Seduction can't be done by orders. Things change, and I need to be able to adjust with them."

He growled and spun away from her. "You seemed awfully chatty with him during the meal. Casual even. What did he say to you?"

"The usual things men and women talk about."

Farrell jerked around. "Are you trying to be funny? You won't ruin this for me, Shara. I won't let you."

"I may have been locked away for six hundred years, but for a thousand before that I was on my own, Farrell. I know men. I remember how to flirt, how to use my body. I did everything right."

Farrell pointed his finger in her face. "You better hope you did a good enough job that he's looking for you tomorrow night."

"I didn't plan on seeing him tomorrow night." She hadn't actually planned anything, but she knew if she saw him again so soon she wouldn't be able to control herself. The failure Farrell expected would be all but his. "The night after will be time enough."

"I knew you were the wrong female for this, but Father was adamant," Farrell said with scorn and dropped his hand.

"When Kiril doesn't see me tomorrow night, he'll return the next night looking. The longer I keep him waiting, the more anxious he'll be to find me."

Farrell looked her up and down with disdain. "You think highly of yourself. Thankfully your glamour helped to add . . . something . . . to your looks, or Kiril might have passed you by."

"I answer to Father, not you."

"Out here you answer to me," Farrell stated tightly. "I'm running this operation, and you'd best remember. Trust me, no one will miss you if you die."

Shara stood in the alley long after Farrell walked away. But it wasn't his words she was thinking about. It was Kiril and his shamrock-green eyes.

Kiril was cranky and on edge when he entered *an Doras*. He should have gone home after his meal with Shara, but if the Dark wanted to play, he was more than willing. He told himself it was because they had sent a female to entice him, but the real reason was his inescapable reaction to Shara.

He hadn't wanted her to walk away. In fact, he had almost followed her.

Kiril wasn't sure what he sought from her, only that he wanted to spend more time with her. And not just because he was spying on the Dark, but because he enjoyed her company.

A Dark Fae.

How his brethren would laugh if they knew.

Maybe it was the past weeks on his own, unable to shift that was making him lose his edge. Which was why he was enlarging the cellar beneath his house. If he couldn't fly, the cellar would at least allow him to shift into dragon form and ease some of his frustration.

"No woman on your arm tonight?"

Kiril ground his teeth to keep from lashing out at Farrell. The Dark had a knack for approaching when Kiril least wanted his company. Which happened to be all the time.

"No' tonight." Kiril walked to the bar and took a vacant stool while motioning to the bartender.

He was known at the pub, so he didn't have to tell the bartender what he wanted. In a matter of moments a glass of whisky—unfortunately Irish—was set in front of him. Kiril drained it in one gulp and lifted the empty glass for another.

"Bad night?" Farrell asked. He took the spot next to Kiril, making himself comfortable.

Kiril shrugged, wishing like hell he could make Farrell disappear. It was bad enough he came to the pub that was infested with Dark Fae every day. That didn't mean he wanted to talk to any of them. He was there for bits of information they didn't bother whispering about. "Just a long day."

"Some more whisky should take care of that. Tell me, my friend, how long are you staying in Ireland?" Farrell asked.

Kiril nodded to the bartender for yet another refill before he swiveled his head to Farrell. "I doona know. I've no' put a timetable on things."

"I'm having a party in a few weeks. I'm hoping you'll stay for it."

It was all Kiril could do not to roll his eyes and laugh outright. He knew exactly what it was—a trap to capture him. If he didn't have the information he needed as well as discovering where Rhi was, he might have to attend.

"Sounds like fun," he managed to say.

"My get-togethers always are. Plenty of beautiful women for you to choose from. Unless you've found someone by then. In that case, feel free to bring her along."

Farrell ran a hand through his chin-length black hair liberally laced with silver. His red eyes locked on him, and he was leaning toward Kiril, too interested in the night and his plans.

That's when realization hit Kiril. It was Farrell who'd sent Shara. It didn't come as that great of a surprise. He speculated that Farrell would go to any lengths to capture him.

With as many Dark as were in the pub, they could try to take him then. The entire town of Cork swarmed with Dark Fae. They could try and seize him without going to such extremes.

What else did they want then?

Kiril almost smiled when it struck him. They searched for something hidden by the King of Kings. If neither Kellan nor Tristan had told the Dark the answer when they used force, the Dark were attempting another tactic.

How sorry they would be when they realized he wouldn't tell them anything because he didn't know the answer. Only two Dragon Kings knew whatever it was the Dark searched for—Kellan and Constantine.

Kellan—because he kept their history—but he hadn't given it away, and Con never would either.

It was going to be a hell of a few days.

CHAPTER
THREE

Kiril rolled onto his back and opened his eyes to stare at the ceiling of his bedroom with a groan. He threw his arm over his eyes to block out the sunlight pouring through his many bedroom windows. Much to his disappointment, Farrell had left the pub early.

It would have been easy to find another Dark Fae to interact with, but Kiril discovered his mind was on other things—more correctly, on another Dark.

Not even in sleep could he get away from her. Shara appeared in his dreams. She would stand off to the side, away from everything. No matter how many times he tried to get near her, he couldn't close the distance.

Kiril sat up and raked a hand through his hair. In the light of dawn, Shara was still on his mind. She was a Dark, a spy sent to monitor a spy. The irony didn't go unnoticed. Still, he wanted more time with her. To hear her laugh, to see her smile . . . to feel her silky skin beneath his palm again. It was madness, but there was no denying the truth of it.

Kiril threw off the sheet and rose from the bed. He walked naked across the large room to the connected bathroom and turned on the shower. He stood beneath the water and let it rain over him.

He didn't know how long he stayed like that as he continued to think of Shara. Finally, he grabbed the soap and washed. When his hair and body were clean and rinsed, Kiril shut off the water and exited the shower, reaching for the towel on the hook as he did.

His gaze immediately went to the large window overlooking the expanse of lawn that extended beyond the house. He briefly tossed aside the towel and walked out of the bathroom to the double doors in his bedroom that led out to a balcony.

Kiril threw open the doors and simply stood there. The Dark Fae were hidden in the trees at the edge of his lawn watching, waiting for him to make a wrong move. He remained there letting them look their fill of him. If they wanted a show, he was happy to give it.

When he felt a push against his mind, he turned away and reentered his room. At the same time every day Con would use the mental link between Dragon Kings to contact him.

Kiril opened his mind to Con's nudge. *"Aye."*

"You're in a foul mood," Constantine said. *"What happened?"*

Kiril briefly thought about leaving out Shara, but if he were taken by the Dark, the Kings needed to know who to look for. *"The Dark tried a new tactic last night."*

"Really? And what would that be?"

"A woman."

There was a pregnant pause before Con said, *"You've made it known that you like a woman on your arm so it doesna surprise me."*

"She used glamour to try to conceal her red eyes and silver in her hair."

Con sighed loudly. *"We should be thankful it's that*

easy to spot the Dark Fae. If the use of evil magic didna change them, we'd be fucked. Tell me about the woman."

"Shara. Her name is Shara." Kiril dressed in a pair of faded jeans and a dark green shirt. He left his room and descended the curving staircase to the kitchen where the cook had left his breakfast waiting.

"That's all you're going to impart?" Con asked, irritation deepening his voice.

"I took her to dinner. Mostly because I wanted to see what she might reveal."

"But," Con urged when he paused.

"I think I might try to flip her to our side."

"Kiril, you're no' known for being reckless, but you're deep in Dark Fae territory. We're a long way from you. Be sure about this before you try anything."

"Warning heard, Con. Shara is our ticket. By the way, any news about Rhi? I've no' heard anything since the night she was taken."

"Nay." The word was filled with fury.

Kiril almost felt sorry for the Dark who had taken her. Balladyn was his name, and he was going to rue the day he ever brought down the wrath of the Kings. *"I'll keep listening around. Something about her will have to surface soon."*

"There's something else," Con said softly.

"What is it? Did you find more clues pointing to Ulrik as the one trying to reveal us to the world?"

Ulrik. He was a Dragon King who had been betrayed by a human and retaliated with war. Ulrik wouldn't relent, and Kiril and the other Kings had had no choice but to bind his magic. Though part of Ulrik's rage was due to the fact they had killed his woman for her betrayal. It had been done out of love and friendship, but Ulrik hadn't seen it that way.

"The Silvers moved again."

Kiril paused as he reached for his mug of tea. Again. The Silvers moved again. The implication was tough. The Silvers were Ulrik's dragons. The four of the largest Silvers had been captured and caged after Ulrik's dragon magic had been bound.

Then the rest of the Dragon Kings had used their magic to put the Silvers to sleep deep in the mountains on Dreagan. As long as the Dragon Kings remained on Dreagan, the magic surrounding the Silvers would hold.

"The first time the Silvers moved Hal fell in love," Kiril stated.

After the betrayal to Ulrik, Con had ensured that no other Dragon King would feel deep emotions for another human. It had taken millions of years, but it had happened starting with Hal and Cassie.

A few months later Guy had fallen for Elena, then Banan for Jane. A year after that Kellan had tumbled head over heels for Denae, and then Tristan followed suit with Sammi, Jane's sister.

The movement of the Silvers had been like a bell tolling the coming apocalypse. The fact they moved again wasn't good news.

"You're the only King no' on Dreagan," Con pointed out. *"I know why you're putting yourself in the middle of the Dark, but I doona believe it's worth it. Come home, Kiril."*

"Worth it?" he repeated in disbelief. *"Kellan was kidnapped by the Dark. Tristan was tricked into coming to them because they had Sammi. And now they have Rhi. You still doona think it's worth it? They'll take another of us, Con. How many more times can we come to Ireland and rescue our brethren before we're seen? How many more times can we get away before the Dark get smart and capture more of us?"*

"They took two of us during the Fae Wars, Kiril. I

know you remember that. Do you want that to happen again? We might be immortal, but they broke the minds of those two Kings and had them attack us. I doona relish killing our own, even if it is a mercy killing."

"I'm no' leaving Ireland. Shara is my way deeper into the Dark world."

"Let me send Ryder or Darius over. They can watch your back."

"No. It's too chancy. The Dark watch me constantly. I can no' have another King here that could be taken. They know what I am, but they doona know that I know. I'm going to use that to my advantage."

"Doona make me regret this," Con warned.

"Until tomorrow," Kiril said before he severed the link.

He stared at his mug of tea and the steam rising from the liquid. The Silvers moving made him think of his own dragons. Kiril often went into the cavern that held the Silvers to see them. There was a chance he might never see his own dragons again, never see the burnt orange of their scales glistening in the moonlight.

Kiril shook his head and closed off those memories. He had to focus on the Dark Fae and their obsession with capturing a Dragon King. It would help if he knew what it was they searched for, what it was that they believed the Kings hid. There was little doubt that Con could have hidden something away if he felt it would cause other beings to gain the upper hand on another race.

The Dragon Kings had been charged with keeping the humans safe. Even with the dragons gone, the Kings kept to their mission—despite how difficult it was at times.

The Kings went out of their way protecting the humans for millennia, fighting wars they never knew about, and yet if the humans discovered them, they would capture the Kings and dissect them.

Kiril often wondered if it might not have been worthwhile to let the humans destroy themselves so the dragons could return and Earth would once more be the beacon of light in the universe.

Though his appetite was gone, he ate the plate of food and drank two cups of tea before he made his way to his office. It was going to be a long day waiting for night to fall so he could see Shara again.

Shara puffed out her cheeks and blew out a breath of air as she tossed aside the book she was trying to read. The hours crept by slower than a slug. It was worse now that night had descended, because she wondered what Kiril was doing. Did he go back to the place they'd first met? Did he walk the streets looking for her? Did she stay on his mind as he remained on hers?

The questions were driving her insane. She rose from her bed and paced the confines of her room. She was no longer locked inside, but there was nowhere else in the grand house that she wanted to go. Unlike humans who struck out on their own as soon as they could, Fae families—both Dark and Light—tended to remain together.

However, this was one time that Shara wished she didn't reside in the same house as her brother, parents, aunts, uncles, and cousins. It wasn't just crowded, but everyone's eyes were on her, watching what she did—or didn't do.

Shara looked around at the walls of her spacious bedroom. They were painted a deep red, as was the rest of the house. The Dark Fae preferred darker colors, shying away from pastel colors because they associated weakness with such colors.

She walked to the mirror hanging on her wall and looked at herself. The red eyes staring back at her didn't hold the cruelty or the malice that her brother's did. Not yet at least. They would eventually if she continued on the path her family had set before her.

It was a path she hadn't thought twice about as she was essentially forgotten while her parents and older siblings played the game of politics and joined in the never-ending wars. Shara had been born nearly a century after Farrell, and her parents quickly thrust her into the care of a nanny.

Shara remembered those days of freedom. Not a care in the world touched her. She was good at her studies, which gave her ample time whenever she wanted. She spent the majority of her younger years right there on Earth soaking up the different cultures and all they had to offer.

She honed her magic, making her tutors proud, even if she never received so much as a message from her parents. They rarely returned to their home on Earth as they schemed the family higher and higher into the social hierarchy of the Dark Fae world.

An already powerful family, the Blackwoods connived and plotted their way right onto the council of the king of the Darks. Now the name Blackwood struck terror in many Dark, though Shara hadn't known that. All she knew was that she never wanted for anything.

She had human friends, and as she grew older, human male lovers. Her tutors taught her the code of a Dark Fae, and the few Fae friends she had never understood why she befriended the humans. Shara hadn't thought anything about it. Until her parents returned.

For over a thousand years she had been ignored, overlooked by the accomplishments of her elder siblings. Shara woke each day hoping it would be the day her family returned to her and took her with them. She hadn't realized how much independence she had until her wish was fulfilled.

Five of her elder siblings had been killed in a war, and

their family had returned to Earth to grieve and regroup. Shara had sat excitedly in her mother's parlor waiting for her to finally bring her into the fold.

She had been beside herself with joy to receive her first assignment. She hadn't blinked an eye when she was ordered to kidnap five human males. That night she completed her task and saw her eyes change from silver to red.

The assignment was easy enough that she was eager for more. Shara had even sampled one of the men herself when prodded by her cousin. The sex had been good, but she hadn't understood why her friends wanted the humans so desperately.

Her second task was to bring five human females to their home on the Fae world. As soon as she brought them through a Fae doorway, the thick lock of silver appeared in her hair.

She knew what was done to the females from her studies, but she had never watched before. After she delivered the humans, she tried to leave, suddenly sick at what she had done. Farrell stopped her, making her watch. It repulsed her to see the souls drained from the women so quickly.

Shara tried to tell herself it was no different from what the female Dark did to the males, but it was. She was so disgusted by what her male family members did that when they finally left the room, Shara snuck inside to release the women. But it was already too late for them. Their souls were all but gone, and their minds were shattered.

Her only choice had been to give them death. She hadn't hesitated in killing them to end their suffering. There had been a measure of relief in what she'd done. But her family hadn't thought the same.

Farrell had demanded her death, as had many others of her family. Her father disagreed, and handed down her punishment of solitude to think about her crimes. For six hundred years she was kept chained in her room. It was only two weeks ago that she had been released. With a new assignment—Kiril.

This was her chance to prove she was part of her family, a valid member who would carry on their ways. A loyal Dark who embraced their ways, taking from the humans because it was their right.

It was also the only way they would ease up on their control of her.

No matter how appealing Mr. Sexy was, she wasn't going to mess up again. She valued her freedom too much. She wanted to come and go as she pleased, and that wouldn't happen until Kiril was delivered into her father's hands.

She flipped the long strands of her hair over her shoulders. It was the use of the black magic full of evil that caused the red eyes and the silver in the hair of Darks. The more silver, the more evil a Dark had done. Her mother's and father's hair were completely silver, and Farrell's was gaining by the day.

Shara didn't fit in with just the single thick strand of silver that ran along the left side of her face. She was a weakness to her family that needed to be smothered out.

If Farrell had had his way, she would have died the night she killed those human females. He hated her, and told her often that she weakened the family name. One wrong move, and she knew Farrell wouldn't wait for the family's decision on her fate.

He would kill her.

She couldn't remain in her room anymore and let such thoughts fill her. When she opened her door, a distant cousin stood guard. Even now she had only so much autonomy.

He raised a brow. "Going somewhere?"

"I want to get a look at Kiril's home while he's gone for the night so I'll know the layout."

Her cousin thought over her words before he nodded. "I'll take you there."

Great. Would she ever be alone again?

That's when Shara realized the only way to get away from the Dark Fae for a few minutes was to be with Kiril. Alone.

In his home.

She bit her lip to keep from smiling as a plan began to take root.

CHAPTER
FOUR

Shara's black sandals didn't make a sound as she walked the woods behind the home Kiril purchased. The entire estate encompassed fifty-three acres. It was a magnificent mixture of mature gardens, manicured lawns, and flower beds. She walked along a quaint path next to a stream with an abundance of wild shrubs and trees. Even in the dead of night, the place was enchanting.

The number of Dark Fae that were scattered about the estate surveying Kiril shouldn't have been surprising, and yet she felt sorry for him—because she knew what it was like to be watched so closely.

Shara faced the house and spotted the pool through the trees. She had the insane urge to strip off her clothes and dive in. What would Kiril do if he came home to find her in the pool? Would he throw her out? Join her?

Kiss her?

She pushed aside such thoughts and glanced at the sky. The sliver of moon afforded her the cover of darkness as she followed the path to the house.

None of the other Dark would bother her. They knew her mission, and her family had kept her indiscretions from getting out to the others. Only the one guarding her knew how tight the rein was.

At least Farrell wasn't there to dog her every step and question her every move. That's how she knew Kiril wasn't at home. Farrell was always near him, always within easy reach of taking the Dragon King.

Shara stepped from the wooded brush onto the manicured lawn. She walked around the pool. Small lights were set in planters around the water and hidden by the flowers and greenery.

She went to the double doors that led to the pool and put her hand on the wood feeling for the locks or security sensors. A smile pulled at her lips when she felt neither. Kiril was either foolish or knew it would take a supernatural being to dare to enter his domain.

That gave her pause, because from what she knew of the Dragon King, he was anything but foolish. What if he knew the Dark were watching him? To come to Ireland where the Fae—especially the Dark—had claimed it as their own was pure insanity.

Which meant . . . he knew he was being watched.

The fact he left his home unlocked revealed that he didn't care who entered. And knew that someone would.

Shara wondered if any of the other Dark had dared, or if she was the first. She hoped she was the first, because it was an invasion of privacy. The others would likely destroy things or use them against Kiril.

Isn't that what you plan to do?

Shara didn't so much want to use anything against Kiril as she wanted to learn more about him so she could carry out her mission.

Same damn thing. Lying to yourself isn't going to make things better.

She really hated when she was right. After a deep breath,

Shara opened the door and stepped inside the two-story house. Inside was as immaculate as she'd expected. The furniture was simple, nothing flashy or too modern. Dark colors, clean lines. The pictures were those of landscapes or buildings. It was the same from room to room, only the colors changed.

She paused when she reached the foyer. The floor was gray marble and a huge chandelier hung above her. The staircase curved elegantly to the second floor.

His bedroom.

Shara slowly walked up the stairs and stopped at the top. She looked to the left down the hallway and saw several doors. The estate had eight bedrooms, but the master suite—the one Kiril would have claimed—would be by itself.

She turned to the right and followed the rug down a short hallway and around a corner. Another set of double doors sat closed. Kiril's room.

Both anxious and nervous, Shara hurried to the doors and opened them. She stood there gazing at the enormous room. It was almost Spartan in appearance. The king-sized bed was set off to the right with a perfect view through the large window to the back gardens. Shara moved to the bed and ran her hand over the black comforter, imagining what Kiril would look like in his bed.

The mental picture flashed of him naked, his chiseled muscles shifting in the moonlight. His shamrock-green eyes focused on her, his wheat-colored hair in disarray.

Shara jerked her gaze away from the bed and swallowed as she tried to get her body under control. Kiril was dangerous—dangerous to her body and her mind. It was something her family could *never* know.

She walked away from the bed and looked around. The walls were painted a soft cream with the baseboards and crown molding a rich, dark chocolate wood. The colors were soothing and complemented the wood floors. Once more the few pictures on the walls were all of landscapes.

There was a small Chesterfield couch in black leather off to the side in front of the fireplace. The table by the bed, and one near the couch were the only other pieces in the room. Shara did a complete circle where she stood, looking for anything she might have missed. And found a sword in the corner leaning against a wall.

She knelt in front of the double-edged broadsword. Her fingers glided over the two-handed hilt wrapped in leather. It almost seemed like any other sword until she spotted the top of it. The pommel was a dragon's head with ruby eyes that looked toward the ceiling.

The blade was clean and sharp with nothing marring the steel until she reached the top where she spotted Celtic knotwork and some language she didn't recognize.

"Dragonnish," she whispered.

She had never heard of the dragons putting their language into a written form, but she wasn't surprised. The words flowed elegantly, with a flourish that bespoke an ancient race and a plethora of wisdom.

Shara wanted to know what the writing said and the meaning of it to Kiril. There wasn't anything in the house that remotely looked like a dragon except for the sword. The sword was left in plain sight. So obvious most people would have glanced right over it and not thought twice about it. But she had been searching for something that was his.

He resided in the home, slept in the bed, ate at the kitchen table, and dressed in the clothes that hung in his closet, but the only thing that was Kiril was the sword.

Kiril looked at his watch as midnight struck. He had flirted with women at all three pubs he visited, and made sure to show his face at *an Doras* where Farrell was once again in attendance.

But he couldn't find Shara anywhere.

Kiril had held onto the chance that he might run into the Dark Fae again, but no matter where he looked, she was nowhere to be found. It was almost as if she was hiding from him.

He was irritated and vexed. It was time for him to return to the estate away from people, but most especially the Dark before he did something stupid like shouting her name up and down the streets.

Kiril slid out of the booth and stood. He didn't bother buttoning his suit jacket as he started for the door. As soon as the summer air hit him, he drew in a deep breath and let the pub door close behind him.

"Leaving so soon?"

Kiril halted, his muscles tightening for a second. Why was it that Farrell was always near? No matter where Kiril was or what he was doing.

He turned to the side and looked at Farrell. The Dark Fae had pulled back his silver-streaked hair. His red gaze looked at Kiril with a mix of cool confidence and certainty, as if the bastard thought he had already caught him.

How Kiril couldn't wait to take him down.

Painfully. Deliberately. Leisurely.

"It's been a long day." Kiril started walking again, hoping that Farrell would let him go. He should have known better.

"There's no woman on your arm tonight. Don't tell me one has snagged you already?"

Kiril stopped again. His mind instantly thought about Shara. She was a setup, and he was pretty sure her absence that night was on purpose. He would play along for the time being, but he needed to keep them on their toes.

"No' at all," Kiril said over his shoulder. "I've no' found a woman yet who has come close to snagging me."

He walked away, letting his comments stew in Farrell's head the rest of the night. Kiril got behind the wheel of his car and started the engine. The roar was loud and deep. He put it in reverse and drove away from the city. Before he turned, Kiril glanced in his rearview mirror to see Farrell staring.

"Give it a rest," Kiril muttered and quickly sped out of the city and over the bridge.

The drive home was uneventful and the weather nice. Still, Kiril didn't put the top down. It was too much of a temptation to see the sky and not be able to take flight. By the time he turned down the road that would take him to his estate, he was in a foul mood. At least no one would see him in such a state. The staff wouldn't arrive until right before dawn as they did six days a week.

Kiril slowed the car as he reached the iron gates blocking entry to the estate. He punched in the code and waited for the gates to open before he drove through, parking the car at the front of the house.

He no longer cared that the Dark watched him. They had become a fixture, just as Farrell had. At least he didn't have to converse with the ones who spied on him.

Normally he loved driving along the roads in his car, but there was a restlessness about him that night he couldn't name or erase. He got out of the car and jogged up the front steps to the door.

Since the day he bought the estate he hadn't bothered to lock the doors or set the alarm system. There was no need. He had nothing worth stealing, and the Dark would get in no matter what he put in their way.

He walked into the house and stilled. With his gaze darting around, he slowly closed the door behind him.

Someone had been in his house. He could smell them, and it was a familiar smell.

Kiril ran up the stairs to his room and burst through the doors. His gaze went to his sword to find it exactly where he had left it. A long sigh left him as relief flowed through his veins. He walked toward the sword, but once he reached the bed he jerked to a stop.

The scent was strong here. Whoever had entered his house spent the most time in his room. Kiril drew in a deep breath and drew in the scent of the sea and . . . primroses.

Shara.

She had been in his home, in his room. His gaze went back to the bed. The previous night he'd dreamt of taking her in his bed, of caressing her creamy skin, of fisting his hands in her long black hair and kissing her until she clung to him, begging him to fill her.

To know that she had been standing in his room, near his bed had his cock immediately hard and aching. Kiril fisted his hands as both need and anger filled him.

If the wench wanted to play tease, he was game to join in. And he'd had much more time to perfect the art.

"Where have you been?"

Shara didn't have time to answer as Farrell pushed her from behind before grabbing her shoulder and roughly turning her around to slam her back against the wall in the hallway of their home.

"I knew you were watching Kiril, so I wanted a look at where he lived to better know my quarry," she answered angrily. The vein at his temple throbbed, an indication that he was beyond furious. Well good, since she was now as well.

Farrell smiled coldly, cruelly. "Is that so? It seems your

charms you were so sure of last night are worth nothing. Kiril doesn't want you."

"He's not a man to shout what he wants or doesn't want, especially to the enemy."

It was the wrong thing to say. The punch came to her side before she could prepare for it. Shara doubled over, the pain making it difficult to breathe.

"You better be right, *little* sister. The next time I won't care if I mess up your face," Farrell said next to her ear before he straightened and walked away.

CHAPTER
FIVE

Forty-eight hours. Forty-eight excruciating, tormenting hours. Kiril experienced every painful second of those hours. And all because of one woman—Shara.

He wasn't going to leave Cork without seeing her again. He didn't care if he had to comb through every business, every pub, and even every house. It didn't matter how many Dark Fae stood in his way.

He. Was. Going. To. See. Her.

Had he not been so wound up, had she not been in his room, he might have realized how close to the edge he was. The fact he knew he was teetering on the brink of losing his control didn't go undetected by him.

Shara wanted something from him, and he wanted something from her. If he allowed it, they could dance around it for days or weeks to come. Kiril wasn't sure how much longer he could remain in Ireland.

He might have told Con earlier during their morning chat that he was fine. He was anything but. It was getting harder and harder to remain in human form, and his work on the cellar wasn't moving along as quickly as he wanted.

Of course, with the Dark watching, he had to take his

time and not let them realize what he was doing. Time was running out. If he didn't learn where Rhi was before it was too late, everything he had done would be for naught.

He drove his SLS Roadster down the same road as he did every night, crossing the bridge into the city center of Cork and parked. The difference was, he didn't park in the same location as he had the last few days. He chose the other side of town.

It was time he changed things up a bit. For the Dark, but more importantly for himself.

Kiril got out of the car, buttoned his suit jacket, and locked the car. He walked along the streets, effortlessly blending in with others—the drunks, the partiers, the tourists, and the locals. He stayed in the shadows, making it look as if it wasn't on purpose. It made it easier for him to see how many Dark followed him.

Three. Two on foot and one on the rooftops.

How many would be watching Shara? Because he knew she would be there. Farrell's anger had been palpable the night before. They thought they had hooked him that first night with Shara, and he made them think differently. They would put her back out that night, just as he had wanted them to do.

Because the simple truth was . . . he was hooked.

She had done something to him. All he could think about was her when he should be concentrating on finding Rhi. There were so many times lately that Rhi had been there to help the Kings out. He couldn't let her down now.

Kiril paused as a group of female college students walked in front of him. Several eyed him, smiling in encouragement. Kiril gave them a nod and continued on once they passed.

His ire grew the longer he walked without encountering Shara. Until he turned a corner and saw her. It was like being punched in the gut, just like the first time he saw her.

She wore a sleeveless dark gold dress that skimmed her curves with a deep V down the front showing ample cleavage. Kiril bit back a moan of approval. Her hair was loose about her shoulders and styled in thick waves. Gold earrings molded in a thin line dangled from her ears, and the only other piece of jewelry was a gold bracelet on her right wrist.

She came to a stop when she saw him, a slow smile upon her lips. As expected, she had her glamour back up, hiding her red eyes and the silver stripe in her hair. It should worry him that her red eyes didn't bother him. It meant she was evil, had done evil, and yet he didn't care.

Was this how he repaid his brethren? Did he betray them so easily? If Rhys, Laith, Con, or one of the others were with him, they would tell him in no uncertain terms to get his head out of his ass and to stop thinking with his dick.

Con was right. He couldn't do this, not by himself. But bringing another Dragon King to Ireland was asking for trouble. There had to be another way to find Rhi and spy on the Dark.

Kiril turned to the side, his back to the building. Shara's smile disappeared and a frown marred her brow. As tempting as she was, he had to walk away. Because if he went to her now, he would kiss her, and one kiss wouldn't be nearly enough.

He started back to his car with purposeful steps. Not once did he stop, not even when she called his name. When he reached the Mercedes, he rested his arms on the top and dropped his head to his chest.

For once he didn't care who saw his conflicting emotions or what they thought of it. They could all go fuck themselves.

"Kiril."

He squeezed his eyes closed. No. She couldn't have followed him all the way back to his car.

"What's wrong?" she whispered as she stepped close. "Talk to me."

"Why?" he asked and lifted his head to glare at her. "Because we know each other so well? Because you're my friend?"

She took a half step back, but she never looked away from him. "Because I asked."

Kiril chuckled wryly. Mainly because he was screwed two ways from Friday. His attempt to get away from Shara had been taken out of his hands. He dropped his arms and faced her before yanking her against him, ignoring how good her arms felt as they rested on his shoulders.

He leaned down until his mouth was by her ear and whispered, "Was seducing me your idea? Or did Farrell send you?"

The slight stiffening of her body was her only response.

"I've known from the first instant I saw you. I can see through your glamour."

She tried to pull away, but he held her fast. Anger sparkled in her eyes. "Why did you take me to dinner then?"

"Because you intrigued me." He ran his hand down her back to rest on the spot above her ass.

"Intrigued?" she repeated, confusion causing her brow to pucker.

Did he hear a tremor in her voice? He splayed his other hand on her back and held her tighter. "Aye, lass. You can tell Farrell that, but the Dark willna capture me."

"You should never have come here," she said and leaned back to look at him.

"Do you even know what's going on? Do you know that the Dark has aligned with MI5 and someone else? The Dark are no' in control. They answer to others."

"You're wrong. The Dark are powerful."

He shifted his hand from her back around to her side. She winced slightly, and he hated the concern that flared. His hand paused for a fraction as it came to rest on her abdomen. Then slowly, leisurely he moved his hand upward, over her breasts, feeling her nipple harden as he did, to her chest until his fingers wrapped around her neck.

"I could kill you right now, snapping your neck in two."

"Do it."

There was no fear in her red eyes, only . . . acceptance. He leaned close until their lips were breaths apart. "You willna beg for your life?"

"No."

He wasn't sure whether to run from her or to her. How odd to encounter a Dark Fae who didn't beg to live or barter with information to prolong their life.

"Take me for a drive."

Her whispered words, and the way she seductively twisted her hips reminded Kiril that they were being watched. "Why?"

"Because I asked."

"Drop your glamour."

"I can't."

"I can see through it."

"So you already said. We can't continue to stand here like this. Are you going to take me for a ride or kiss me?"

He was going to do both, but the ride wasn't going to be in his car. Kiril released her. "Get in."

Shara was shaking as she walked around the car. She was so rattled that she didn't even realize Kiril was behind her until he opened the car door for her. She met his green gaze, but the anger she saw earlier was gone, hidden once more. He waited until she was seated in the leather seat before he closed the door and walked around to the driver's side.

He moved as fluidly as a lion, as stealthily as a tiger, and anyone who didn't see the primal beast held tightly within was a fool.

She couldn't take her eyes off him as he slid behind the wheel and started the car with a push of a button. It was a chance she was taking going off with him. He recognized she was Dark Fae, and worse, he discerned she had been sent to seduce him.

For all she knew, he could take her somewhere he planned to shift into a dragon and take her to Scotland. Odd how that didn't bother her as it should. Family meant everything. Right?

She had thought being released and being allowed to join her family would sort out the conflicting thoughts that had plagued her all those centuries of her confinement. Sadly, it was only getting worse now that she had met Kiril.

He drove them easily through the city streets until they reached a main road to take them out of town over one of the many bridges.

"Are you new to the Dark ways, or are you just young?" he asked in a bored tone.

Shara fingered the stripe of silver in her hair. "Neither."

"It doesna take that long for silver to show up in a Dark's hair. The first use of evil magic does it. You just have the one stripe, although it is thick. That tells me you have no' been at this long."

She didn't owe him an explanation, and yet she found herself saying, "I was the last of nine children between my parents. They concentrated on turning my siblings into what a perfect Dark Fae should be while advancing the family socially and politically. I was born a century after Farrell, and my parents didn't have time for a baby. I was left with a nanny and tutors and allowed to do what I wanted."

The lights from a passing car glanced off his face showing her a stony visage.

She took a breath and continued. "I was but a small child when the Fae Wars occurred, but I still recall how others spoke of the Dragon Kings and how they shifted into fierce and impossibly large dragons."

"The Fae Wars were thousands of years ago."

"Five of my siblings were killed in the Fae Wars. My parents joined in the fight as well, and I was left behind again. I ran wild those years, doing whatever I wanted whenever I wanted."

Kiril wore a frown when he briefly looked at her. "The Fae Wars lasted hundreds of years."

"I know. When my family returned, I thought things would change, but they didn't. Once more my parents focused on having the best Dark Fae children and having them close to Taraeth. Two more of my siblings died in battle with other Dark for placement next to our leader. For every child my parents lost, the more they focused their attention on the next one."

"Forgetting about you."

"Yes. I had been waiting for the chance to be a part of the family when my mother finally deemed it time."

"Is that what I am? A chance?" Kiril asked.

Shara smiled sadly at her hands clasped in her lap. "My chance was luring men into our world. When that proved easy enough, I was told to bring women. So I did. Then my brother made me watch what they did to the humans."

Kiril grunted. "You cared? I find that hard to believe."

"My parents thought it was because I wasn't disciplined early enough."

"What happened?"

She cut her eyes to see Kiril with one hand on the wheel and his head turned slightly to her. "I ended the suffering of the humans. Since it was all done within our house, none of the other Dark knew. My brother wanted to kill me, my mother wanted to banish me, but it was my father who handed down the punishment."

"And that was?"

"I was locked in my room for six hundred years."

"Is that supposed to make me feel sorry for you?"

Shara laughed as she looked out the passenger window. "Of course not. You asked why I had so little silver. I explained."

"And I guess I'm the assignment that will put you right with your family?"

"Yes."

"It's no' going to happen, lass."

She turned her head to him. "Then why did you bring me with you tonight?"

"Something I've been asking myself."

CHAPTER
SIX

Kiril knew he wasn't thinking clearly. Why else would he bring Shara back to his house? It was a grave mistake, and yet he didn't turn around and drive away.

He got out of the car.

Shara was slow to follow suit. Kiril waited for her at the top of the steps watching her every move. She swallowed and glanced around before she came to stand beside him. "I would've thought you'd take me elsewhere."

He wanted to hate the sound of her voice, but he found himself looking forward to hearing the Irish brogue. Kiril turned the knob and pushed the door open. "We have the most privacy here."

She paused, worry flickering over her face. "Privacy?"

"Well, besides the many Dark Fae eyes scrutinizing me."

"How long have you known?"

"That they've been watching? Since the first moment I stepped onto this isle."

Her lips parted in surprise. "Then why have you stayed? Do you want to be caught?"

Kiril walked past her into the house. He knew she would follow. It was her curiosity that would drive her inside. When he heard the door close softly, he smiled inwardly. But was it because he knew what her actions would be? Or was it because he now had her all to himself?

"I thought the Dragon Kings were smarter than this."

Kiril tossed the keys to the Mercedes on the entry table against the wall and laughed. He braced his hands on the table. "Do I look as if I'd make a stupid decision?"

"You look like you're holding back a tide of rage."

Rage. Aye, that's exactly what flowed through him. Rage and . . . desire. He briefly squeezed his eyes closed and tried to shove back the need clawing through him. Tried and failed. "Two of my fellow Kings were taken recently."

"They escaped," she said softly.

"A friend was taken. I have to find her."

"Her?"

Was that a hint of jealousy he heard in her voice? Kiril straightened and walked into the front room without looking at Shara. He stopped at the sideboard with various crystal decanters filled with liquor. He poured two glasses of whisky and turned around.

Shara stood in the doorway, her expression closed and her body rigid. Good. He wanted her off kilter. He wanted the Dark to wonder what he was up to. He held out the whisky.

She didn't move from her spot. "Aren't you going to turn on the lights?"

"Why? You've already walked through my house last night."

Her eyes flared. "How did you know? There are no cameras. I used my magic to search."

"Your scent was everywhere." Kiril inhaled, pulling her smell deep within him. His cock swelled, need heating his blood.

Shara regarded him a moment longer before she walked to him and accepted the proffered glass of whisky. "You said you were looking for someone. Is she . . . is she your lover?" she asked and quickly lifted the glass to her lips.

"Would it matter if she was?"

"If the Dark have her, you should just forget her. Humans never last long."

"I never said she was human."

Shara took a hasty step back. "Fae? You're looking for a Fae? But Dragon Kings hate all Fae."

"Who told you that? Your family? We despise the Dark. The Light . . . we've come to work with on occasion." She didn't need to know it was a very rare occasion and only with Rhi.

"It doesn't matter. Whoever the Dark takes is never the same, even if you do find her."

Kiril glanced around the darkened room. He walked to a leather chair and sat, stretching his legs out in front of him and crossing his ankles. "Did you know that during the Fae Wars the Dark took two Dragon Kings? At different times, of course."

"I suppose they escaped as well? Are you telling me we don't know how to hold a Dragon King?"

"The Dark did . . . things to my brethren. One completely lost his mind and attacked us, which is what the Dark wanted. He had to be killed. The other King knew what was happening to him, but he couldna stop it. He came to us and begged to be killed before he could harm one of us."

Shara sipped her whisky before she said, "You lost two Kings and I lost seven siblings."

"And the Light the Dark took?"

"The Dark take the Light and the Light take the Dark."

Kiril let his gaze drift down her body. How he itched

to have her long legs wrapped around him. Things would be so much easier if he didn't desire her as he did, but there wasn't a switch he could flip to turn off his body's reaction. The more he tried to ignore the growing desire, the more it raged uncontrollably within him.

He gave himself a mental shake and returned to their conversation. "What's the plan, then? Will the Dark storm in here and try to capture me?"

Shara walked around the room, her hand skimming along the backs of the chairs. "No."

"No?" Kiril set aside his glass on the table next to him and silently rose to his feet. He followed her as if a string tied them together. "What then?"

"You don't really want to know."

Kiril spun her around so hard that her glass flew from her hand and landed upon a rug, spilling the whisky but not breaking the crystal. "Tell me," he demanded in a soft, deadly voice.

"My job is to seduce you." She held her stance for a heartbeat before she retreated, taking two steps back.

He tracked her until she was once more in the entryway. The shadows darkened everything, and yet the smallest sliver of moonlight found her, illuminating her in a pale blue glow.

No longer could he deny what he wanted. Perhaps it was her confession. Maybe it was because he hadn't taken to the skies in weeks. Whatever it was, all he knew was that he had to have her or go up in flames.

"Then seduce me."

That halted her. She held her ground as he drew closer. He bit back a smile when he saw the pulse at her throat beat erratically. She wasn't immune to him. It was a victory, though a small one. She was as dangerous as her mission, perhaps more so. And yet it didn't matter. There was no turning back for him. He knew it with a calmness that he had only felt once before—when he had taken over as King to his dragons.

He looked into her eyes, hating that her glamour prevented him from seeing her as he wanted because of the faint but unmistakable flicker of her magic. "First, drop the glamour."

Her lips lifted slightly in the corners. The shimmer he had seen around her, indicating the glamour, vanished.

"Better," he stated.

His cock swelled. Her beauty was so astonishing that it held him dumbstruck, immobile to do anything but drink in her splendor.

She tugged at the silver lock of her hair. "This? And these?" she asked as she pointed to her red eyes. "This is better?"

"Aye, lass." For once, he wasn't going to lie to himself or to her.

Her gaze lowered for a moment, and the next second she closed the small space between them and laid her hands upon his chest.

Kiril had to stop himself from grabbing her. His breath came faster, his blood pounding in his ears. Saying he wanted her didn't come close to describing the utter craving, the absolute necessity that hounded him, drove him to claim her. There was no running away from it or denying it. She had gotten into his blood, and he would have a taste of her if it were the last thing he did.

Shara knew she was walking on dangerous ground. It wasn't Kiril she feared, but her own reaction to him. He sent her careening toward desire and passion at a speed that was bound to destroy one of them.

And he would be the one left standing when it was all over.

Not even that knowledge could make her leave. She didn't remain because it was her duty to her family or her mission. She remained because of him—the Dragon King who had seen through her glamour and still wanted her.

She slipped her hands under the edge of his navy jacket. Even through his shirt she could feel the heat of him. It made her stomach flutter in anticipation. With her palms flat against his taut stomach, she slid her hands upward over hard sinew. Her mouth went dry as she imagined what he would look like naked. Her hands were shaking by the time she reached his thick shoulders and pushed the jacket off. He loosened his arms and let it fall unheeded to the floor.

Her gaze snagged on something on the left side of his neck just peeking past the collar of his light blue shirt. She couldn't believe she hadn't seen it before, but then again, her eyes had been on that incredible face of his.

His green eyes were hooded as he watched her, and yet he let desire flare in his depths for her to see. It made chills rush over her. Chills and . . . longing.

Moving slowly, Shara undid the buttons of his shirt one by one until she reached the waist of his slacks. She was breathless by the time she slid her hand inside his shirt and rested her palms against his warm flesh. His stomach clenched and she felt all the hard muscles move beneath her hand.

Shara could no longer wait to see his body. She pulled his shirt out of his pants and jerked it open, the last two buttons flying to bounce along the wood floor. Her lips parted as she took in the spectacular display of hard sinew and the dragon tattoo. Unable to help herself, she traced the tat, startled by the black and red ink mixed together.

But it was the dragon design itself that made her skin prickle with awareness, appreciation.

Soul-sucking desire.

The dragon took up most of Kiril's impressive chest. It looked as if it were climbing his chest with its wings half-spread and the tip of his long tail curling to the left side and disappearing into his slacks. The head of the dragon, inked on his right shoulder and neck, was lifted toward Kiril, as if seeking him.

She raised her eyes to Kiril and sucked in a breath when the heat, the hunger of his gaze slammed into her. It was scorching, searing. Sizzling.

It wasn't as if she hadn't experienced desire before, but whatever was happening between them was on another level completely. The intensity of it frightened her. Yet she couldn't leave no matter what her mind cautioned her to do. Because she wanted him with a desperation that bordered on insanity.

Shara couldn't draw enough breath into her lungs. She ached, she burned.

She *yearned*.

His heat only fueled her growing passion to new heights. As dangerous as it was, she grasped it with both hands and held on.

Shara gradually caressed her hand up his washboard stomach, over his hard chest to his thick shoulders just as she had done to remove his jacket. Except this time there was nothing between her and his skin. She wanted to see more of that sun-bronzed skin and feast her eyes on his virile form.

She pushed his shirt over his shoulders and down his arms to join his jacket on the floor. He wore the suit like a man born to it. It had hinted at the physique beneath, but nothing could portray his incredible form like the man himself bare of everything.

What madness it was for her to think she could seduce a man like Kiril. He exuded sex and sensuality as if he created them for his arsenal alone. He was the one who had seduced her—with a single look.

Why it had taken her until that moment to realize, she wasn't sure. In the confines of his house, in the heat of his nearness, her worries and concerns about her family and future crumbled away. She looked into his eyes and became powerless, impotent to think of anything other than him.

Finally he touched her. Shara couldn't stop the shiver of anticipation that ran through her nor the sigh that escaped past her lips. His smug smile only made the desire burn brighter.

His hand slid around her neck to the back of her head where his fingers closed in her hair. He tugged her head back at the same time he pulled her forward so that her breasts scraped against his chest.

Shara was breathless, panting as she anxiously waited for what he would do next. All the while she lowered her hands to the waist of his slacks. The feel of his thick arousal against her stomach had her reaching for his cock. She wrapped her fingers around his rod through his pants and squeezed.

He yanked her head back farther, causing her back to arch and her breasts to push against his chest. Shara watched the desire darken his features, watched the passion take him in its grip.

She ran her hand up and down his length twice before she unfastened his trousers. His pants hung precariously on his trim hips as she slipped her hand down the front to once more wrap her fingers around him.

He was velvet and steel, fire and fervor.

With one hand on his cock, she reached around and rested her other hand in the middle of his back. She held there for a moment before she leisurely stroked downward until she reached his rock-hard ass.

He lowered his head, his gaze locked with hers. Their breaths mingled, their bodies touching from thigh to chest. Shara tried to raise her head to his lips, but he wouldn't release his hold.

Her lungs seized, her body tingled when he hovered his lips above her, just grazing her mouth.

CHAPTER
SEVEN

Kiril was singed inside and out, and he had yet to claim Shara as he longed to do. She touched him, touched his tat, and it set him on overload. Her breathing was erratic, her skin flushed, and yet she was nowhere near as aroused as he wanted her—nay, *needed* her.

He gazed down at her with her head held back and her breasts pressing against him, and he knew there was no turning away from her now—if that had ever been an option. He hadn't accepted the truth until that minute.

His hold on her kept her immobile and, to an extent, exposed. She didn't fight it. No, she accepted it as if she yearned for it as much as he did.

Kiril felt as if a rug had been yanked from underneath him. He had been searching for something to hold onto in the dark. And found it in the most unlikely of people—a Dark Fae sent to seduce him.

Seduce him she had, with merely a smile and a look. She wrapped him around her finger with ease. Kiril just prayed she never realized it.

"Kiril." His name was but a whisper upon the wind, a sigh upon her lips.

Her gaze silently begged him while her hands continued their magic upon his aching cock. As if he could deny her—or himself—the pleasure that awaited.

He placed his lips on hers, a moan filling his chest at the softness of them. He tilted his head and slipped his tongue past her lips.

The first taste of her was heady and intoxicating. She sent him reeling, careening down a path of longing he hadn't realized existed. He deepened the kiss that quickly grew fiery and intense. The more he tasted of her, the more he had to have.

It was too much, too fast. Kiril had to keep his head about him—or at least attempt to. He ended the kiss and released his hold on her hair, but kept her tight against him.

Her dark red eyes blazed with passion, and her swollen lips begged for more kisses. He touched the indent of her neck. His eyes held hers, daring her to look away, as he caressed a finger down her chest between her breasts to stop at the V of her dress.

The swell of her breasts beckoned. He let that same finger glide over the portion of her breast that peeked out of the dress. His balls tightened when he saw her nipple harden.

He kissed her again, hard and punishing. She wrapped her free arm around his neck and returned his kiss with all that she had. She pumped her fist over his rod in time with their kisses, sending him spiraling out of control quickly.

Kiril reached down her leg and began to gather her skirt in his fingers until he reached the hem. Then he slid his hand beneath the dress to cup her butt. He felt only skin, and his arousal twitched as he thought about her wearing a thong.

He moved his hand to her hip waiting to feel the edge

of her panties, but once again encountered only skin. To know that she was naked beneath the dress undid him.

Kiril ended the kiss long enough to yank her dress over her head and toss it away. She wrapped both arms around his neck and kissed him passionately, fervently.

There was no more waiting, no more teasing. Kiril had to be inside her, had to feel her around him. He kicked off his shoes at the same time Shara did hers. Before he could shove his pants down, she used her toes to grab the material of his pants at his knees and tug. His trousers pooled around his ankles.

She leaned forward, sending him backward and tripping over his pants. Laughter exploded from them as he fell hard on his back, still holding her. The laughter died when they looked into each other's eyes. Kiril rolled her onto her back and leaned over her. Her wealth of midnight hair was spread around her, the moonlight hitting upon the silver strip.

His eyes, however, were on her body. Her breasts were full without being overly large. Her nipples, a dusky rose, puckered beneath his gaze. He trailed his hand down her side to the indent of her waist and over her flared hips to her long, lean legs. With a touch on her thigh, she opened her legs. The black curls between them were trimmed neatly and gave him a good view of her sex, which glistened with arousal.

Kiril moved so that he lay between her legs and looked up at her. Her hands roamed over his face, her nails scraping his whiskers. She sucked in a breath when he leaned forward and wrapped his lips around a nipple.

He suckled it hard before moving to the other peak. Her hips ground against him, reminding him there was another part of her he wanted to taste.

With his lips trailing kisses down her stomach, Kiril moved her thighs onto his shoulders. Her head lifted as she stared at him. The first touch of his tongue on her sex and her head dropped back, a soft moan falling from her lips.

Kiril enjoyed her reaction, but he wanted her screaming. He teased and sucked and licked until she was squirming. Her back arched, lifting her torso off the floor as her hands delved into his hair and held his head.

Her moans quickly turned into soft cries filling the still house. He lifted her hips in his hands and held her still as he tongued her clit. She put her feet upon his back as her cries turned louder.

And then she was screaming his name, her body jerking with the force of her climax. Kiril kept licking her, prolonging her orgasm until she went limp.

He rose up over her, intending to enter her when she suddenly sat up and shoved at his shoulders. He fell onto his back with a grunt. Shara was on all fours, her hair tousled, as she crawled toward him.

In all his millennia of life, he had never seen anything so sexy. His cock twitched, and her gaze lowered to his engorged arousal.

She stopped beside him and raked her gaze over him. Kiril fisted his hands by his sides so as not to touch her. She was a sexual creature, and the confident, assertive woman next to him was driving him wild with need.

Her hands roamed freely over his chest and abdomen. She spent a lot of time looking at his dragon tattoo. Her soft, gentle touch was hurtling him toward his own orgasm, and she had yet to touch his cock again.

No sooner had the thought gone through his mind than she took him in hand. He sucked in a breath, steeling himself for her hands. His breath hissed through his lips when her mouth slid over him.

Kiril was stiff, his muscles locked as she bobbed her head up and down his staff, her hands massaging his sac.

He intended to allow her all the time she wanted, but it became clear that he couldn't take her sweet mouth anymore.

He grabbed her by her shoulders and lifted her up. There was a smile on her lips as he set her down so she straddled his hips, her back to him.

She rose up on her knees until she hovered over his arousal and lowered herself down. Kiril grabbed her hips and squeezed. She was tight and wet. The feel of her sliding down him was exquisite.

He closed his eyes and simply enjoyed the feel of her. Once he was fully seated, she rotated her hips. Kiril moaned and moved his hands upward to cup her breasts. He rolled her nipples between his fingers and pulled her back against him.

Using his feet as leverage on the floor, he pumped his hips with long, slow thrusts. She groaned and arched her back. Kiril reached between her legs until he found her sex and circled his thumb around her swollen clit.

She peaked instantly, her body convulsing around his rod so that he had to clench his teeth or spill. With the walls of her sex still clenching, he rolled them over and came up on his knees.

He raised her hips and took her arms to hold them behind her back. Kiril pulled out of her until the tip of him remained, and then he slid deep.

She moaned his name and pushed back against him. He repeated the move and then held still. She whimpered and swiveled her hips to entice him to move.

Kiril let his free hand roam over her ass. She was utter perfection. No other woman had ever matched him during sex as she did. He was loath for it to end, because he feared once it was over—it would be over for good.

But his body demanded release. No longer could he hold back. He began to move, building his tempo with each plunge. He went harder, deeper and still she leaned back against him.

Kiril released her arms and grabbed her hips with both hands as he mercilessly drove within her. He tried to hold back, but it was as if she knew and would rock her hips.

And then he was lost.

He fell forward over her as he pounded her ruthlessly. When the walls of her sex clamped around him, it sent him spiraling to his climax. Kiril thrust deep and spilled his seed as he rode the waves of bliss from one peak to another.

When he opened his eyes, they were on their sides, their bodies still joined. Kiril held her close and pretended that she wasn't his enemy and that he wouldn't have to leave her.

Her hand rested on his and she idly traced his fingers with her own. Minutes went by as they remained as they were without uttering a word.

It was the sound of faint footsteps at the back of the house that had both of them separating. Kiril didn't bother with clothes as he kept to the shadows and ran to look out the back.

There were two Dark who peeked through the windows to try to get a look at them.

"How about another drink?" Shara said loudly from the living room.

The two Dark backed away immediately. Kiril waited until they were once more in the cover of the trees before he turned and walked back to the entryway. He dressed quickly, roughly tucking in his shirt that gapped because the buttons were gone. He walked into the front room to find Shara sitting in one of the chairs, dressed, with her legs crossed and a drink in hand.

"Why did you do that? That could've been your chance to capture me."

"My chance was when you were orgasming," she said and looked away.

"You still have no' explained why you spoke and sent them away."

She shrugged nonchalantly. "I can't answer that. And before you ask me what I'm hiding, I'm not. I can't answer it because I don't know."

He walked around her, never taking his gaze off her. She was a mystery to him. Her actions made him want to trust her, but that would be the first—and last—mistake he made.

"Who is she?" Shara asked.

Kiril frowned. "Who?"

"The Fae you're looking for."

"Rhi. She's one of the Queen's Guard. At one time she and a Dragon King were lovers."

"Was it you? Were you her lover?" Shara asked and lifted her gaze to him.

Kiril slowly shook his head. "Nay, it wasna me, but she's a friend. She was taken by Balladyn."

She cringed when he said the name. "Balladyn has a vicious reputation even among the Dark. She is lost to you."

"I doona believe that. I'm going to find her and return her to the Light. Help me."

Shara stood and lifted her chin. "Just kill me now, because if I help you, that's exactly what my family will do if Balladyn doesn't get me first."

Kiril walked to her and traced a finger along her jaw. "We can protect you."

Her smile was full of sorrow. "Like the Kings protected Denae and Sammi? Yes, I know of the humans caught by my people. I can't, and I won't help."

"Then why no' walk out there now and let them come for me?"

"I'll answer that if you can answer why you brought me here tonight."

Kiril backed away. He'd had the best night of his extremely long life, and it was going to end on a sour note. "We're at a stalemate."

"That means it's time for you to return me to Cork."

"To your family." He touched her left side so quickly she didn't have time to step away or hide her wince. "Is that who hit you?"

Shara turned and walked to the front door. "I'll walk back."

Kiril bit back a curse and grabbed his keys as he followed her out. It was going to take a lot more than good sex to flip Shara to his side, but he wasn't going to give up.

CHAPTER EIGHT

Rhi wondered how long she'd been Balladyn's prisoner. The Fae she had thought of as friend, mentor, and brother.

The darkness was sucking the life from her breath by breath. She longed to see the sun, to feel its rays upon her skin. Every time she woke after Balladyn tortured her, it became more and more difficult to remember what the warmth of the sun felt like. What would go next? Remembering what it looked like?

Would she forget her family? Her friends? The Dragon King who had stolen her heart, only to shatter it?

She tried to hold back the tears that filled her eyes as she thought of her lover, but one still escaped and fell onto her cheek.

When they had been together it had been wonderful and perfect. It had come out of the blue, blindsiding her when he had ended things. Her world had been crushed, her heart destroyed. It didn't matter what she said or did, he wouldn't take her back. Remaining on the same realm had been too much. Rhi walked into a Fae doorway, intending never to return.

Because of her preoccupation, she didn't realize where

she was until the Dark attacked. She managed to get away, but not before being wounded. She wandered endlessly, dying slowly as she searched for a way out.

And then her body had quit on her.

The next thing she knew, she was back with the Light, her wound all but healed with Balladyn beside her. No matter who she asked how she got home, no one would tell her. Then it no longer mattered.

She let herself mourn the loss of her lover as Balladyn guarded her door. He looked in on her often, always there to hold her while she cried. Until all her tears were dried.

Or so she thought. How was it dozens of centuries later that she could still cry over a King who had turned his back on her?

She tried to move her hand to push away a strand of hair stuck to her chin, but she couldn't even lift a finger. Rhi turned her head and used her shoulder to stop the hair from tickling her.

If she remained in Balladyn's fortress much longer, she would lose the glow within her. The fact he didn't bring even a candle or light the room with his magic told her he knew that as well. He wanted her to suffer.

All because he blamed her for Taraeth taking him and turning him Dark. The Balladyn she knew before wouldn't blame her.

When she eventually turned Dark, would she do the same? It was a fact that no Light Fae ever ventured into the Dark's realm. Who else would come? The Dragon Kings?

Rhi almost laughed at the thought. Constantine, the prick, would prevent anyone from even thinking about it. Never mind that she had risked her life by helping to rescue Denae and Kellan, and had been helping the Kings when Balladyn took her.

As for her lover . . . that was just wishful thinking.

Whatever paradise they had found had only been on her end. He hadn't loved her as she'd thought, hadn't opened his heart to her as she had done.

She had been duped, suckered.

The laughable part is that she had begun to help the Kings again. Now, when she needed them the most, they were nowhere to be found. She should've known that's what would happen. Once more, she had been tricked by them.

Would it be the Dragon Kings that she focused her hatred on? Would she go after them when she turned Dark? Would she even remember the Fae she had been when the evil took her?

Rhi hurried to dash away any trace of tears when she heard the sound of Balladyn's boots hitting the stone as he approached. The last bout of torture had felt as if it lasted an eternity. She had been hanging onto the last of her hope when it finally ended. How many more sessions of torture could she endure?

The door of her prison opened and Balladyn walked in. He didn't bother to close it behind him. She couldn't raise her arms, much less stand, so escaping was out of the question. Thanks to the Chains of Mordare holding her, any time she tried to use her magic, an electrical shock went through her that felt as if she were being split in half.

"I didn't think you could look any worse," Balladyn said as he squatted beside her. His Irish accent was thick, making her long to hear a Scot's brogue.

"Kiss my grits," she said with as bright of a smile as she could dredge up.

"Still doling out the insults, I see."

She forced a laugh that sounded crackly to her ears. "Me? Go eat yourself, douche canoe."

Balladyn's cold smile was his response.

Rhi inwardly shrank away, because she'd pushed him too far. Perhaps he would unintentionally kill her and end the hell she was living in.

Balladyn's red eyes held hers as he stood and took a few steps back before he spread his legs and held out his hands, palms facing each other level with his chest. Rhi whimpered when the black cloud billowed from his hands, but it was drowned out by the deafening sound of evil yawning toward her.

She thought about the first time she had seen her lover, her magnificent Dragon King. The thought was barely in her mind before she was thrown across the room, her body slamming against the stone.

A scream tore from Rhi as bones shattered.

Shara entered her family's home, her heart still pounding with excitement over her time with Kiril. After Kiril dropped her off in Cork, she was surrounded by Dark who had escorted her home.

She walked to the kitchen and looked around. They, like so many other Dark, had taken residence in a human home. Shara didn't even want to know what her family had done to the original occupants.

The manor was large, the design ancient, and yet her family kept it updated with modern conveniences. Three hundred years ago, her mother had decided to give the manor a facelift and had the entire outside redesigned to look more modern.

The Fae—both Light and Dark—once fought to claim Earth as theirs, but the Dragon Kings hadn't stepped aside. The Fae had relented to a truce when the Kings began to pull ahead. The truce stated that no Fae could venture into Scotland or remain on the realm for long periods of time, but there was something about humans that drew them. None could stay away for long. And somehow, someway the Fae began to integrate with the humans in Ireland. They kept themselves separate, but always near the humans.

As Shara looked around the house, it gave the appearance of humanity, but there wasn't a scrap of good within the walls. Evil lived, breathed, and bred there.

She lived there.

How was it that she didn't feel evil after spending time with Kiril? She was born into a Dark family, had done evil herself as was evidenced by her eyes and the silver in her hair. As she looked around, she felt like a foreigner in her own home.

"You're back early," Farrell said as he sauntered into the kitchen, his eyes raking over her. "Your hair is messed up. Did you get him in bed?"

She wasn't sure why she made the decision to lie, only that she did the instant the words came out of her mouth. "Kiril has a convertible, if you'll remember. Of course my hair is going to be messed up."

"You were at his house. Didn't you use your wiles?" he asked in a mocking tone.

"I did. He kissed me."

"Kissed you?" Farrell twisted his lips in a smirk. "Is that all you managed with your *seduction*?"

It was on the tip of her tongue to tell him to go screw himself. Instead, she smiled sweetly. "I suppose you're used to the whore's seduction, brother dear. Would you even know what it was if a lady seduced you?"

"You're no lady."

Her smile grew. "Oh wait. You don't know because you don't know how to get a woman without using your name or the family money."

"You little bitch," Farrell growled and came at her.

He wrapped his hand around her neck, much as Kiril had done earlier in the night. The difference was, Kiril had held her firmly without hurting her, but Farrell was squeezing painfully. Shara stared into his eyes, daring him to do what he had wanted for decades.

"Farrell," their mother said from the doorway. "Release her."

Shara didn't rub her neck as she longed to do when Farrell's hand finally dropped away. She kept her arms by her sides and watched their mother all but glide into the room. Her completely silver hair was cut in a bob at her chin, not a hair out of place.

Her eyes blazed in red fury as she looked from Farrell to her. "Shara, you know this is your last chance to prove you're one of us, our blood."

"I'm making headway, Mother. Kiril knows I'm not a whore, so I can't just go barreling in there."

Her mother nodded regally. "Quite right. You're being smart about this. For once. I'm happy to see that. I'll be even happier when I see more silver in that hair of yours. If this assignment wasn't so important I'd have you working for me and gaining silver in your hair by the day."

Shara looked at her mother calmly. Had she been switched at birth? Why did the idea of hurting someone make her uncomfortable? She was a Blackwood. Evil should be second nature to her. If anyone had a hint what she was thinking they would strike her down where she stood.

Everyone in the house made her feel inferior, as if she hadn't been born into one of the most powerful Dark families of the Fae. It wasn't her fault she had been forgotten by them, and now it was all up to her to prove herself. There were times, like now, that she wanted to disappear.

Or better yet, have them disappear.

But that was never going to happen. She either completed her mission adequately or she died. It all came down to having Kiril captured or continuing to live.

It had been an easy choice yesterday, but now things were more . . . complicated.

Shara started to move past her mother when her hand reached out and her long fingers griped Shara's arm painfully. "You're testing my patience with that color you dare to wear."

Shara glanced down at the dark gold dress. "I needed him to see me even in the shadows. It's still a dark tone."

"Black, Shara. Don't make me remind you again, or it won't be Farrell who has a hand around your neck."

Shara bowed stiffly, her anger barely contained, before she pulled her arm free and stiffly walked to her room. Wearing dark colors had always come easy because she liked them. It had nothing to do with viewing pastels as weak colors, they just happened to be colors she didn't care for. But there were times Shara saw a red dress, a white shirt, or even a bright pink skirt she liked. It felt like blasphemy to even think of those colors.

She kept her pace controlled as she walked into her room. Shara turned to shut the door and glanced into the corridor to find her guard take his place.

Once the door was closed she rested her forehead on it. Even now when she was doing what they wanted, they kept her cousin guarding her. Wasn't she proving herself by doing what was asked?

How much longer would she be followed? Would it even make a difference if Kiril were captured with her help? She had a sinking feeling that it wouldn't, not until her hair was more silver than black.

Shara thought back to when she killed the human females after her brothers and cousins had sucked their souls dry. There was no way she could witness that again, or even be party to it. Her family must know that as well. Why else would they keep her under guard?

She had remained under their thumb for centuries,

locked in her room isolated from everyone and everything. She refused to allow that to happen again.

"Never," she whispered and straightened.

There was strength and confidence within her that hadn't been there before that night. She thought about Kiril, about how his kisses had weakened her knees while his touch had stolen her breath.

He had taken her wildly, passionately.

Completely.

And he might very well have changed her forever.

CHAPTER NINE

Laith walked into Constantine's office to find the King of Kings standing at his window staring out at the rolling land that the Dragon Kings had called home for eons.

"So much stayed the same for so long that it's hard to grasp the changes taking place here," he said.

Con's shoulders lifted as he inhaled deeply. "You've the right of it."

"What troubles you?"

"I've got an uneasy feeling about Kiril remaining in Ireland." Con turned around and walked to his desk. He sat in the leather chair and regarded Laith.

Laith leaned against the doorjamb and crossed his arms over his chest. As usual Con was dressed in a suit, though his jacket hung on a hook on the wall. It was an appearance Constantine had taken two hundred years before, and it had stuck.

While the other Kings were content to wear comfortable clothing—no matter what time period they were in—Con was different. Always had been, and always would be.

"You think we need to go after Kiril?" Laith asked.

Con's forehead furrowed, his onyx eyes serious, thoughtful. "That would speed the war coming. Nay, I just want him home."

"He will soon enough. As much as I doona want him there either, he's spying."

"They know who he is."

Laith grinned. "Perhaps, but they willna expect him to know that or to respond to them as I imagine he will."

"They're using a female Dark to seduce him."

That caused Laith to pause. "I know Kiril. He willna fall for something so obvious."

"I doona think he will either, but that doesna mean the Dark doesna have other tricks."

"I'll go to Ireland."

Con shook his head. "I can no' send another King into that nest of evil."

"Then who? You certainly can no' send a human." When Con merely returned his look, Laith pushed away from the wall. "You're no' really thinking of asking the Warriors?"

"Who else is there? Rhi? She's already been taken by Balladyn."

"I know. I was there," Laith stated coldly.

"Phelan calls for updates on Rhi. He asks every day if he can join in the rescue when we find her."

Laith rubbed the back of his neck. "You did remind him that no Light Fae has ever come back from the Dark the same? Most likely Rhi is already . . . Dark."

"I know," Con said quietly, too quietly.

"Phelan has Aisley, Con. The Warriors may be immortal

with powers thanks to the primeval gods inside them, but they can be killed."

"So can we."

"Only by another Dragon King. Anyone can take a Warrior's head."

Con stood, his hands on the desk as he leaned forward. "Kellan and Tristan were already taken by the Dark. I can no' and willna have another King in the hold of those malicious beings."

Laith tilted his head to regard Con. "Tristan said the Dark was asking for something. They believe every Dragon King knows where it's hidden, but we doona. Only you know."

"And Kellan," Con said.

Of course. Kellan would know everything since he wrote the history of the Dragon Kings. "What is it the Dark are after?"

"Leave it, Laith."

"What could it possibly be?" he pressed.

Con sucked in a breath and went back to gazing out his window. "If my predecessors thought it important enough to keep secret, who am I to argue?"

"It was kept secret from the rest of the Kings?"

"Aye. The first King of Kings hid it, and each of us who have taken the position has kept it hidden."

Laith shifted uncomfortably. It had to be great indeed if Con felt the need to conceal it from all of them. "Is it dangerous?"

"Extremely. Trust me. We doona want it to fall into the hands of the Dark."

"That shouldna be a problem if only you and Kellan know the location."

Con looked at him over his shoulder. "Doona underestimate the Dark. Ever. They'll figure out a way, and I need to be prepared for that."

* * *

Kiril was sitting on the sofa in his room staring out the window at the dawning of a new day. It's where he had gone after returning from dropping off Shara.

It had been everything he could do to drive away from her. Every instinct he had told him to bring her back with him—and he didn't mean the estate. He meant Dreagan.

His gaze went to the cushion beside him when his mobile phone vibrated. He always kept the phone with him, but none of the Kings contacted him in that manner when they could converse through their link without fear of the Dark ever intercepting the call.

Kiril lifted the phone, frowning when he recognized Rhys's number. He took the call and lifted the phone to his ear. "Hello?"

"Well, I didna wake you," Rhys said, a smile in his voice.

"Nay. I'm awake."

"Did you rise early?"

Kiril focused his gaze back out the window though he didn't see the trees or the flowers. "In a manner."

"You didna sleep at all, did you?" Rhys asked, irritation deepening his voice.

"Nay."

"I can be there in a few hours."

Kiril smiled despite himself. "No' even funny, you reckless bastard."

"I'm no' joking."

The smile left Kiril. "I know, but it's no' wise."

"Neither is you being there by yourself."

"As I told you before, it's better if it's just one of us."

"It should've been me," Rhys grumbled.

Kiril could practically see Rhys's aqua eyes narrowed in exasperation. "It was fair and square."

"It was a fucking rock, paper, scissors game, jerk."

"Quit your complaining, dick." Kiril found the tension easing in his muscles. Rhys had always known just what to do to bring him out of any kind of funk.

"Are you all right?" Rhys asked, his voice serious and hard.

Kiril sighed. What did he do? If he lied, Rhys would know and come to Ireland. If he told the truth, there was still a good chance Rhys would come anyway.

"Truth, jerk," Rhys said, as if sensing that Kiril was weighing his options.

"What has Con told you?"

Rhys grunted loudly through the phone. "He keeps it brief, as he always does. He did mention a female Dark. I told him there wasna a chance in hell that she could seduce you."

Kiril squeezed his eyes shut and rubbed them with his thumb and forefinger. He then dropped his hand onto his leg and went back to staring out the window.

"Fuck me sideways," Rhys hissed. "Are you kidding me?"

"She didna have to seduce me. I went right to her knowing exactly who and what she was."

"All right." Kiril could practically see Rhys nodding his head as he spoke. "Do you think you can turn her to our side as Con mentioned?"

Kiril thought back over his conversations with Shara. "No' a chance. I gather I'm a test. If she sets things up so I can be captured, she's back in with her family. If she doesna . . ."

"They kill her," Rhys finished, his voice tight.

They sat in silence for a minute, their minds running through every possibility.

Rhys cleared his throat. "If she has to prove herself to her family, that means she did something they doona approve of."

"Aye."

"Use that against her. Turn her, Kiril. We need to know what the Dark are up to, or more importantly what they're searching for."

"I like her, Rhys."

"You'll be fine if you have no' bedded her yet."

Kiril blew out a breath. He wouldn't lie to Rhys.

"Oh, fuck."

And that was putting things mildly. Kiril dropped his head back on the sofa. "Aye, my friend."

"No wonder you've no' slept. What can I do?"

"Remain at Dreagan. It's nearly time for Con to contact me for our morning chat."

"Are you going to tell him about the female?"

Kiril lifted his head. "Nay. It might have happened millennia upon millennia ago, but I remember vividly what we did to the human female that betrayed Ulrik."

"So you think this female Dark will betray you?"

"It's likely. It's her family. What else is Shara to do?"

"You have two choices, my friend. Walk away. Or get her to fall for you."

Kiril leaned forward and dropped his head into his free hand. "I can no' walk away from her."

"Then you have just one choice." Rhys sighed loudly. "I'd feel better if I was there watching your back. I could remain hidden."

"They're already onto me. To bring another King here would be like offering up a buffet to a starving man."

"It should've been me," Rhys repeated.

Kiril shook his head, and then remembered Rhys couldn't see him. "Nay. This is playing out just as it was meant to."

"I wouldna be falling for a Dark," Rhys ground out.

That made Kiril smile. "I'll bet you my new Mercedes that you'll fall for someone soon enough."

"Bite me, jerk wad."

"Ah. Did I hit a sore spot?"

"I'm hanging up now."

"I did hit a spot." Kiril sat up, on instant alert. "Who is she? What does she look like?"

"There's nobody."

"I think you protest too much."

"Whatever. Be safe, jerk."

"Always, dick."

"I'll call soon," Rhys said, right before he disconnected the phone.

Kiril set the mobile phone aside, a smile on his face. For a few minutes Rhys had taken his mind off the situation—and off Shara.

Yet he couldn't help but wonder who it was that Rhys had found. Did the others even know yet? The fact Rhys wouldn't even talk about it spoke volumes. No one else knew, and had he not been joking about it, Kiril was sure he wouldn't have even put the pieces together.

He was smiling when he stood and walked into the bathroom, disrobing. That smile soon faded as he caught sight of the scratches on his shoulders in the mirror. Instantly a vision of him and Shara rolling around on the entryway floor sprang to mind. His cock hardened. He wanted inside her again, to feel her tight walls, to hear her scream as she peaked.

It wasn't just his need. He was worried about her. There was a chance that everything she'd told him was a lie, but he knew when she was acting and when she was herself.

It was the way she held herself so stiffly, as if she were waiting for him to call her a liar. She was much more relaxed when she spoke the truth. Of course, just because she might be telling the truth didn't mean he still wasn't being led into a trap—a beautiful, beguiling trap, but still a trap.

He looked himself in the eyes through the mirror and grimaced. He was in way over his head.

"Shit."

CHAPTER
TEN

Shara walked out of her room expecting to see her dutiful guard. Except the corridor was empty. She looked one way and then the other before she shrugged and walked down the stairs to the kitchen.

She was turning into the kitchen when her name was called. She pivoted, surprised to hear her father's voice. He was a busy man keeping their family ranking high among the Dark, which meant he was rarely home. If he was, she normally didn't see him.

It wasn't always a good thing when he wanted to see her, and after the secret she kept from her family about her time with Kiril, she couldn't stop the thread of fear that knotted in her stomach. Had they somehow found out? Would this be the day she died?

She walked down the hall until she reached her father's office, then stopped at the doorway. "Yes, Father?"

He smiled in greeting, his thick hair pulled back in a queue, not a strand of black to be seen in the silver. He rose to his feet and motioned her inside. "Come, Shara. Let's take a walk."

A walk. This could either be really good, or really, really bad. She refused to show fear, however. Shara walked around his desk to his side. He held out his arm and she looped hers through his. A smile still in place, he led her through the opened glass doors outside to the manicured gardens.

There wasn't a flower in sight. Everything was green. Flowers meant color, and color, especially bright or pastel, equaled weakness. A Dark Fae wouldn't be caught dead with flowers anywhere near their homes.

"I always had such hope for you, Shara. I knew, despite being the youngest of my children, that you had the potential to exceed all of them," he said.

They had the appearance of being alone in the expanse of the yard, but there were Dark everywhere guarding her family—but mostly her father—from any kind of threat.

She looked into her father's red eyes and smiled. This was the first time she'd ever heard anything like this from him, and her anxiety kicked up a notch. "I'm glad you think so."

"It's because of your resolve and persistence with the Dragon King that I've made the decision to remove everyone from dogging your every step."

She almost tripped she was so surprised.

"Farrell and your mother disagree with my decision, but they will abide by it," he said in his calm, deep voice that commanded such obedience. He led the family with an iron fist, and everyone knew not to go up against him for they would lose—and lose badly.

She looked out over their view of the water. All she could think about was her freedom to do what she wanted, when she wanted. She could see Kiril as often as she wanted.

"Farrell had taken my orders too far," her father said, breaking into her thoughts. "How could we expect you to aptly seduce a Dragon King without giving you some room to do what you must?"

"Exactly. I tried to tell him the same thing."

"Farrell just wants to ensure the rise of this family. He's made me proud. I expect you will do the same."

She nodded when he stopped and turned to her. "Of course," she added when he looked at her expectantly.

His gaze was full of pride. A first that she could remember. "Just as I assumed. It's no mean feat what you're intending to do. The Dragon Kings are dangerous, my daughter, but they can be brought down. Your name will be remembered for all eternity for what you're doing for the Dark and this family."

"Why do you want the Dragon King?"

His gaze turned shrewd while he studied her. After a long pause he seemed to come to a decision, because he said, "They have hidden something we want."

"A weapon?"

"In a way. It can be used against the Kings."

Now Shara was confused. "Our magic can be used to make a Dragon King revert to his human form, but that's all that can be done to them. Nothing can kill them but another Dragon King."

"Or so they want us to believe." Her father spread his arms to encompass the scene of the ocean, their garden, and the rocky land around them. "We've conquered Ireland, but it was always our intent to conquer this realm, not one measly isle. We will succeed, but first we need what they've hidden."

"And you believe Kiril will tell you."

Her father laughed, the sound cold and evil. "Ah, my dear girl. I think with the right motivation any Dragon King will give us what we want. Taraeth managed to have two in the depths of his stronghold, but our family will be the one who delivers the next one. We'll be the one to keep him trapped, and we'll be the one to break him."

Shara thought back to the story Kiril had told her of the two Kings taken during the Fae Wars. "How will we break him?"

"His mind. It will take a long time, but then we have you."

"Me?"

"You'll make him fall for you, make him care. We'll lead him to believe that we have you and will torture you."

She might be considered young by some Dark, but she wasn't naïve or stupid. "You mean you will actually torture me."

Her father shrugged nonchalantly. "We'll have to prove to him we'll be willing to do anything to you. The Kings are meant to protect humans. It's in his nature to protect the very woman he believes is human that he cares for."

"And then?" She wasn't about to tell him that Kiril knew she was Dark.

"We break him. We'll have to fake your death, of course, but he will feel as though he failed. That will speed his descent. Once he's broken, he'll tell us anything we ask."

Shara had longed for her father to bring her into the fold of the family. He was giving her that chance. "I want to be there when we find whatever the Dragon Kings have hidden."

"I can arrange that," he said with a nod of pleasure.

Her mind drifted back to the breathtaking kisses and toe-curling sex she'd had with Kiril. "How did you know Mother was the right woman for you?"

"That was easy." He began walking along the stone path again, keeping ahold of her arm. "When it came time to marry I had my pick of women because of the family and the name I'd made for myself, much like Farrell is doing. Your mother was one of many."

"Why did you choose her?"

"She had a quick, devious mind that far exceeded any other, and her desire to advance to the top was as great as mine. We had the same ambitions."

Was it as simple as that? Is that how she was supposed to look for a husband? No. She was to stand meekly, but confidently, and wait for her husband to choose her.

"Don't worry, Shara. Farrell has already lined up men that I'm considering for you. Many wanted you before, but now that they know what you're doing, more are clamoring for your hand. I'll choose wisely."

It was how it had always been done with their people. Why then did she wish she had a choice in picking the male who would share her bed?

Silence in the wake of such a statement was rude. Shara smiled tightly. "I trust your judgment, Father."

"Farrell told me he hit you hard enough to bruise. Did the Dragon King take note of the bruise?"

Shara focused her mind on the conversation. The last thing she wanted was to be caught in a lie, and that's what her father was trying to do. "He wrapped his arm around me, and I pulled away. When he asked if I was hurt, I thought it prudent to let him know that I was bruised."

"Did he ask how you had been hurt?"

"He did. I told him that I ran into a counter, but I made sure the lie was told badly enough that he saw through it."

Her father patted her arm. "Very good. Aye, very good indeed."

She nodded expectantly when he looked at her. "I want to fully be a part of this family. I'm proving myself, Father. Please tell me everything."

His lips pursed as he considered her words. Seconds stretched into minutes as he remained quiet, their stroll circling back to the house. The closer the house came, the more anxious Shara was to learn all the Dark were planning. For herself, of course.

"I thought you said I was proving myself? I made one mistake, and I served out my punishment. I'm bringing a Dragon King to you."

"You did serve out your punishment with dignity. However, I've told you all there is for now."

Shara gave her cheek to her father to kiss as they reached the doors to his office. "Thank you for your approval, Father."

His red eyes went hard as he stared. "Now that you have it, if you botch anything up, Shara, only your death will make up for it."

"I won't disappoint you."

With a nod, he released her arm and walked back into his office. Shara turned to look at the sea once more. It stretched endlessly before her, and yet, Scotland wasn't that far away.

Why was she even thinking of Scotland? Just because she had felt good in Kiril's arms? He was a Dragon King, enemy to the Dark. Her family was all she had, and she had to remember that. At the end of the day, if Kiril had to choose, he wouldn't choose her. It was a dose of reality that she needed. She would do as her family asked.

But she also knew her brother was a first-class arse. He hated her, had always hated her. No matter what he said, he would do his utmost to ensure that she failed somehow while still managing to capture Kiril.

That meant she had to think for herself. Farrell would likely strike before she could ever have her father's ear, which meant she needed someone with more power than her family.

She briefly thought about Taraeth, but quickly dismissed the idea. As ruler of their people, there were countless females looking for his favor. No, she would need something more immediate, someone who would notice her sooner.

Her mind immediately snagged on a candidate who had power that even her father feared—Balladyn.

It was a huge chance she was taking, and he might not even notice her. Yet she wouldn't know unless she tried. First, she would need a look at him and his infamous fortress.

A part of her thought about asking for Kiril's help, but she knew there was nothing he could do for her. If she was to come out of this at all, she had to have the help of a Dark Fae.

Shara turned on her heel and walked around to the back of the house where a lone Fae doorway was located. It was kept separate because it would bring her right inside Balladyn's compound. She hesitated for just a moment before she stepped through.

Gone was the brightness of the sun. There was nothing but darkness and shadows and gloom. A Dark Fae's perfect world. She ignored the looks of the Dark soldiers guarding the doorway. They knew exactly what family that doorway led to on Earth, and because of that, they didn't stop her.

She kept her shoulders back and her head high even though she didn't have a clue where she was inside the fortress. It was time she learned what was going on. Being kept locked away for centuries made her ill-prepared, and that was the worst thing for a Fae in her position.

Her wandering through the hallways brought her to the great hall, reminiscent of the castles dotting Ireland, which was crowded with Dark Fae. Tall, slender cages hung from hooks on the walls or dangled on chains from the ceiling. Inside the cages were humans—males and females.

They were naked, waiting for a Dark to take notice of them. The males were in a constant state of arousal as they desperately tried to reach out to any female Dark to take pity on them and have sex.

Many of the human females stared blankly around them, a sign that a Dark had already begun to suck out their souls. They weren't the worst. The worst was seeing the human females sitting huddled in the cages crying as they begged for someone to help them. Those were the females that every male was focused on, because they hadn't yet been touched by a Dark.

In the middle of the hall stood a Dark she didn't recognize. His black-and-silver hair was trimmed short as he shouted to the occupants. And then the bidding for the newly kidnapped human females began.

That could be her up there except for the fact that she was born a Fae. The Dark weren't particular about the humans they snatched. Pretty, ugly, fat, skinny, old, young. It didn't matter. Because a Dark male would kill just for the taste of a human soul.

Shara shifted her gaze to the grouping of Dark females as they looked at their choices of caged males. The Dark females rarely took the souls of the humans as the Dark males did. A Dark female had more . . . refinement in how it was done.

They were slow in their taking of the soul, just sipping at it. It helped the human males last much longer than the females.

"Find something to your liking?"

She turned to see a handsome male with black-and-silver hair that hung down to his waist. This wasn't a Dark warrior. This was a Dark used to power, money, and influence. A Dark who let others steal what he wanted.

He smiled and bowed his head. "I'm X."

"X?" she asked. "An odd name."

"It's a nickname. Put an X on it, and I find a way to get it for you. I wondered when you might find your way into Balladyn's fortress, Shara Blackwood. I had been hoping."

"I've been . . . away."

"So your family has said. I'm glad you're back."

Shara drew in a deep breath and returned his smile, making it as seductive and inviting as she knew how. "So much has changed while I've been gone. I've heard whispers of Balladyn. Is his legend as great as they say?"

"Greater," X said and held out his arm for her.

Shara eagerly took it. "Tell me everything."

CHAPTER
ELEVEN

Kiril knew if he remained in Cork he wouldn't be able to remain away from Shara, and he needed to have a clear head if he was going to keep out of any kind of trap. He dressed and left the estate in short order. Kiril didn't have a destination in mind at first until he spotted a sign mentioning the Jameson whisky distillery. Kiril turned down the road and drove toward the distillery.

Dreagan whisky was the most sought-after Scotch in the world, but he wanted it to be the number one whisky—Irish, Scots, or American. It was Dreagan that began making whisky well before any human ever thought to. Because the Dragon Kings didn't like to leave Dreagan, and because their methods for whisky were proven, they hadn't taken any other company seriously.

Yet Kiril needed his mind occupied with something other than midnight hair and red eyes. If he had to visit every distillery in Ireland, he would. It was imperative that he get a handle on himself.

Kiril drove down the winding roads with the top down. His mind drifted to Shara as he wondered what she was doing.

And wished like hell that he could trust her.

He pulled into the Jameson distillery and parked. The sheer size of the distillery was impressive. The tour didn't take as long as he'd hoped, and the fact that he couldn't focus on what was being said didn't help. Even when it came to tasting the whisky, he couldn't remember it since his mind was so ensconced with Shara.

After three more distillery tours, Kiril gave up and just drove. Hours passed as he meandered around Ireland, never venturing too far from Cork—and Shara.

Kiril eventually pulled over and chuckled as he found himself at a tourist spot. He shook his head as he took in the view of the beautiful cliffs. They weren't of Scotland, but they were majestic just the same. Across the wide expanse of dark blue waters of the Celtic Sea was Wales. It wasn't near enough to being Scotland to calm his restless heart however.

"It's pretty enough, I suppose, but it isna Scotland."

Kiril briefly closed his eyes as the voice registered as belonging to Phelan. Kiril turned his head to look at the Warrior. "What are you doing here?"

"No hello or anything?" Phelan asked with feigned hurt. "I should've expected that from a Dragon King."

"Phelan," Kiril said in a low voice, his anger rising by the second.

Phelan signed dramatically. "Tristan called, but never said why. A day later so did Con, giving me the same response. It was Rhys arriving at my home that got me worried."

"What did Rhys tell you?" He prayed it was nothing about Shara, though if anyone could understand it was Phelan. He had taken a *drough,* or evil Druid, as his mate.

Aisley had saved her own soul from Satan and reverted back to being a *mie,* a pure Druid, but before that happened Phelan caught all kinds of hell from his fellow Warriors and their Druid wives.

Phelan crossed his arms over his chest and faced him. "It wasna so much what Rhys said as what he didna."

"So you came because you think I'm in trouble? Please remember that I've been alive since the beginning of time."

"You think way too highly of yourself, Dragon," Phelan said with a flat stare. It vanished a moment later. "The truth is, all three are worried, but when they wouldna tell me why, I knew then it had to be bad."

"I can no' find out anything on Rhi."

"I might care for Rhi as if she were my sister, but that's no' the entire reason I came."

Kiril watched the continual roll of the sea hoping it would help calm him. It didn't. It was Rhi who had found Phelan and told him he was part Fae. They had developed a strong, unbreakable bond, a bond Kiril understood fully.

"The Dark are onto you," Phelan stated. "Everyone is worried."

"I've been handling things."

"No doubt. It's just . . . things can get out of control quickly."

Kiril narrowed his eyes as he swung his gaze to Phelan. His words held a deeper meaning. "Rhys told you about her."

"Only after I pestered him. He's concerned. The Dark managed to get their hands on two Dragon Kings recently. It was by pure luck and strategy that both Kellan and Tristan were able to get away. And here you are smack in the middle of the Dark Fae nest, almost daring them to try something."

Kiril shrugged. "Dreagan must be protected, as all the Dragon Kings should. Our enemies are growing, and I can no longer sit idle and hope that the few allies we have discover something for us."

"Your fellow Kings want to be here with you, but it isna safe. No' the same for a Warrior. I'm no' saying what you're doing is wrong. I'd be doing the same." One side of Phelan's lips quirked in a smile. "Besides, I loved to irk Charon as often as I could."

Kiril laughed. He couldn't help it. Phelan had spent most of his immortal life away from MacLeod Castle where the Warriors resided. He had a different take on life than they did, but he also understood what it meant to be a part of a family.

They sat in silence listening to the wind swoosh around them and inhaling the sea air. Kiril closed his eyes and relaxed for the first time in days. He didn't know if it was because Phelan had arrived, or if it had something to do with Shara. Either way, it allowed him to push past the blinding need and clear his mind.

"Who is she?" Phelan asked. "More importantly, how significant is she?"

"Her name is Shara, and she's a Dark Fae." Kiril met his gaze to see a frown form on Phelan's brow. "She tried to use glamour to hide that fact, but I saw through it."

"So you knew she was Dark?"

"Aye."

"Did you walk away?"

"Nay. I took her to dinner."

Phelan nodded absently as he dropped his hands to his sides. "I imagine because you wanted to see what she was after."

"That's how it began."

"You've seen her since?"

Kiril rubbed the back of his neck, debating how much to tell Phelan. No other Kings could be there to watch his back—or remind him he was treading on dangerous ground with Shara. But Phelan could.

"Aye. I went looking for her. I had to."

Phelan let out a slow breath. "She ensnared you already?"

"It only took one look at her."

"Damn. Have you slept with her?"

Kiril paused a beat too long.

Phelan let out a string of curses as he paced away. When he turned back to Kiril, his face was hard as stone. "How deeply are you in? I'm going to stay regardless if you accept my help or no'. The more I know, the more I can assist you."

The fact Kiril knew he needed aid told him just how far he had treaded on risky ground with Shara. He wanted to believe everything she said, but it could all be a lie to lure him into a trap—a trap that would be useless since he didn't know the location to whatever it was Con had hidden.

Kiril considered Phelan's words for long moments before he said, "I'm in too deep."

"That's what Rhys thought. Let me help in whatever way I can."

Kiril looked around him to see the many tourists stopping to see the cliffs. "Where is your car?"

"I doona have one. Fallon jumped me here."

Of course Fallon would teleport Phelan. It was the quickest mode of transportation, damn them. "How are you going to get back to Cork?"

"I'll figure it out. Does this mean you'll accept my help?"

Kiril didn't spot any Dark observing him, but that didn't mean they weren't there. "They watch me always. We can no' be seen together again."

"How do I contact you if I need to?"

"We'll figure it out as we go. I bought an estate no' too far from Cork. Doona come there. I go into the city every evening for dinner and then to the Dark's pub *an Doras*."

Phelan nodded and turned so his back was to Kiril. "Understood," he murmured and walked away.

Kiril walked to different spots along the tourist location, and just as he hoped, others spoke to him as well. He thought his plan was working until he saw two Dark out of the corner of his eye standing behind a tour bus.

There was no way the Dark could know about Phelan. Kiril pivoted and started toward the bus. If the Dark knew what he planned they would teleport away before he could reach them. The tourists milling about didn't help, but their attention was on the majestic scenery, not him.

Kiril stopped to talk to the bus driver as he covertly swiped one of the canes set against the outside of the bus. He then walked around the tour bus and spotted the two Dark. They were facing each other, one with his back to Kiril, talking.

He threw the cane, pegging the Dark who faced him squarely in head, knocking him to the ground instantly. Kiril moved with lightning speed to get behind the second Dark as he began to turn around.

Kiril grabbed the Dark around the back of the neck. Before he could break the Dark's neck, the glint of sunlight off the blade of a push dagger caught his attention. Kiril leaned to the side to avoid the small but lethal blade and grabbed the Dark's hand that wielded the weapon while continuing to apply pressure around his neck.

Kiril kicked his feet out from underneath him, dropping him to the ground on his arse. He had more leverage since he was kneeling and used that to his advantage as he used his strength to turn the Dark's hand toward his own chest. Kiril ground his teeth together and gave a shove, sending the push dagger right into the Dark's chest. The Dark jerked, his eyes widening as the life drained from him.

Kiril pulled out the push dagger and looked at the blade to realize it wasn't just any weapon. It was a weapon from a Light Fae, forged in the Fires of Erwar. It was a weapon that would kill a Fae—any Fae.

He flipped the dagger in the air and caught it deftly as he stalked to the second Dark and plunged the blade into his throat before he had time to wake. After tucking the push dagger in his pocket, he pulled in a deep breath and called forth his dragon magic. As the breath passed his lips, it was pale blue, making ice coat his lips.

When his breath touched the two Dark, they were frozen instantly. Kiril heard the approach of footsteps and punched both of the icy corpses, shattering them into millions of tiny pieces. He stood and walked to the back of the bus, a smile on his face as the strong sea wind lifted the shards of ice and scattered them.

There was no trace of either Dark, and neither had then reported back about Phelan. Not to mention Kiril had worked off some of his aggression. It was a win-win in his book.

He returned to his car and started the drive to his estate feeling much more in control of things.

Shara was surprised at how orderly Balladyn ran things in his compound. She tried to see everything, but spending an entire month there wouldn't reveal everything. There were too many passages, too many rooms even X didn't know anything about.

After passing so much time on her own while her family was dealing with Dark Fae politics, wars, and who knew what else, and then being locked away for her screwup, she was so out of the loop of what the Dark were doing.

Because she knew it was much more than just taking the souls of humans. The Dark were always planning something, always trying to take over one realm or another.

It was odd to see the Dark in all their sinister beauty, lounging on the floor amid huge pillows and reclining on chaise lounges while the music of Pitbull thumped through the speakers and humans—male and females—either begged for attention or prayed to be ignored.

"We're going to rule them," her companion stated when he caught her gazing at a human male.

Shara nodded absently. A human male with wheat-colored hair caught her attention. He was handsome enough, and at a quick glance resembled Kiril. The more she looked, however, the more she spotted the differences.

The human was thinner, not having nearly the bulk or definition of Kiril. The human's hair was short instead of having Kiril's long waves. The human's eyes were a plain brown and not the shamrock green of Kiril's.

The differences continued, but Shara stopped noticing them. Her heart had accelerated at the thought that Kiril could end up in the compound, and that alone, alarmed her.

She wanted to be a part of her family. It had been all she thought about those six centuries of her imprisonment. She was willing to do anything to once more belong instead of being locked away. Already she had put herself in an untenable position by telling Kiril the things she had and keeping other things from her family.

If her family discovered where she was and what she had planned, anything could happen. They might praise her for taking action, but most likely she would be punished for thinking she could make her own decisions.

How was she to follow the wishes of her family so blindly after living over a thousand years on her own? She craved her freedom, yearned to make her own choices about what she wore and who she spent time with. Most of all, she wanted to decide who would be her husband. That shouldn't be her father's choice. She should have the final say, regardless of whether it was Dark tradition or not.

Her father thought confining her for six hundred years would rein her in, and for the most part it did. Until she was back out in the world. Until she met Kiril.

Kiril made her hunger for things she had forgotten, to desire the one thing she was meant to betray—him. How had she gotten into such a horrible position?

Choices. Her choices. That's how she had ended up there. That and the fact of who her family was. To go against them would be like declaring war on them, and in order for her to live, she couldn't do it alone. She had to have allies, strong allies.

"Are you all right?" X asked her.

Shara swallowed her fears and flashed a bright smile. "Fill me in on everything and everyone. I want to know who are the strongest Dark, the ones everyone fears. I've been away for so long."

X hesitated, a look of uncertainty filling his face. "But your brother—"

"Isn't master here," she interrupted him. Shara stopped and faced the Dark. "Who do you answer to? Balladyn or Farrell?"

"Balladyn, of course," X hastened to answer. "But Farrell is coming up through the ranks quickly."

"Quickly enough to defeat Balladyn?"

The Dark laughed low and deep, a sinister smile upon his thin lips. "That will never happen. If anything happens to Taraeth, Balladyn will be the one to lead us."

"Then why are you afraid of my brother? If you serve Balladyn, then he will protect you."

"I will protect X from what?" came a deep, gravelly voice behind her.

Shara's heart plummeted to her feet as she turned and found a tall Dark with red eyes narrowed at her. His hair was long, hanging midway down his back, with thick strips of silver running through his black hair.

His bare arms, crossed over his chest, showed chiseled muscles. As menacing as he looked with his black leather vest and pants, his strength couldn't compare to that of Kiril's. Thinking of her Dragon King, Shara found her heart calming, her breath evening. She had an opportunity here. She couldn't let it slip through her fingers.

"I'll ask you again, female, why are you declaring that I, Balladyn, will protect X?" he demanded, his arms dropping to his sides as he took a menacing step toward her.

CHAPTER
TWELVE

Shara couldn't speak for a full minute. She'd never expected to come face-to-face with Balladyn during her first visit. She wasn't prepared to speak to him, but she had no choice. Most Dark in his position didn't mix with the hangers-on that littered his fortress; the fact he did was another revelation.

She wanted to run back to the doorway that would take her home. That was the girl she used to be. Her family had forced the woman to come forward. If she were going to take her life into her own hands, then she needed to begin to act like a Blackwood.

"I'm Shara Blackwood."

His angry demeanor vanished. It was replaced with a look of delight and satisfaction. His gaze raked her head to toe in a slow perusal. "Your family allowed you to come here?"

"I didn't ask their permission."

Balladyn chuckled, his body relaxing. "A female who knows her mind. That's not like a Dark. I like it."

"It shouldn't come as a surprise if you know my family."

His gaze flared with desire. "There is talk that you will marry soon."

"So I've been told. Apparently, there are some who wish to align with my family."

"And have you as a wife."

Shara's smile was slight, barely turning her lips upward at the corners. "There are very few worthy of my family. Or me."

She wasn't sure what she was doing. Flirting with a male like Balladyn who served as Taraeth's right-hand man was as mad as being attracted to a Dragon King. Maybe that was her problem. She was crazy. It was the only explanation for her recent actions.

Balladyn's gaze shifted to the Dark next to her. "Leave us."

X bowed his head and hastily walked away. The power and respect Balladyn had was remarkable. People feared her family, and therefore feared Farrell. All around her she could see the admiration and influence Balladyn had. If there was ever a Dark who would dare to go against her family besides Taraeth, it was Balladyn.

He moved closer, crowding her so that she had to choose to move away and appear weak or stand her ground. As difficult as it was, Shara decided to stand her ground. Balladyn stood so close his chest brushed her breasts. He peered down at her, and then touched the silver strip of her hair.

"Why are you in my compound?" His demand, asked in a soft voice, didn't hide his doubt as to her reasoning.

She turned her head away from his intense gaze and motioned to the room at large. "I've heard a lot about what goes on here."

"No you haven't."

Shara shifted her gaze back to him and raised a brow. She didn't know how he knew she lied or if he was testing her. Either way, she was going to allow him to win. It was intuition she followed instead of certainty regarding the situation. "The truth isn't as neatly tied up."

He backed her against the wall and put an arm on either side of her. "But it's the truth I want."

"Farrell told me I couldn't come without him. I am tired of being told what to do."

Balladyn's gaze held her for several tense moments. "Once you marry, it'll be your husband who tells you what to do."

"There has to be a Dark out there who would appreciate a strong woman and her opinions."

Just as she hoped, his eyes lowered to her lips. "Aye," he murmured.

Shara had been nervous with Kiril, but she had never been terrified. She was that and more with Balladyn. And yet she found herself considering him because she had no other choice, regardless that she wished Kiril was a choice. The fact was, he wasn't. Any female who managed to tie Balladyn into marriage would find herself elevated above almost all.

She would no longer be under the thumb of her family. As Balladyn mentioned, she would be under his. Except he didn't seem like the type who wanted to control her. He seemed to appreciate her strong will. That could be to her benefit.

A Dark female without family was shunned from everyone and everything. So walking away from her family wasn't an option. She wouldn't live out the week. Farrell would see to that.

Since she couldn't leave everything behind or go to Scotland with Kiril, this was all that she could do. Shara didn't want to marry Balladyn any more than she wanted to trap Kiril, but no matter where she looked, she couldn't see another way for her.

Her flaunting of her family's rule and taking control excited Balladyn. She could see it in his gaze and the way he stared at her as if he was holding back from throwing her over his shoulder and taking her through one of the many doors she saw down the various corridors. She would always have to watch herself with Balladyn. The first hint of deceit or dishonesty and he would kill her.

On the other hand, she was able to truly be herself with Kiril. No lies, no deceptions . . . just herself.

Marrying Balladyn would make my family accept me as well as get me out from under their thumbs while ranking me high in the Dark society. It would also stop my mission with Kiril.

It was settled. She set her sights on Balladyn.

Balladyn leaned back slightly and caught her gaze. "Your family will come looking for me once they discover where you are."

"Are you afraid of them?"

"No." He said it with a heavy dose of wrath.

She smiled and took a deep breath, causing her chest to expand and her breasts to make contact with him. "I don't think there is much you're afraid of."

"You don't know what you're trifling with, Shara."

His warning caused her heart to miss a beat in fear, because she had no clue what she was stirring. She wouldn't let him know that, however. "I guess it's time I returned home then."

She started to turn away only to have him grab her arm and jerk her back against the wall roughly. His nostrils flared as he leaned his face close to hers. "I don't like being teased," he said angrily.

"I'm not teasing." She swallowed and knew she had one chance with Balladyn or all would be lost. There would be no second chances with him. "You're what a Dark is supposed to be. Not what others pretend to be. You lead and rule with power unlike anything I've ever heard of. I had to see you. I never expected to talk to you, much less have you notice me."

He eyed her skeptically.

Shara rested her hand on one of his biceps and felt it flex beneath her palm. "Say the word, and I'll return home."

"I don't want you to leave."

She didn't smile. Balladyn might not have sent her away, but she had a long way to go before she was his.

Kiril's face flashed in her mind.

Damn, but why couldn't the Dragon King stay out of her head? He was going to mess up everything, and if she wasn't careful, he was going to get her killed.

"I'm glad," Shara said to Balladyn. "Show me more of this fortress you rule. I want to see what you do here. I want to see the power you command with a single look."

"This is no place for a female of your rank."

Shara should have known she wouldn't get close to Balladyn. No matter his power, her father would claim he wasn't Dark enough to offer for her. All because he had been turned from Light to Dark instead of being born into a Dark family as she had.

She wasn't sure why it mattered since the Dark began as Light Fae before they turned.

"I should return you to your father immediately," Balladyn said as he ran a finger along her chin. "But I won't."

He stepped away from her and held his arm out to the side, offering for her to walk beside him through the fortress. Shara trembled with excitement. At least she preferred to call it excitement and not dread.

She was acutely aware of how close he stood and how often he brushed against her. He wanted her. He didn't try to hide it or play coy. It was there for her—for anyone—to see as he walked her through the great hall.

The looks of fury and jealousy from the female Darks made her grin. None had been bold enough for Balladyn. They thought to gain his attention by lounging around. He was a different breed altogether, just as Kiril was.

Damn!

She really was going to have to stop that. No matter what, she was going to make sure she ended up with Balladyn. At least then she wouldn't have to trap Kiril. Perhaps she could make sure he was gone from Ireland so she never had to worry about him being captured.

They walked from corridor to corridor, up stairways and through towers, and though Balladyn stayed close, he kept a tight rein on his desire. Shara managed to get his attention, but she was going to have to keep it. If she didn't do something . . . wild . . . he was liable to forget her when she left.

She waited until they were walking down the winding steps of yet another tower with Balladyn in the lead before she faked a stumble. Her effort had been done so she could fall against him, but she wasn't prepared for how quickly he moved.

One moment she was pitching forward, and the next he turned and had his arms around her. Shara found her face even with his. She didn't give herself time to think on it, just leaned forward and kissed him.

There was a split second when he didn't respond, and then his arms tightened as he held her and deepened the kiss. He was a skilled kisser, but her body didn't stir as it had when Kiril kissed her.

Truth be told, it only took Kiril's green eyes on her to send her blood pounding and need tightening low her in her stomach.

Balladyn, for all his handsomeness and power, stirred . . . nothing. She continued to kiss him as if she enjoyed it. It was something she would have to get used to no matter who she married. That thought had her sliding her fingers through the thick strands of his black and silver hair. A moan rumbled his chest in response.

It was long minutes later before he ended the kiss and looked at her. "You're very bold, Shara."

"Was I wrong to think that's what you wanted?"

"No," he said with a pleased smile.

He touched her silver stripe again. Shara moved out of his arms and gave him a stony look. "Is my lack of silver an issue?"

"Did I say it was?"

How she hated when people answered a question with a question. "It's a problem with my family. I should've known you'd be the same."

Shara attempted to walk around him, but once more Balladyn stopped her with an arm across her midsection. She turned her head to find his eyes burning with anger. "Don't make the mistake of thinking you know my responses. I'm not like others."

"I'm Dark. I was born into a Dark family who all have more silver than black."

"That doesn't make you less," he said and tugged on the strip. "It makes you stand out."

"Not in a good way in our world."

"Our world is what we make it. We live between two realms—the Fae and Earth. Look at the Dark around you. More and more are choosing to live in the human world, wearing their clothes, listening to their music, and in some cases pretending to be human."

"All a ruse to kidnap humans for their pleasure," she said, unsure of where he was going with his talk.

He took her hand and led her down the stairs. "Is that what you think? Look closer next time. Aye, some use it as a ruse, but others don't."

"My family lives in a human house. It was given to my

family by Taraeth because my father controls the Dark in the lower half of Ireland for Taraeth."

Balladyn shrugged as they reached the bottom. "Look around, Shara. Take a look at all Dark—even your family."

She stopped, her heart thumping wildly. "I've been . . . gone . . . for some time."

"Imprisoned by your family, you mean?"

Shara took a step back, pulling her hand from his. How could he possibly know? It was kept within the family, an order given by her father that no one in the family would dare disobey.

"I know much," Balladyn said as he leaned a shoulder against a wall. "It was Farrell who brought my attention to your family, and it was Farrell who told me about his young sister and how she was locked away."

Buckets of shame descended upon her. It mixed with fury directed at Farrell. Her brother should never have spoken about what happened, and if he had disclosed that much, she was sure Balladyn knew the cause of her imprisonment.

"So you've been toying with me all this time?" She should've known. It had been too easy to get close to Balladyn.

"I warned you not to think you know me. Yet," Balladyn added smoothly. "I had no interest in Farrell's sister until I overheard you today. Now, I fear that I may never let you return to your family."

CHAPTER THIRTEEN

Dreagan Industries

Rhys entered the gift shop and came to an abrupt halt when his gaze landed on Lily. Lilliana Ross. Her coal black hair fell over one shoulder in a long braid that came to rest at the top of her breast.

She was bent over looking into a box. Despite her wearing clothes several sizes too big for her, there was no mistaking the outline of her curves. Rhys swallowed.

Hard.

"Do you need something?" Elena asked as she walked around him to the counter, a clipboard in hand and a pencil stuck behind her ear.

Rhys looked into her sage-green eyes that now watched him curiously. He'd had no reason for coming into the shop other than for a glimpse of Lily as he had many times. But this time he had gotten caught.

His gaze darted to Lily to see that she had straightened and turned at Elena's voice. Lily's black eyes held a smile. When she first arrived at Dreagan she had looked fragile and . . . scared.

Now she just looked . . . gorgeous.

The sweater Lily wore was so large that it fell off her shoulder, revealing more of her skin. Rhys inhaled and shifted his gaze back to Elena quickly. "Nay. I didna need anything. I was looking for Guy."

Elena set down the clipboard, a knowing smile upon her lips. "He's with Tristan and Sammi at Laith's pub. Sammi is going to start working for Laith. It should be good for everyone involved. By the way, when you see my husband, tell him he better be showered before he arrives for lunch."

"Will do," Rhys said and promptly turned on his heel to head out to the pub the Dragon Kings owned on the outskirts of town on the edge of Dreagan land.

He managed to walk out without another look at Lily. She wasn't his type. He liked his women tall and well endowed. He preferred women who understood their dalliance lasted a single night only—and sometimes not even that long.

Just like the two women who would be accompanying him into Inverness for dinner that evening. They were the type of women who knew there could never be anything between them.

Lily was the type who had forever stamped on her. She was the kind of woman a man never left.

And Rhys was not that type of man.

The pebbles crunched beneath his boots as he walked around the thick hedges to the manor hidden in a way that no visitors who toured the distillery ever saw. He entered by the side door through the conservatory. Rhys hadn't taken two steps before his mobile phone buzzed. He pulled it out and saw the text was from Phelan. It read: FOUND KIRIL. I'M STAYING.

Four words, but it was enough for Rhys to know that Phelan had spoken with Kiril, and Kiril had accepted his help. Rhys was relieved.

"By the smile, I imagine it's good news."

Rhys looked up to find Con sitting upon the two-foot-tall wall of stones that encompassed the fountain that stood in the middle of the conservatory. He pocketed his mobile and walked to Con. Rhys rested a foot on the barrier next to Con. "It was."

"Kiril agreed to Phelan helping?"

Rhys glared at Con. "What did you do? Follow me?"

Con merely raised a blond brow. "Kiril wanted to make sure you didna come to Ireland. Since that meant the two of you had spoken, it wasna a large leap to imagine you would go to Phelan."

"I suppose you doona agree with my methods?"

"No' at all. I had already called Phelan once, and I planned to visit and ask the verra same thing. You beat me to it."

Rhys dropped his chin to his chest. "I've a bad feeling about Kiril."

"So do I. He willna come home. No' yet, at least."

"You know it's just a matter of time before they find a way to capture him." Rhys tilted his head to meet Con's black gaze.

Con nodded, his face grim. "Aye, I know. It doesna help that he's no' only spying, but trying to find word about Rhi."

Rhys leaned an arm on his knee. "So you knew I'd do something about Kiril. What have you been doing? Because I know you've no' been sitting on your hands."

"I do what I've always done—protect Dreagan and keep who we are secret."

Rhys wasn't buying it for a moment. Sure, Con did those things, but there was more. Always. And Rhys knew that somehow it involved Ulrik. Con had said he was going to talk to Ulrik, but so far it hadn't happened. Maybe because Con knew if he did, the battle between the two that had been brewing for eons would finally come to a head.

Ulrik. Once best friends with Con, Ulrik was the only other Dragon King who had the magic powerful enough to fight Con to lead all Dragon Kings. Ulrik hadn't wanted to lead, so he'd stepped aside and the role went to Con.

It was years later after humans were suddenly on Earth with the dragons that Ulrik—like many Dragon Kings— took a human as his lover. Her betrayal of Ulrik and all dragons mushroomed into a war that nobody won.

After Con sent Ulrik off for some dragon business, Con and the other Dragon Kings had found Ulrik's woman and killed her for what she did. When Ulrik returned and discovered what had happened, his fury was immense— both against the humans and his own kind. It wasn't long after that the Dragon Kings had no choice but to bind Ulrik's magic when he wouldn't stop killing humans.

For hundreds of thousands of years Ulrik had walked the Earth immortal, but without his magic and unable to shift into dragon form. It was Con's belief that Ulrik was the driving force behind MI5 and other humans wanting to reveal them to the world. The evidence pointed squarely to Ulrik.

Con stood and adjusted the gold dragon-head cuff links at his wrists. "I'm keeping a closer eye on Ulrik. He's remained in Perth at his shop, but eventually he will screw up."

"And you'll be there to stop him."

"Kill him," Con corrected coldly. "It was something I knew I should've done when we bound his magic."

Rhys set his foot down. "It was unusually cruel of us to allow him to remain immortal but no' to be who he really is—a dragon."

"I didna want to kill a man I thought of as my brother."

"But you will now?"

Con lifted his chin, his black eyes fathomless and chilly. "I do what's best for all of us. No matter how messy or distasteful it might be."

"I'm surprised you have no' just gone to Perth and done away with him already."

"I must have proof or I lose the trust of all of you."

Rhys watched Con walk away. Each Dragon King was strong-willed, fierce, and powerful in their own right, and it took a strong man like Con to bring them all together. He had done it on multiple occasions. Con had a silver tongue when it was needed, but he didn't hesitate to put an end to anything he saw as a conflict between them.

Rhys had completely agreed with binding Ulrik's magic at the time, but he didn't agree with Con's wanting to kill him now. If it turned out that Ulrik was the one plotting to expose the Dragon Kings then he might have to reevaluate his opinions.

Until then, Ulrik was one of them, no matter if he could shift into a dragon or not.

Besides, if he were in Ulrik's place, he would crave revenge as well.

The fact that everything pointed to Ulrik was damning. The Kings' enemies knew things about them only another Dragon King would, and knew locations on Dreagan land that no one save a Dragon King should know.

Rhys walked out of the conservatory into the main house. The sound of female voices coming from the kitchen area let him know that at least a few of the mates to his friends were busy preparing a meal.

He took the stairs three at a time until he reached the third level. Rhys turned left and made his way to the back of the corridor and the large room set up with numerous computers.

A blond head peered over one monitor when he walked into the room. Rhys nodded to Ryder as he came around the half moon–shaped desk to see a box of donuts sitting on the desk.

"Still observing Ulrik?" Rhys asked.

Ryder stuffed the last bit of a chocolate donut with sprinkles in his mouth and pointed to four of the ten computers. Rhys stood behind Ryder's chair and crossed his arms over his chest when he saw the angles of the cameras directed on Ulrik's place of business from the front, sides, and back.

"He willna be able to make a move without it being seen," Ryder said, a note of exasperation in his voice.

"You doona agree with Con?"

Ryder turned his chair around to look up at Rhys with hazel eyes. "Ulrik is a Dragon King. I wouldna agree no matter which one of us Con wanted to spy on."

"And if Ulrik is the one aligning with the Dark Fae, MI5, and who knows who else?"

Ryder scooted his chair away from Rhys and stood. "I doona want to believe it's Ulrik."

"The facts say otherwise."

Ryder shrugged and lifted the lid on the box of donuts to search through them. He pulled out another pastry, this one jelly filled. He let out a whoop and lifted the donut. "My favorite!"

Rhys shook his head, though he couldn't hide his smile. "You and those damn donuts."

"They're amazing," Ryder said right before he took a big bite, leaving strawberry jelly on the sides of his mouth.

Rhys moved his gaze back to the monitors focused on Ulrik's business. He glanced at the other computer screens to see buildings and homes of people thought to be in alliance with Ulrik.

"He doesna leave that building for long," Ryder said, speaking of Ulrik. "Though he does leave."

"Where does he go?"

"Around Perth to get groceries or to eat."

"Is he alone?"

Ryder polished off the donut and nodded. "Always."

"That's odd. If he was aligning with others, they would come to him or he would go to them."

"Aye. Con wants one of us to get inside and put a bug in his phones."

Rhys frowned as he studied the monitors. "Ulrik willna be so stupid as to allow that to happen."

"Con believes that is how he's communicating with others."

"I'm sure it is, but Con can forget about it. It willna happen, not with Ulrik."

Ryder sat in his chair again and leaned it back. "Ulrik was always a crafty one. If he is doing this, it'll be hard to pin it on him."

"He told Banan he wanted revenge."

"Wouldna you?" Ryder asked. "I sure as hell would. In some ways Con was right. He should've killed Ulrik back then. I wouldna want to live as Ulrik has all these centuries alone and unable to be the one thing he is—a dragon."

Rhys blew out a deep breath just as Hal walked into the room.

The Dragon King looked at him with moonlight blue eyes before lowering his gaze to Ryder. "Any movement from Ulrik?" Hal asked.

Ryder shook his head. "None."

Hal stood beside Rhys and crossed his arms over his chest. "I think I'll go pay Ulrik a visit."

"He told Tristan to keep all of us away," Rhys reminded him.

Hal merely smiled. "When has that stopped us?"

He had a point. Rhys chuckled and faced Hal. "I think I'll go with you."

"Are you both trying to start a shit storm with Con?" Ryder asked.

"That is usually Rhys's job, but I thought I'd give it a try," Hal said with a wide smile.

"Both of you can bite me," Rhys said, though he was smiling as well.

Ryder swiveled his chair to face both of them. "I'm coming with you."

Rhys raised his brows. "Well, this will certainly piss Con off. Too bad I willna be here to see it."

CHAPTER
FOURTEEN

Kiril reclined in a chair outside by the pool and looked over the garden. Part of him hoped Shara suddenly showed up.

And another part prayed she didn't.

If she was truly seducing him in order to trap him, then when he didn't show up in Cork, she would come looking for him. The last time Kiril had wanted something so badly was after the last of the dragons was sent away and he prayed he and the other Kings would be able to bring them back.

That was thousands of millennia ago. The dragons were never going to return to this realm. He would never see his beloved Burnt Oranges again. He would never fly high with them around him, hearing their roars.

Even after all this time, it was still hard to accept. There were times he couldn't. Would the same happen with Shara? Would he continue to try to earn her favor even if she turned out to be evil as his friends believed?

Kiril swirled the whisky in his glass. Dreagan. It had arrived just two hours before by courier. He'd had it shipped in from one of their distributors. It was a small taste of home, but it did nothing to ease the knot in his belly.

His mobile rang shrilly into the silence. Kiril palmed it and briefly thought about tossing it in the pool when he looked at the number. He didn't recognize the caller, but whoever it was was in Ireland.

He answered with a curt "Aye?"

"I've got a lovely redhead who's dying to meet you."

Farrell. Kiril slowly sat up. "Do you now?"

"I told her you'd be here as you are every night."

He set down his glass of whisky at his feet. "How did you get my number?"

"I'm connected. If there's something I want, I get it."

"I'm beginning to believe that."

Farrell chuckled. "Are you . . . occupied?"

"Nay."

"Good. You must get down here."

"I'm going to pass."

There was a beat of silence, and Kiril could practically hear Farrell's anger growing. "How about I bring her to you?"

Kiril wasn't in the mood to play games or pretend that he liked Farrell, when he couldn't stand the bastard. "What? You love my company so much you're looking for ways we can spend time together? I'm thinking you need that redhead much more than me."

He ended the call, and though he should have handled things better, Kiril found that he really didn't care. Being around so many Darks was like rubbing a wound raw.

Evil festered, gnawed. Being so close to so much maliciousness corrupted and infected everything around it. That's what was happening to him. He could feel it eating at him from the inside out.

Where was Shara? He didn't care what her reasons were as long as she came to him.

Kiril remained outside for the time it took him to toss back the last of the whisky in his glass. He rose and walked inside the house and slammed the doors behind him. He then turned on the stereo and cranked up the Thousand Foot Crutch CD with "Fly on the Wall" blaring through the speakers.

He kept the lights off as he hurried to the door of the cellar. It was meant to be nothing more than a wine cellar, but Kiril had been expanding it since he'd purchased the estate.

There wasn't a single piece of furniture in the cellar. It was far from his cave in the mountains on Dreagan, but it kept the Dark Fae from seeing him.

And he desperately needed to be hidden.

He let out a bellow, his hands fisted as he bent his arms, releasing the pent-up frustration, rage, and aggravation. The cellar wasn't quite as big as he wanted it. The plan had been to come work on it, but now he knew he needed to be there for another reason entirely.

Ever since he arrived in Ireland he had been tamping down his urge to shift. This time, when the need hit, he eagerly sought it.

One moment he was human, and the next he shifted. The cellar was cramped, barely leaving room for his body to fit lengthways. With his tail tucked against him and his wings as close to his body as he could manage, he was hunched over. He couldn't stand upright, but he didn't care. He was in his true form, and that alone helped to alleviate most of what bothered him.

Kiril lay down, resting his head upon his paws. To think he had been tired of hiding at Dreagan, tired of never being able to stay away from it too long.

What he wouldn't give to return. Except he had his brethren—and Rhi—to think about. He had to remain in Ireland for as long as he could.

Though he feared he wouldn't be able to stand it too much longer.

Shara wasn't concerned with the passing of time. Though her thoughts often turned to Kiril, she quickly thought of something else. As long as she was with Balladyn, no other man would dare offer for her nor would her family bother her.

She watched a female Dark go up to a cage that held a human male and grab his engorged cock. His face was a mask of euphoria from that simple touch. That was something she understood all too well. It's what she'd experienced in Kiril's arms.

Damn, she was doing it again. She had to stop thinking about him. If everything went to plan, she would never have to face Kiril again, never have to ignore the burning desire or pretend that she wasn't aching for his touch.

"Shara," Balladyn said as he wrapped an arm around her, his fingers digging into the bruise on her side.

She hissed in a breath and hastily covered it as she smiled at him. His gaze, however, was narrowed and ire hardened his features.

"You didn't tell me you were injured."

She lifted her shoulders helplessly. "It's just a bruise. I'm fine."

"And how did you get this bruise?"

"It's of no concern."

He smiled, though it was hard and cold. Balladyn turned her to face him. "Farrell has a habit of using his fists against females when words would work better. Is that how you got your injury?"

If she admitted to it, then Balladyn would want to know why Farrell had hit her. And Shara wasn't going to tell him anything about Kiril.

Her silence, it seemed, was answer enough when a

muscle in Balladyn's temple throbbed. "I'll have to have a word with him."

Shara had to think quickly and say something before Balladyn could ask anything else. "You surprise me once more. I never thought you would mind a female getting hit."

"If a female hits me, then I will hit back. For a brother to hit a sister? Nay, I don't agree." His face softened. "If your slack jaw is any indication, I really have surprised you."

She closed her mouth and reconsidered him. "What surprises me is that you haven't already found a wife."

"I hadn't found anyone worthy. Until now."

Shara smiled, delight spreading through her. He cupped her face, his thumb brushing her bottom lip. How different her life would be with someone like Balladyn.

Or Kiril.

She once more took Balladyn's arm. They had been around his fortress already, but she knew he wasn't leading her for another tour. He had something else in mind.

Regardless of her reluctance to share her body with Balladyn because it felt like a betrayal to Kiril, she had to think of her future. Whatever had happened between her and Kiril was in the past. There was no future for them. He couldn't live in her world, and she could never live in his.

Another option had presented itself in the form of Balladyn. If only she had ventured into the doorway sooner and found his fortress, then she might never have had that night with Kiril and long for something that would never be hers.

"I want some time alone with you," Balladyn said. "I don't want to have anyone looking at us or trying to hear what we're saying. The only place I can ensure that is my chamber."

Her feet stopped of their own accord. She kept her gaze on the floor, because she couldn't form a reason for halting.

"Don't worry. As much as I want to take you to my bed, I won't. Not tonight."

Another surprise. Shara looked at him, wondering if he was telling the truth or was as adept at lying as her brother.

"I will take you," he promised in a low, deep voice. "Hard. Often. Until you can't stand. But not tonight."

She shivered, but she wasn't sure if it was because his words scared her. Or thrilled her.

He gave a tug of her arm that got her moving again. "Are you pleased with what you've seen here?"

"I am. Tell me more about what Taraeth is doing. The two Dragon Kings that were captured is all anyone can talk about."

"I imagine it's more that they can't stop talking about how the Kings escaped."

"Both. Is it true that there will be another war?"

"War is inevitable. It's just a matter of when, not if. As for Taraeth's plans, I can't speak of those." They reached the door to his chamber then. He pushed the heavy wood door open and motioned her inside.

Shara walked into the room to find more of the stuffed pillows tossed in piles on the floor. A massive four-poster bed sat in the middle of the room with sheer red drapes hanging at all four corners.

"Speaking of plans," Balladyn said as he closed the door. "I hear a rumor Farrell has some of his own."

"Farrell always has some kind of plan," she said offhandedly.

"I'll be visiting Cork soon to see what's going on. These rumors have reached Taraeth, and he isn't pleased."

Shara turned to face Balladyn. He was leaning back against the door, blocking her way out. Had Balladyn been playing her all along? Did he only want information about her family? Anxiety soured her stomach. "If you have a question for me, ask. I'll answer."

"Did Farrell send you here?"

She laughed, and then hastily cut off the sound when Balladyn frowned. "Apologies. If you knew our relationship, then you would know that I try hard to do the exact opposite of what Farrell wants. I'm sure when he discovers where I am, he'll be furious."

"I'll take care of that. Are the rumors true that Farrell is going to capture a Dragon King?"

Shara prayed she kept the surprise from showing on her face. "As I said, Farrell always has some plan he's talking about. He's ambitious. He wants to be in a position of authority as my father is."

Balladyn rubbed his chin. "I'm not going to Cork just for your brother."

Shara's heart began a slow, sickening thump in her chest. She wasn't good at hiding her emotions, which meant her fear showed plainly. She had to think of something to explain it. "Is it because I came here?"

"Nay." Balladyn's face broke out in a smile. "Though I will include a stop at your house for a chat with your father. If that's what you want."

Was it? This was her last chance to change her mind. "I do."

"I want you by my side while I'm in Cork."

Damn. How would she explain to Kiril? Would she even get a chance to? "Of course," she said when she saw his expectant look.

"My main reason for going is because of the Dragon King who has dared to come to our land."

Shara grabbed ahold of one of the posts of the bed to keep herself standing. She didn't want Kiril caught any more than she wanted to be locked away again.

Balladyn took a step toward her, but stopped when a knock sounded on the door. He threw it open angrily. "It'll have to wait."

"Forgive me," one of his men said as he glanced past Balladyn to her. "You said to remind you of the time no matter what you were doing. It's time for another interaction with your prisoner."

Balladyn sighed and looked over his shoulder at her. "I won't be gone long. There's an old . . . friend . . . I must have another chat with."

CHAPTER
FIFTEEN

Rhys glanced at the sign above the store with an exact drawing of the Silvers kept at Dreagan.

"Even in exile he flaunts who he is," Hal said with a wry twist of his lips.

Ryder shrugged. "I'd do the same."

"We all would," Rhys said as he crossed the street and walked to the door. He opened it and stepped inside the store, his gaze scanning the room until he spotted Ulrik behind the counter toward the back of the store. Behind Rhys, Hal and Ryder entered and moved to either side of him. Ulrik lifted a brow and set down some papers he had been reading.

"I told Banan that none of you were welcome here," he stated and riffled through more papers.

His dismissive attitude didn't surprise Rhys. "I wouldna want to see us either. We've no' visited."

"I've no' thought much about it."

"Liar," Ryder said.

Ulrik's head slowly lifted to pin Ryder with a withering look. "What is it you three want?"

Hal stepped forward and inspected a painting that sat on an easel near the door. "I wanted to see you."

"Forgive me if I doona believe you," Ulrik stated sarcastically.

"It's true." Hal turned to face him. "Whether you believe it or no', I've stayed away for you."

Rhys watched the way Ulrik's face lost all emotion, as if he had just erected some wall around him.

"I didna want to rub it in your face of what you had lost," Hal continued. "I know now it was wrong. I'm sorry."

"You've had your say. Now get out." Ulrik once more went back to his papers.

Rhys drew in a deep breath and released it. "Are you conspiring with the Dark Fae against us?"

"Ah," Ulrik said with a chuckle. "So the real reason comes out."

Ryder walked to the counter and slammed his hand on the papers Ulrik was looking over. "Look at us!"

That got Ulrik's attention. His golden gaze fastened on Ryder. "Or what? You'll kill me? Is that no' what you've come to do?"

Ryder reared back, affronted. "Nay."

"Con can be such the coward. He should be here himself."

Rhys remained by the door. Ulrik might no longer have his magic, but he wasn't going to underestimate him. Whether he was the mastermind of the plot to bring them down or not, Ulrik was never one to be misjudged. "If Con wants you dead, he'll have to do it himself. I'm no' here for that. None of us are."

Ulrik looked at each one of them. "What do you want?"

"If it is you conspiring with the Dark, MI5, the Mob, or whoever, we're asking you to stop," Ryder said.

Hal moved to the next painting and glanced at Ulrik. "We're no' saying it's you, but we're asking that if it is, you give it up. Nothing good can come of what is happening."

"We know you want your revenge," Rhys said. "You've a right to it after what we did."

Ulrik's smile was cold. "Is that right?"

"We're your brethren," Ryder said.

"Brethren," Ulrik repeated. "Where were you when I needed you? Where were you when Con deceived me and killed my woman, which was my right after what she'd done? Where were you when the humans were killing our dragons, and I was the only one who retaliated?"

"You were no' the only one," Ryder said softly.

Rhys and Hal exchanged a look as Ulrik chuckled.

"One battle, Ryder. That's all you lasted before Con convinced you to turn against me."

"It wasna against you. We vowed to protect the humans," Ryder argued.

Ulrik's brows rose. "Protect the very beings who were killing us, slaughtering us? All of you are all right with that? Is that why so many Kings still sleep in the mountains?"

"Enough," Rhys said. "You've made your point, Ulrik. We've all made mistakes. Hold on to your hate, let it eat away at you. You want your revenge on us, then come at us."

"Oh, I want my revenge, and I will have it," Ulrik stated calmly. "Con might want me dead, but I want to see the breath leave his body as well."

Hal shook his head. "You two were as close as brothers."

"Aye, and that's why his betrayal cut so deep." Ulrik's gold eyes flashed angrily.

"He's looking for a reason to come here," Ryder said.

Ulrik merely smiled. "Let him come. He knows where

I am with all the cameras watching me and following me."

Rhys ran a hand down his face. "If it isna you trying to reveal us to the world, would you consider helping us?"

"You have a lot of nerve." Ulrik made a sound at the back of his throat. "I didna come to any of you when I was alone, without my magic, and unable to shift into my true form. Doona come to me now looking for help. I've none to give."

Ryder said not another word as he stormed out of the store. Hal followed a moment later, leaving Rhys. He and Ulrik locked gazes, both refusing to look away.

"A war is coming."

Ulrik lifted one shoulder in a shrug. "It's inevitable."

"Dragon Kings could die."

"Why do you care? You know you'll never see your dragons again. Are you truly happy here without them? Watching over humans who would rather kill you than live with you?"

Rhys knew it was pointless to continue the conversation. He turned on his heel and walked out, but he couldn't forget Ulrik's words.

Mostly because he had already thought of them himself.

Kiril woke and opened his eyes. The CD had finally stopped playing sometime in the middle of the night, and silence met him. He would prefer to remain in dragon form for the rest of the day. Yet there were things he needed to see to, and with his mind clear once more, he could focus as he was supposed to.

He grudgingly shifted back into human form and walked naked up the stairs into the main house. Dawn was just creeping over the horizon when he went upstairs. He turned on the water to the shower. While he waited for it to heat, he looked out his window to where he knew the Dark watched.

It was time he rattled them a bit, just as he had flustered Farrell the night before. Kiril was smiling when he stepped under the water and began to wash. By the time he stepped out of the shower, he was putting a plan together. The first part would bring him to Cork for the entire day—and night.

He was buttoning his shirt when he felt Con push against his mind. It was time for their daily talk. Kiril knew that to ignore him would send Con and other Dragon Kings straight to Ireland, but he also couldn't let Con know his plans.

"*Con*," he said after he opened his mind to the King of Kings.

"*I understand Phelan has taken to sightseeing in Ireland.*"

"*Aye.*"

"*And you didna send him away?*"

Kiril stared at his reflection in the mirror. "*Why? He wouldna have left anyway.*"

"*You've been there long enough putting yourself in danger. It's time for you to return to Dreagan.*"

"*I've no' learned anything about Rhi yet since the night she was taken.*"

"*And you probably willna,*" Con replied wearily.

Kiril frowned and set his hands on the top of the dresser. "*So you've given up? I know you hate her, but after all she's done to help us, you're just going to leave her? With them?*"

"*A Light Fae doesna come back from that. If she's no' dead, they will turn her into a Dark.*"

"*It's no' right, Con.*"

"*What's more important? A Fae, or ending our enemies who are trying to expose us to the world?*"

Kiril turned away from the mirror. Damn him for making it as simple as that. *"You're one cold son of a bitch, Constantine."*

"Someone has to be."

"Phelan willna turn away from looking for Rhi. I'm no' going to tell him that we've given up."

There was a stretch of silence before Con said, *"Phelan can no' be caught by the Dark. If they learn he's half Fae and a prince to the Light, they'll take him in an instant."*

Kiril had been so caught up in his own problems with Shara that he hadn't thought much about what it could mean if Phelan was caught. *"Give us two days. No matter what, I'll have him back by then."*

"Two days."

Kiril blew out a breath when the conversation ended and Con's voice was no longer in his mind. He had just two days. Two days to discover if Shara was lying or not. Two days to find out anything about Rhi.

It wasn't nearly long enough.

He wasn't worried about himself. The Dark couldn't kill him no matter what they did, and he'd be damned if he allowed them to mess with his mind as they had others. Phelan, however, was different. If Rhi were there, she'd have Kiril's head on a platter for involving her prince.

"Dammit, Rhi. Why did you have to get taken? And who is the ass who took you?"

Kiril ran a hand through his hair and gathered the length at the back of his neck. He wrapped a piece of leather around it to secure it and grabbed his jacket. He slid his arms in the coat and shrugged it on. After adjusting it with a shift of his shoulders, Kiril walked downstairs to the entryway and grabbed his keys.

With a firm tug, the door slammed shut behind him. He got behind the wheel of the Mercedes and put the roof down. A moment later and the car roared to life as he drove down the drive and through the iron gate that closed automatically behind him.

A calm settled over him that morning once he'd decided on his course of action. First things first. He needed to get word to Phelan to be ready to leave at a moment's notice. Since he had no idea where Phelan was, that wasn't going to be easy. Then again, when was anything?

He reached Cork and chose to park along the street away from *an Doras*. Eventually that night he would end up at the pub. Until then, he would stay away. Kiril exited the car and stood on the sidewalk looking at the businesses around him. Humans had no idea they walked, lived, and worked alongside the pure evil of Dark Fae. There were parts of Cork that the Dark tended to prefer, but they infested every inch of the city in some way.

It was going to take most of the day to get the address he wanted, but Kiril didn't mind. He liked stirring the pot, especially when it involved Farrell.

He went into the first business he came to and left almost immediately when he didn't see any Dark working. Business after business, building after building, Kiril walked the streets making a mental note of where the Dark congregated and where there were none.

By noon he had only covered half the city. He was looking in the window of a jewelry store when he spotted the two Dark Fae males following him. Out of the corner of his eye, he saw movement. Phelan was sitting on a bench talking to an elderly lady. His gaze lit on Kiril for just a moment, but that's all Kiril needed to know that Phelan was also following him.

Kiril turned and crossed the street into a pub for lunch. He chose a table in the back that gave him a clear view of the door. After placing his order, Kiril saw Phelan walk into the pub alone. Phelan smiled and leaned on the bar to talk to a pretty bartender while other customers came in and began to fill up the tables. Phelan's conversation was brief however. He straightened and ambled over to the only table available—the one behind Kiril.

Kiril spun the cocktail napkin on the table as he listened to Phelan place his order. The many conversations made the atmosphere loud and difficult to hear. Unless you were a Dragon King or a Warrior.

"What are you up to?" Phelan whispered as he leaned back in his chair, nearly touching Kiril's.

Kiril didn't see a single Dark in the pub, but that didn't mean there weren't humans willing to spy for them. He wasn't sure what made him think it was a possibility. Perhaps it was the way a man in his late twenties furtively looked at Kiril.

"I'm searching for someone," Kiril said.

Phelan snorted. "You're stirring shit."

Kiril bit back a smile. "That, too."

"Two Dark are trailing you."

"Spotted them already. By the way, you need to be ready to leave Ireland."

Phelan set all four legs of his chair back on the floor. "Why? Have you learned something?"

"That's what today is about. It willna be long before they realize who you are."

"It's a chance we take."

Kiril smiled to the waitress as she brought his sandwich. He waited until she walked away before he said, "I refuse to face Aisley because you were an idiot."

"You think I want to be the one to tell Con you were captured?"

Kiril bit into his sandwich and swallowed. The human male's gaze was on him again. Kiril returned the stare until the human quickly looked away. "Under no circumstances let yourself be discovered by the Dark."

Phelan's food arrived. He chatted with the waitress, making her blush. She looked back at him when she walked away. When she was occupied with another customer, Phelan said, "Ditto. Except you can no' get taken."

"That's no' my plan." But it might very well come to that. How else was Kiril going to learn what he needed? "If I am, contact Rhys first."

"Fuck," Phelan murmured.

There was nothing else to say. Kiril ate his meal, not tasting anything as his mind was on something else entirely—Shara. Even while he slept in dragon form, he had thought of her. She hadn't come to him last night. There were numerous reasons as to what could have kept her away, but he continued to think of the worst ones.

Assuming she wasn't lying to him and she didn't want to have him captured by the Dark.

Then again, she could be the ultimate seductress by using timidity mixed with her sweet allure. It could all be an act to pull him completely under her spell. And damn her, it was working.

"Watch yourself," Phelan whispered as he tossed down some money and walked out of the pub.

Kiril ordered a mug of ale and decided to remain in the pub for a little longer. He got a pen from the waitress when she brought his drink and used the back of the cocktail napkin to draw a map of Cork.

He marked with an X the places where he'd found more than two Dark. What it showed more clearly than anything was how the Dark weren't just living in Cork—they were taking over.

Several businesses were owned by the Dark, and several more had Dark working amid humans. Why? Why would the Dark who think of humans as toys put themselves so close to them?

Kiril remained in the pub until he finished his ale. He then paid his bill and left, stuffing the napkin in his pocket. He turned to the left and continued his exploration of the city. Except this time he wasn't just studying things.

Four Dark looked up as he walked into a souvenir shop. Kiril gave them an aloof smile. "Who can point me to the home of the Blackwoods?"

Their eyes went wide at the mention of Blackwood. Just as he'd expected. Shara's family was as powerful as she'd led him to believe.

"Nothing?" he asked.

When they only stared at him blankly with their red eyes, Kiril walked out and went into the next building. There was only one Dark inside, and she was shopping. With a nod at the human owner, Kiril went to the next shop.

Every time he encountered Dark that were working at the businesses, he asked about Blackwood, and each time he got the same response—fear. A few Dark dared to look at him as if he were digging a hole for himself. They had no idea who he was. Kiril was fine with that. The fewer Dark who realized he was a Dragon King the better.

It would be easier for the Dark to capture him if all of them knew who he was, but it reaffirmed his suspicions about Farrell. The jackass was trying to capture him on his own. Kiril was going to make him pay for thinking it was that easy to take a Dragon King.

The sun was dipping low in the sky when Kiril walked into a store with several Dark Fae about. He made his way to the cashier and asked, "Do you know the address of the Blackwood residence?"

The female Dark quickly shook her head and disappeared through a door to the back. Kiril turned and started to walk out when a Dark stepped in front of him.

Her black and silver hair was trimmed close to her head, and she wore a nose ring. Heavy makeup covered her face, especially her eyes. She tapped the toe of her combat boots on the floor in time with the smacking of her gum. "Why do you want the Blackwoods?"

Ah. Finally someone willing to talk. Kiril knew it would happen eventually. "It's business."

"You know they're a family you don't want to mess with, right?" she asked in her thick Irish accent.

Kiril smiled. "I appreciate the warning. Will you give me the address?"

She chomped on her gum for a few seconds before she too smiled. "If you're senseless enough to go there knowing what awaits you, who am I to stop you?"

Kiril walked out of the shop with a destination—and a purpose.

CHAPTER
SIXTEEN

Shara woke from her position in the high-backed chair and turned her head. To lock gazes with Balladyn.

His red eyes blazed with a craving a blind woman could see. She swallowed, unsure what to say. It had been hours since he had left her to attend to his business. When he held out his hand, it never entered her mind to refuse him. In the time she had been with Balladyn she'd learned that no one refused him *anything*.

"You remained."

She glanced at their joined hands. "You asked me to." What else was she to do? Leave after he'd told her to stay? Return to her family? As if.

"You didn't leave my chamber."

Shara tilted her head as his words sank in. "You had someone guarding me?"

He was no better than her family keeping watch over every move she made. The fury that erupted within her was fierce and overwhelming.

Balladyn simply raised a black brow. "The guard was there to ensure that no one bothered you as well as to see to anything you needed."

Shara looked away. Her chest heaved from the anger swirling within her. She wanted to believe him, but she wasn't sure she could. Would she be trading one prison for another with Balladyn?

"There are . . . things . . . in my fortress that could harm you should you encounter them," he said into the silence.

She smiled tightly, still refusing to look at him. The fact he wouldn't release her hand was all that kept her next to him. "Right. Just as my family locked me away for my own good."

Balladyn tightened his fingers on her hand and pulled her closer until their bodies touched. Then he placed his other hand against her chin and turned her face back toward him. He looked intently into her eyes. "You'll know if I ever imprison you, Shara."

"Because you'll tell me?"

"Because you'll be in chains."

Shara held back a shudder. Barely. "Do you hold many prisoners?"

"A few. Most are Dark who have gone against Taraeth or need . . . persuasion of some kind."

She couldn't believe she was even considering asking him about Rhi, but she hadn't been able to forget Kiril's words. He had called the Light a friend. She didn't think any Fae—Light or Dark—were friends with the Dragon Kings. At least that's what she had been taught.

"What else do you have here?" she asked.

He smiled and loosened his hold on her hand. "An enemy of mine. A Light Fae."

Her shock wasn't faked. She had thought Kiril might be wrong in who he thought had taken Rhi. But he hadn't been. She grabbed his arm with her free hand, her eyes widening. "Are you serious? You actually have a Light?"

"Why is that so surprising?"

"I've never seen a Light Fae." It wasn't a lie. "Are they as silly as we're taught?"

Balladyn studied her carefully. "I was Light."

"I know."

"I was one of their fiercest warriors, Shara. Do I look silly?"

Of all the words she could have chosen, she had to use that one. Just great. "You're Dark now. I assumed you became who you are once you came to us."

"I didn't come to this side. I was taken wounded off the battlefield," he said softly, severely.

No wonder he considered Rhi an enemy. Had she been with him when he was injured and left him to be taken by the Dark? Shara didn't want to feel sympathy for Balladyn, but she did. She cupped his face before she could think twice about it. "I'm sorry you were taken from your home."

He covered her hand so that he held each of her hands in his. "A Dark who feels compassion?"

Shara looked away, suddenly fearful of the empathy she had shown him. It wasn't what a Dark would do, should do. She pulled away from him and took several steps back. The fact that he had released her couldn't be a good sign. She fisted her hands to stop them from shaking. Associating with someone like Balladyn could either mean good things or very, very bad things.

One little comment could seal her doom.

His arms dropped to his sides. "Stubbornness, willfulness, and compassion. The first two are traits pushed for in the males, but certainly not females. Nay," he continued in a calm, smooth voice. "Females need to be compliant, subservient, and respectful."

She held his gaze while trying to figure out what he was going to do with her. He was so composed and unruffled that it set her on edge.

"You, a daughter of a high-ranking family, killed human females that were in service to your family. Why?"

Not once had she ever thought she would have to defend her actions outside of her family. Yet here she was. Was it a simple question, or was she on trial? "Does it matter?"

"It does to me," Balladyn answered and crossed his arms across his chest.

Shara had once tried to explain herself to her family, but they hadn't wanted to listen. Balladyn would be the same, she was sure of it. No matter what, she had to give him an answer.

"I was with them on the streets of Cork. I ate with them, drank with them, and kidnapped them for my family. I knew the vivacious women that they were before they were reduced to crying masses begging me to help."

"Begging?" Balladyn asked with a frown.

Shara laughed as she recalled how two of her female cousins had each held one of her arms to keep her immobile. "Didn't Farrell share that part? They made me watch. Farrell thought it would affirm what it was our family did."

"And you had never seen a Dark male take a human female before?"

"No. I knew it occurred. I just didn't realize what it would do to the females."

"So you killed them."

"Yes. Farrell wanted to kill me right then and there, but my uncle brought me before my father."

"Obviously your father disagreed with Farrell."

Shara loosened her fingers. If she were going to die, then she would do it with courage. "Is that why you kept me with you? You wanted to know everything? To see if I would screw up and prove that I wasn't a true Dark?"

A full minute passed in silence before Balladyn

dropped his arms and turned on his heel to walk to the door. "Follow me."

Her legs were shaky and her feet heavy, but she fell into step behind Balladyn. His strides were long, making her quicken her pace to remain with him. He took her downstairs below the great hall to the dungeon. Balladyn didn't stop until he stood in front of a solid metal door. Shara looked from the door to him.

"Go inside," Balladyn said in a hard voice.

So this is what was to become of her. He had said she would know when he imprisoned her. From one prison to another. She clenched her teeth when he made her open the door. Only a certified ass would make a prisoner open their own cell door.

The heavy door swung open silently. Shara peered inside the dark prison to see someone chained at the far wall. The prisoner's head hung to their chest as they were half-lying, half-sitting up.

"Meet Rhi," Balladyn said from behind her.

Shara was aghast at the sight of the Light Fae. She jerked her gaze to Balladyn. "Why did you bring me here?"

"To show you what I'll do to anyone who dares to say you're inferior."

Shara blinked, thoroughly confused. "You aren't . . . disappointed in me?"

"Quite the opposite. Most Dark go blindly quenching their needs and desires. They think of no one and nothing but themselves. You have a strong mind and a strong will to do what is right for your people."

Why then did she want to rush back to Cork so she could tell Kiril she knew where Rhi was being kept? That had nothing to do with the good of the Dark, and everything to do with . . . Kiril.

"You think instead of just acting on what is expected of you."

Shara looked back at Rhi. The Light Fae was covered in filth, her black hair hanging limply around her. At first glance, Rhi looked dead. She didn't have to ask to know that Balladyn had spent the night torturing Rhi. Was that what was needed to turn a Light to the Dark side? Is that what had happened to him?

"Do you remember being Light?" she whispered.

"It's like it happened to another person, but I do retain some memories."

"How do you turn a Light to Dark?" She really didn't want to know, but she had to have the information. For herself and for Kiril.

"Torture is always a good start. It takes decades, and sometimes centuries for a Light to turn."

Shara closed her eyes. Balladyn said it with such matter-of-factness that she didn't doubt him. "And no Light can withstand this torture?"

"It's not just the torture. We get in their heads and learn what they care about the most. Then we use it against them."

"Who does Rhi care about the most?"

"Her Dragon King lover."

Shara's eyes snapped open. So it was true. She looked at Balladyn. "Why are you the one with Rhi? Why doesn't Taraeth have her?"

"Because I want my revenge," Balladyn said through clenched teeth.

She took a step back and ran into the door. She knew she should leave well enough alone, and yet she asked, "For what?"

"She was my friend, the only family I had. She left me on that battlefield to be found by Taraeth."

"Do the Dragon Kings know you have her?"

"I doubt they'll care. Her lover left her," Balladyn said with a triumphant grin. "They don't care about her no matter what she might hope for."

Shara looked at Rhi again. If only Balladyn knew the truth he wouldn't be so cavalier. Shara had seen the look in Kiril's shamrock green eyes. He would find Rhi. What she wouldn't do to have someone feel that way about her.

Balladyn suddenly took her hand, turning her attention back to him. "I want you as mine, Shara. I want you to rule this fortress beside me."

He was offering exactly what she had hoped for, and yet she was finding it difficult to say yes. Thankfully, he didn't give her a chance to answer.

"It starts tonight," he said and pulled her out of the cell to close the door. He had his hand on her back as he guided her out of the dungeons.

"What starts tonight?"

"Us seen together."

Together? Hadn't they already been seen by everyone in his compound? And then it hit her. "Seen where?"

"I thought it was time I visited *an Doras*."

"Farrell will be there," she said as she reached the top step and walked down the long corridor to enter the great hall.

Balladyn chuckled and wrapped his arm around her. "Exactly. I think it's time he and I had words. He needs to know it won't be him who captures the Dragon King in Cork. It'll be me."

CHAPTER
SEVENTEEN

Kiril had no trouble finding the exclusive residential community on the outskirts of Cork's city center. He drove through the neighborhood until he found the address.

The white house was three stories and had sweeping views of the countryside with the River Lee edging the back gardens. It was grand and imposing. Exactly the type of house a Dark would occupy.

He parked the car in the drive and stared at the house for a moment. Kiril half expected Farrell to come rushing out demanding that he leave. The quiet belied the evil that resided within the house.

Kiril walked to the front door as the last light of the day faded. He didn't have to wait long after his knock. A female Dark in a black dress and white apron opened the door. The image she presented was so stereotypical that Kiril had to fight not to laugh.

"Yes?" she asked haughtily.

"I'm here to see Mr. Blackwood."

"He's not in," she said and tried to close the door.

Kiril stuck his foot in to stop the door from slamming

in his face. "He's going to want to hear what I have to say. Get him. Now."

She glared at him with red eyes before she looked down at his foot. "I'm not letting you in. Move your foot so I can close the door while I find him."

He removed his foot. A heartbeat later the door shut. Kiril stared at the black door. If he had to, he would break it down to get their attention.

As the minutes stretched on, he was getting ready to do just that when the door opened again. A male with short silver hair combed back stood in the doorway regarding him with narrowed red eyes. He wore a thin black sweater with the sleeves pushed up over his elbows and khaki pants.

By the absence of black in his hair, Kiril guessed the Dark to be several thousand years old. Just a drop in the bucket of the years Kiril had walked the Earth.

"How did you find me?" Blackwood demanded.

Kiril lifted his shoulders with indifference. "Does it really matter?"

"It does. They'll be taken care of," Shara's father said coldly. "Just as you will be."

Kiril narrowed his gaze on the man. He held the youth and beauty of a Fae, but evil left marks that couldn't be hidden like the silver hair and the fading radiance of a Fae. "I doona take kindly to threats."

"It's not a threat."

"You want to do this here?" Kiril asked and swept his arm to indicate the quiet neighborhood. "Amid all the proper humans? I'll be happy to."

The Dark crossed his arms over his chest, his nostrils flaring. "What do you want?"

"Shara."

"So she did get to you," he stated with a triumphant grin.

"I want to see her."

"She's not here."

Kiril bristled at the icy tone. As much as he wanted to see Shara, it wasn't why he had really come. Nor did he believe Blackwood would send Shara out if she were home.

"Is that all?" Blackwood asked with a snort. "You came here begging for my daughter like a lovesick fool?"

Kiril merely smiled. "Nay. I came for something else entirely. I just wanted to see if Shara was about."

"And what might that be, Dragon King?"

"The games Farrell are playing are getting old. If he wants to attempt to capture me, tell him to get on with it."

Blackwood dropped his arms and stepped out of the house. "You have some nerve coming to my home and threatening me."

Kiril laughed and shook his head. "Ah, the thought process of a Dark never gets old. And just so we're clear, that isna a threat."

He turned on his heel and walked to his car. Kiril wished the arse would try to take him then, but nothing happened. He got into his car and drove away with Blackwood still standing in the doorway.

Kiril hoped Phelan remembered his words of caution from earlier. There wasn't enough time to warn him now. His actions weren't the smartest thing, but he was tired of waiting. He needed action and a response.

And he refused to leave Ireland without some idea of where Rhi was. No matter what Con said.

Kiril wouldn't be captured. He had no woman they could use against him, because though he hungered for Shara, she was one of theirs. They wouldn't harm her.

He had nothing to lose and everything to gain. It was why his plan was going to work so perfectly. The words exchanged with Blackwood would put things into motion.

Farrell was greedy and wanted the recognition for being the one to catch a Dragon King.

As for Shara . . . her actions would prove her innocence or guilt with her family.

Kiril drove into Cork and parked. He closed the roof before he walked into the steakhouse. He sat at the bar and ordered a pinot noir as he waited for his table. His glass was barely half empty when he was seated at a secluded booth in a corner.

He lifted the menu to look at it when someone slid into the seat opposite him. Kiril lowered the menu to see none other than Farrell.

"You want a war, Dragon King?" Farrell leaned over the table and spoke through tight lips. "I'll give you one."

"The Dark already began the war, imbecile. Had you no' been playing at leading, you might know that."

Farrell's left eye began to twitch at the corner. "Playing? You think I've been playing?"

"Some are born to lead. Others to follow. I've known what you've been about since the first time I met you."

"Liar."

Kiril leaned back and rested one arm on the back-side of the bench. "Your skills at deception are in need of work."

"You don't know everything," Farrell said with a smirk.

Kiril wondered if he had ever been so young and stupid. "You mean Shara? I saw through her glamour immediately."

"Liar." There was little heat in his voice, just wariness.

Kiril rolled his eyes. "Come up with another word."

"You brought her to your house. You asked for her today."

"All to make you think she had gotten to me. Shara is beautiful. For a Dark. But she didna seduce me."

Kiril hoped Farrell bought the lie, because it sat like

acid on his tongue. If they knew how deeply Shara had wormed her way into his psyche, they would be more than willing to use it against him.

Farrell stared at him as the minutes stretched by. "I promised my father that I'd capture you, and I don't give a vow I can't keep."

"You willna keep this one."

"We'll see about that," he said and left the restaurant.

Kiril was finally left alone to eat his meal. Or so he thought. He was nearly done with the steak when he caught sight of a Dark standing outside the restaurant waiting for him. Kiril rose and walked to the kitchen where he handed his waiter a wad of money.

"Sir?" the waiter asked in confusion.

Kiril nodded to the money. "That's for the meal, with a hefty tip. I need the back exit."

The waiter pocketed the money. "Right this way."

Kiril followed the man, palming the push dagger in his pocket. He gave a nod of thanks to the waiter as he walked through the back exit and softly closed the door when he spotted a Dark lounging against the corner of the building.

He walked up behind the Dark and plunged the dagger into his neck. The need for battle sat heavily on his chest, making Kiril long to shift and take to the sky, billowing ice and fire.

There would be no shifting, no air rushing along his scales. There was only darkness and evil, only rage and death. The Dark thought they could defeat the Kings. If Kiril had to take them out one at a time, he would prove that the Kings wouldn't be defeated.

Kiril walked toward the front of the restaurant. He was nearly upon his foe when the Dark turned and saw him. The Dark instantly sent a ball of magic straight at Kiril, causing him to dive to the side. He came up on his knee as the dagger flew from his hand and embedded in the Dark's chest.

He looked around, waiting for more Dark to attack. Kiril stood and retrieved his dagger, ducking into the shadows as humans came rushing out of the steakhouse at the sight of the dead Dark.

Shara smoothed her hands down the black gown that molded to her body like a second skin. The front draped becomingly at her breasts, showing just a hint of décolletage. Her hair was piled at the back of her head and fell in long, loose curls around her.

She looked in the mirror once more to check her makeup when she spotted Balladyn gazing at her in the mirror. Shara turned, surprised to see him since she hadn't heard him enter.

Balladyn pushed away from the doorway and nodded in approval. "You look gorgeous."

"Thank you for the dress," she said, still nervous about being seen with him. It would cause an uproar in her family, but that's not what she worried about.

It was Kiril. What if he was at the pub as he always was? Would she be able to ignore him, to pretend she didn't know what his kisses tasted like, that she didn't know how good it felt to have him deep within her?

Balladyn's smile grew. "My pleasure. I enjoy giving you things."

He had also changed into a black silk button-down shirt and black slacks. His hair was once more left down with only braids at his temples pulled back to keep it out of his eyes.

"Ready?"

He wanted a strong woman, so she couldn't falter now no matter how frightened she was of the outcome. "Yes."

She accepted his arm and walked from his chamber at

his side. As soon as they descended into the great hall, Shara noticed that the cages filled with the humans were gone as were all the Dark lounging about. Dark soldiers—both male and female—filled the hall now.

"They're for when the Dragon King is brought here. I'm not taking any chances," Balladyn said.

"And Taraeth can't afford to have another King escape his clutches."

Balladyn gave a slight nod as they walked through the great hall and ten soldiers fell into step behind them. "There is that as well."

"I don't advise taking your men into the pub," she said and glanced at them over her shoulder. "Farrell will attack you immediately."

"I didn't think your brother was that dumb."

"He's not usually, but he considers the pub his domain."

"It's about to be mine," Balladyn stated as they reached the Fae door that would take them into the middle of Cork.

Shara took a deep breath and stepped through the doorway. Balladyn's fortress faded as the sights and sounds of Cork filled her senses. The sun had set and the streetlights chased away the shadows. The pub was only a couple of streets over. She stood still while Balladyn directed his men to split up and surround *an Doras*.

While she walked with Balladyn to *an Doras,* her gaze darted about, hoping she didn't see Kiril and wishing like hell that she did. Her heart thumped in her chest the closer they came to the pub. All she had wanted was to fit in with her family, but she learned too late that they wanted her to be something she wasn't—something she couldn't be.

They would never accept her for who she was, and nothing she did to prove her worthiness would be enough for them. It left a bitter taste in her mouth. Was it her love for her family that had blinded her to the truth?

More importantly, why couldn't she have realized this when she was with Kiril?

Balladyn didn't slow his steps as he reached the pub door. The Dark standing guard tripped over his feet to open the door for them. Everyone knew Balladyn and his reputation. No one dared to go against him in anything.

How this would infuriate Farrell.

Shara couldn't wait to see the outcome. She raised her chin as they stepped inside the pub. The place went deathly quiet except for the music playing as talk ceased and all heads turned to them.

Balladyn merely smiled and guided her to the bar. He pulled out a chair for her and ordered them drinks. Shara didn't want the wine he ordered for her, but he hadn't asked her opinion.

He'd picked out the dress, told her how she would wear her hair, and ordered her drink. Was this a clue to how her life would be from now on? He wanted a woman who knew her mind, and she was going to give it to him.

Shara pushed the wineglass back to the bartender. "I'll have a whisky."

Balladyn's eyes crinkled at the corners as he grinned at her before the smile faded and he looked around the pub.

Her glass of whisky was set in front of her by a fearful bartender who kept looking at Balladyn. Everyone who worked at the pub was Dark. The only humans were the ones who dared to come in for a drink.

Balladyn glanced at her as he leaned one arm on the bar and kept the other on the back of her chair, caging her in. He winked at her, ignoring the bartender. The conversation throughout the pub gradually picked up again.

It didn't take long for the news to reach Farrell in his office at the back. He threw open the door and met her gaze. There was a subtle shift in Balladyn when he took notice of Farrell.

Her brother strode angrily to her. Farrell nodded at Balladyn before he turned his red gaze to her. "Where have you been?"

"That's none of your business," Balladyn stated and took a sip of his whisky. "She doesn't answer to you."

The muscle in Farrell's temple twitched, signaling his fury. "She's my sister. It's my business."

"Not anymore," Balladyn said calmly. "She'll no longer answer to you or anyone else in her family. She's mine."

CHAPTER
EIGHTEEN

Not two blocks from the steakhouse, Kiril found three Dark trailing him. It had taken over an hour, but with some help from a group of college students and a change of clothes he managed to get far enough away that they never saw him jump to the roof of a building.

Kiril remained there long enough to determine that they didn't know where he was. From there he made his way to *an Doras*. He smiled when he spotted them gathering outside *an Doras* talking hurriedly, their hands moving agitatedly as they spoke.

It never occurred to the idiots that he might show up at the pub. A few seconds later and the three split up again. None wanted to tell Farrell that they had lost him.

Kiril remained in the seclusion of the shadows in a narrow alley between two buildings, giving him a perfect view of the door of *an Doras* so he could see who was coming and going.

The sheer number of humans, especially females, who entered the club boggled his mind. As a Dragon King, he was sworn to protect mankind, but how could he when they could be so incredibly stupid?

Didn't they sense the evil of the pub? Didn't they notice how few females walked out of the pub unchanged in some way? Didn't they think the red eyes weird?

It was times like these that made Kiril think Ulrik was right in wanting to wipe out the human race. They hadn't wanted the protection of the Dragon Kings, had instead sought to kill the dragons.

And yet, time after time across the millennia, the Dragon Kings had kept the Earth safe and the humans from knowing the horrors that existed on other realms.

The Kings did it while hiding who they really were. If the humans discovered everything there would be few who thanked the Dragon Kings. Those few would be outnumbered by those wanting to kill or enslave the Kings, and still others who wanted to dissect them.

It made Kiril sick. To know the Dragon Kings had gone to such lengths—including sending their own dragons away—for the humans made him want to hit something. No human would ever understand what it had done to each Dragon King to watch the dragons fly through the Dragon Bridge to another realm.

There was a piece missing from each King, and had been since the dragons left. It was a piece that would remain lost until the Kings were reunited with the dragons. And that would never happen on Earth as long as the humans inhabited it.

Kiril didn't hate humans. He felt nothing for them. The only ones he could tolerate were the females who had mated with other Dragon Kings.

Cassie, Elena, Jane, Denae, and Sammi were different than other humans. Their compassion was immense, their minds open to possibilities, and more than anything, each had risked her life for a Dragon King.

There wouldn't be such a human female for him. Kiril knew it in the very depths of his soul. Other Dragon Kings like Rhys sought out the females for nothing more than to relieve their bodies, but Kiril was perfectly content to never have one in his bed.

His gaze sharpened on the pub when a Dark couple rushed out of the building, looking over their shoulders as they did. Just what was going on inside? Kiril intended to make his entrance eventually, and he was thinking the time was about right.

The sound of high-heeled shoes on the cobblestones pulled his attention from the pub. A woman with red hair in tight curls and a blue dress that barely covered her ass approached in a drunken stumble. He thought she might pass him by, because no one could see that deeply into the shadows. Yet the woman came straight to him.

"There you are," she practically purred in a thick Irish accent. When she reached him, she rubbed her body against his side, her hands everywhere.

Kiril kept his arms at his sides and turned his head away. She would go away as soon as she realized he wanted nothing to do with her. "I think you have the wrong man."

"I'm sure I don't."

He looked down at her to find that though her voice and actions were seductive, her gaze was sober and direct. "You found me. What do you want?"

"To give you a message." She pulled his head down and kissed him.

The kiss was nice, but nothing that stirred him as Shara's had. Kiril didn't pull back as he let her lead the kiss. Everything so far had been for show by the human. He suspected the kiss was as well. Either way, his concentration on what was going on around him didn't wane.

She ended the kiss and wrapped her arms tightly about his neck so her mouth was even with his ear. "Phelan says Balladyn is inside."

"How interesting." He tried to pull back, but she held tight.

"That's not all. Balladyn isn't alone. Shara is with him."

Kiril's gaze jerked to the door of *an Doras*. Balladyn and Shara? Is that where she'd been? With that bastard?

The woman released him and stepped back. "That's all I have."

"Thank you. I suggest you get out of the city tonight."

"I don't know what's going on, but I see you looking at *an Doras*. I wouldn't suggest going inside. That place is . . . wrong. Two of my friends went in. One we've never seen again, and that's been six months ago. The other isn't the same person she once was."

"Why remain here then?"

She shrugged and hugged herself. "I stop as many people from going in as I can. I just thought I should warn you."

Kiril considered the woman for a moment. Here was a human risking her life by urging others not to enter the pub. "If those running *an Doras* discover what you're doing, they're liable to kill you."

"I know."

"And you're willing to risk it? Why?"

"Others should know. My friends didn't, and look what happened to them. Maybe if someone had warned them they wouldn't have gone into that place."

If the Dark weren't in Ireland, the woman wouldn't feel the need to risk her life every day to save others. The Dark. They were a plague that had been allowed to breed in Ireland unchecked.

"I'm sorry," Kiril said.

The woman cocked her head to the side, her curls shifting with her. "For what?"

"For letting evil multiply."

"Evil is evil. It's everywhere. It's not your fault."

How wrong she was. The blame lay with every Dragon King. The Fae Wars had gone on for thousands of years, and when the Dark and Light Fae finally admitted defeat and signed the treaty, the Kings had just wanted to get back to days that didn't involve constant fighting.

Their apathy allowed the Dark to remain in Ireland, trusting the fiends to abide by the treaty. The Light had to some extent, but not the Dark. They always tried to find a way around things.

Kiril grabbed the woman's arm when she went to turn around. "Go home tonight. Trust me. You doona want to be here."

"Perhaps you should go home as well?"

"Oh I am. Verra soon."

She smiled and slumped over as she stumbled drunkenly out of the alley, her act once more in place.

Kiril shook with rage. He had told Shara about Balladyn, had told her it was the Dark who took Rhi. She hadn't said she didn't know him. In fact, she had admitted to knowing who Balladyn was. He began to suspect that Shara had played him more than he'd realized. And damn it all, he still craved her touch.

Still longed to hold her.

Still hungered to fill her body.

"I heard Balladyn is in there," a Dark male said as he rushed past the alley where Kiril hid.

A second Dark with him rubbed his hands together. "In Farrell's place? This should be interesting. I never thought Farrell would be a good leader for us."

The first punched the second in the arm. "Don't be stupid and say those things out loud. The Blackwood family has a lot of allies."

"And a lot of enemies."

They two continued their conversation, but they were

too far away for Kiril to hear the rest. It seemed that Balladyn's appearance was causing quite the stir. Dark Fae from all over Cork were coming to *an Doras.*

"Oh, please let it be him," said a whiney female voice coming closer with every word.

Kiril remained still as he focused on the conversation.

"It is," said another female, with a husky voice. "I know it. He's going to be mine."

A third snorted. "I heard he's found his woman."

"Who?" demanded the second as they walked past the alley.

The first smiled excitedly. "Yes, who?"

"Farrell's sister, Shara," stated the third.

Kiril stopped listening. He wanted to rip something apart, to shift into dragon form and let loose a ball of fire right at the pub. So what if Shara was with Balladyn? He'd had one night with her. It hadn't meant anything.

Liar.

"My father hasn't given permission," Farrell told Balladyn. "He's head of the family and ultimately decides who Shara will marry. It won't be you."

Shara sipped her whisky. For the first time, she knew Farrell wasn't going to win. And neither was her father. It was hard not to contain her joy or the smile that threatened. Would they feel as helpless as she had? Would they know the futile fury that nestled like a cold mass in their gut? She hoped so, especially when it came to Farrell. He was a weasel, a bastard of the first order.

"Is that right?" Balladyn said and faced Farrell. "You think you're someone important because of your family."

Farrell gloated, his smile cruel. "I know I am. No one goes against a Blackwood."

"And who is Taraeth's right hand? Who commands the respect of the Dark army? Who is undefeated?"

"That will change soon enough," Farrell stated confidently.

Balladyn grinned, but it didn't reach his eyes. In the short amount of time Shara had been with him, she knew it was a sign that he had almost reached his limit. Her brother, the dumbass, didn't know that.

Farrell thumbed his nose at her. "Besides, I thought after what I told you about her that you would know enough to stay away. It's a matter of time before I get to kill her."

"How many others have you told your family's secret to?" Balladyn asked in a quiet voice, belying the fury she could sense.

Farrell shrugged, uncaring that he was treading on thin ice.

Balladyn closed the small distance between them until he was glaring down at Farrell. "How. Many?"

"Enough to make sure that stupid bitch is forever alone."

The whisky glass slipped from her numb fingers to shatter on the floor. Her secret that was never supposed to leave the family had been bandied about all over Cork. Shara felt sick.

But she was also furious.

"You gave your word to Father," she told Farrell. "You betrayed him, me, and the entire family."

Farrell roughly grabbed her arm and dragged her out of the chair yelling, "He should've let me kill you!"

Whatever else he was going to say was cut off when Balladyn slammed a fist into his jaw. Farrell crashed to the ground, pulling her with him since he still had ahold of her arm.

Balladyn gently pulled her up and sat her in the chair. Then he turned back to Farrell. "As Shara said, you've betrayed your family. That is unforgiveable for a Dark."

Farrell was holding his jaw as he leaned up on one elbow, blood seeping from his busted lip. "It's accepted when it's deserved."

"And you thinking you could capture a Dragon King all by yourself?"

At that, Farrell climbed to his feet. "I will succeed. I was gaining ground."

"By having drinks with him?"

"Shara was seducing him."

She wanted to kick Farrell in the balls. Didn't he ever know when to keep his mouth shut?

Balladyn's gaze slowly turned to her. There was murder in his eyes—for her.

CHAPTER
NINETEEN

"You know this Dragon King?" Balladyn asked in a frosty tone that threatened to suck all of Shara's courage from her.

She refused to cower to Balladyn. He could kill her with one blast of magic. How could she have even *considered* him her salvation?

"Yes," she answered.

Balladyn faced her, his red gaze promising pain for her omission. He lowered his chin, his lips pulled back in a vicious sneer. "Who is he?"

Shara parted her lips, her mind rushing with options when Farrell chuckled loudly. Balladyn's gaze slid to him, a dangerous glint in his eyes.

Farrell leaned on the bar behind Shara's chair grinning like a cat that had gotten into the cream. "The bitch knows to keep her mouth shut. The Dragon King is ours to take."

For once Shara was grateful for Farrell's arrogance and brazenness. Everyone's gaze in the pub was on Balladyn. He grabbed Farrell and jerked him back, only to slam him against the bar.

Magic swirled around Balladyn as he gathered it in one of his hands. "I think it's time you and I came to an understanding, Farrell. My understanding."

Shara jumped when the first round of magic hit Farrell in the stomach. He screamed, his eyes squeezed shut against the pain. A few brave Dark snuck out of the pub and made a run for it while others remained transfixed with either grins or masks of fear as they watched Balladyn.

Shara used the opportunity to slide off the bar stool and slowly move away. Any moment now, Balladyn's men would come into the pub, and she wanted to be long gone by then.

She reached the end of the bar without Balladyn noticing her. Another two steps and she turned the corner out of his sight. She didn't wait another second to teleport out of the pub.

Shara appeared on the docks. She cringed when she was immediately soaked in the pouring rain. A glance around showed she was thankfully alone. She wrapped her arms around herself and was about to disappear again when she realized she had nowhere to go.

Wherever she went, Balladyn or someone from her family would find her. She just wanted a few minutes to herself to think without worrying about who was going to do her harm.

And then she remembered there was one place she could go, one place where she felt safe and secure.

Kiril was irritated that his plan to confront Farrell in the pub had come to a screeching halt. He wouldn't mind confronting Balladyn as well, but he wasn't the reckless kind to go busting into the building and face all those Dark alone.

No, that was something Rhys would do.

Kiril heard the crackle of thunder just before the skies

opened up and drenched everything in sight. Dark came rushing out of *an Doras* as if something were coming for them. A heartbeat later, Kiril heard the screams within.

It was time to reevaluate his plan. Facing Farrell or Balladyn was one thing, but if he walked into the pub with both of them together then they would join forces against him. Kiril refused to be locked away in any type of Dark prison. He wouldn't let it happen, which meant he had to go about things differently.

"It's time to leave," Phelan's voice reached him from behind.

Kiril didn't bother to turn around. "Because Balladyn is in there."

"Because you are many things, Kiril, but no' a fool. Balladyn came to teach Farrell a lesson. That's who is screaming."

"Good. I never liked that arse anyway. By the way, how did you know it was Shara with Balladyn? You've never seen her."

"I'm smart like that," came the cocky reply.

"So she's with Balladyn." The idea still rankled him, like rubbing salt in a wound.

"Forget her. If you try to get to her, you'll only end up in one of their dungeons."

"No' going to happen."

"Good. Now get out of here. I'm soaked and in need of something besides the nasty Irish whisky."

Kiril waited a few more moments in the rain, hoping to catch a glimpse of Shara. He just needed to know that she was all right. When that didn't happen, he turned on his heel and strode to his car.

It had taken all day to find the address of Shara's home, but the result had been exactly what he wanted. However, the final bit of his plans dissolved like sugar in the rain. He was ready for a glass of Dreagan whisky and another night in dragon form in the cellar when he drove through the gates of his estate.

More Dark were watching the house, which meant he would have to take time tomorrow to lose them in the streets of Cork once more, but he liked the challenge. As well as making them look stupid.

He walked into the house and immediately recognized that he wasn't alone. Shara's scent was strong, filling him with need so overwhelming he was drowning in it.

Kiril tossed his keys on the table and quietly closed the door. He walked to the left and reached in the dark to wrap his hands around her throat. She gasped and grabbed his arm, her shoes dropping from her fingers as he dragged her into the entryway.

"I thought you'd found a new man. Was Balladyn lacking in bed somehow?"

She opened her mouth, but he squeezed her throat to keep her from talking. Her midnight hair hung in damp strands around her with some stuck to the side of her face. The black dress clung to her body as water beaded along her skin.

"I doona want to hear anything you have to say," he ground out. "I held out hope that you were something other than you are, but you gave me all the answers I needed tonight."

Her eyes silently beseeched him to listen to her, but Kiril was beyond that. He was angry—at himself and her—for falling for her. He had been prepared to take her to Dreagan with him, and damn whatever consequences followed.

Yet she'd betrayed his trust, disdained his offering.

Scorned his affections.

The fact that he'd dared to help a Dark was something that would remain with him for all eternity. Shara had reminded him that none could be trusted, that the Dark were evil to their very core.

Some were just better at hiding it than others.

"Kiril," she squeaked.

He squeezed harder, but dammit, he found he couldn't harm her more than that. No matter how much he wanted to hit something, it wouldn't be Shara.

"Rhi," she wheezed.

Kiril instantly loosened his grip, his anger dissipating. "What about Rhi?"

Shara coughed and sucked in huge breaths, but she held his gaze. "I saw her," she whispered.

He briefly closed his eyes before he released Shara and turned his back to her. Looking at her hurt too much. He remembered the taste of her lips, the feel of her smooth skin, the heat of her sex clamping around his cock.

Why couldn't he forget her as he had every other woman that he'd had sex with? The simple truth was that Shara was different from any other female across all time. Her fake innocence and passion had caught him more securely than any kind of trap.

"Rhi. Where is she?" he demanded.

"Balladyn has her in his fortress."

"How do I get there?"

There was a pause. "I don't think you can."

Kiril should have known she would try some kind of trick. He laughed hoarsely. "Of course no'."

"You don't understand," she said hurriedly.

How he had missed the sound of her sweet Irish accent. Kiril took a step away from her, but turned to face her. "Explain it."

"I went through a Fae door in my family's garden. Balladyn's fortress is hidden. There is another doorway near the pub, but it's heavily guarded in Balladyn's compound. I don't know of any other way to reach it."

"Then take me through the doorway that you do know."

"Are you insane?" she asked, her voice rising. "If I

bring you to my family's home, they'll try to take you captive."

"The operative word there is *try,* sweetheart."

"Kiril, please."

He braced himself as she came closer. She licked her lips, her arms wrapped around her middle. Her back was hunched a little and she looked frightened. Good. She should be afraid of him after what she had done. It was all a ruse on his part though. As cunning as she was, she would most likely discover very soon that he wouldn't—couldn't—hurt her.

"Every Dark is going to be hunting you by morning. If Farrell survives Balladyn's attack, then he will come here himself. You must leave."

He raised a brow. "If you think I'm going to let a Dark—any Dark—take me as a prisoner, then you doona know me at all."

"I know you," she said softly. "I know you're an honorable male who is trying to save your friend. Balladyn brought me to her cell. I saw the form that was Rhi. She's . . . broken, Kiril. No Light can survive what the Dark do to them. Think of yourself and the other Dragon Kings and return to Scotland."

"I'll leave soon enough, but no' without Rhi."

"You'll never get to her," Shara said with a small shake of her head.

Kiril advanced on her, making her backpedal quickly. "Do you forget who you're talking to, Dark? I'm a Dragon King. I've been alive since the dawn of time. We were the ones who won the Fae Wars. We've been the ones protecting this realm. We're the biggest badasses around. Perhaps the Dark need reminding of that fact."

"I know."

"Nay. You doona. Tell me, when is the last time you saw a King in dragon form?"

She swallowed loudly and whispered, "Never."

"Shall I show you?"

"You do and they'll come for you in an instant." She straightened her spine and lifted her chin. "Be angry at me, but think. You want to hurt me, then do it, but don't be foolish."

Her words helped to cool his growing ire. There was something about Shara that made him protective, obsessive even. Yet, with a touch or a word she could calm him—or send his desires into overdrive.

She dropped her arms to her sides. "Balladyn has an entire army at his disposal. They're waiting at his fortress for when he brings you. He didn't tell me specifics, but . . . he's put things in place to ensure that the next Dragon King he captures doesn't escape."

"How many men does he have?"

"Hundreds. Thousands," she said with a shrug. "I only got a glimpse. I didn't have time to count."

He walked around her to the front room and poured himself a glass of Dreagan whisky. Kiril didn't have to look to know that Shara followed him into the room, though she only stood at the doorway.

"Why are you telling me this?" he asked.

"What Balladyn is doing to Rhi . . . it's not right. No one should have to suffer that way."

"And yet you tell me that I should leave her."

"Because she's lost to everyone."

"She's a friend. We doona leave friends behind no matter what."

"Rhi is very lucky then."

Kiril turned to face Shara. "So, what sort of trap have you set for me?"

CHAPTER TWENTY

Shara couldn't believe the difference in Kiril. He wasn't the same charming man as before. The undercurrent of danger was still there, but a deadly thread had been added to it. It saddened her, but at the same time she couldn't blame him. She was the enemy. He thought she had deceived him, and in some ways she had.

"I don't know of a trap."

His smile didn't reach his eyes. "I'm supposed to believe you?"

"Believe what you want. I came to tell you about Rhi because . . . well, I don't really know why. If you happen to find your way to Balladyn's compound, he will capture you."

"And you'll be standing beside him, I suppose? Do you often jump from one man's bed to another?"

His words stung so badly that she wanted to lash out verbally and physically. It was the absence of his smile and smooth seduction that froze her, keeping her immobile as her heart hammered against her ribs.

"No," she answered simply when she finally found her

voice. "Regardless of what you think, I didn't share Balladyn's bed. He wanted me there, and for a short period I considered him as a means to get away from my family."

"I suppose that's why he attacked Farrell?" Kiril asked casually before taking a drink of the whisky.

She watched the deep gold liquid tilt in the glass before flowing past his lips. Her gaze traveled to his throat to see him swallow. She lifted her gaze to find him watching her coolly.

Shara had known coming to him was going to be a mistake. She couldn't think straight around him. He was purely male, utterly sexual. And for one brief moment in time, he had been hers.

Everything she had done after that had pushed him away. Fear of being without her family, and worry of trying to fit in with the Dragon Kings had stopped any thoughts of a future with Kiril.

Knowing what she did now, she would change every decision she had made. Yet there was no going back. She had put herself in this predicament, and she would get herself out of it. Somehow.

"He attacked Farrell because Farrell was going after you."

Kiril lifted one shoulder in a shrug. "I can see that. Balladyn doesna want his position threatened by anyone, least of all by one of the most powerful families in the Dark world. It still doesna explain why you're here. You could've left me a message about Rhi. By the fact your clothes are no longer soaked, you had to have waited here quite awhile for me."

"I did," she admitted. "I left the pub right after Farrell told Balladyn that I knew you."

Kiril raised his glass. "Ah. So you deceived the great Balladyn as well. You're running out of men, Shara."

"I didn't tell him about you because I knew he would force me to help him get to you."

Kiril threw his glass against the wall, his thunderous expression darkening his face as the crystal shattered. "No one can make you do anything you doona want to do! Quit using that as an excuse!"

"Fine!" she shouted in return. "I'll tell you the truth. I flirted with him because I thought he could be my way out from beneath my family. I have to marry anyway, and I knew Balladyn was the only one my father couldn't say no to. I was using him. Is that what you wanted to hear?"

"Finally, the truth."

Shara slapped her hands against her legs and blew out a frustrated breath. "You want more truth? I came here to see you one last time. Are you satisfied, damn you?"

She gasped as he was suddenly before her, slamming her against the wall with her hands held over her head by one of his and his hard body covering hers. His face was breaths from hers, the anger gone from his gaze, replaced with desire.

"Say it again," he whispered savagely.

Her breaths were coming faster, her chest rising erratically. But she had never felt such passion burning through her veins. "I wanted to see you."

He searched her gaze, and as always with Kiril, she found herself opening to him. There was nothing she could hide from him, nothing she *wanted* to hide from him.

His head lowered, and when he paused she lifted her face trying to reach him to get another of his searing kisses. Yet he pulled his head back. She stared at him, trying to decipher what it was he wanted from her.

He wasn't even attempting to hide the desire sparking his green eyes. Water beaded at the ends of his long hair before dropping onto his shoulders, soaking into the material of his jacket.

Shara tried to lean against him, needing to feel more of his body, but once more he didn't allow it. She had never wanted someone so much only to have them push her away. What she didn't understand was why? He desired her.

Suddenly he released her arms and took a step back. She slowly lowered her arms to her sides, confounded that he hadn't made another move to kiss or touch her.

Shara was swiftly losing her confidence. Her emotions had been on a roller coaster since they'd made love. Arriving tonight, she had been uncertain, but sure that she had to tell him what she knew.

Then he pushed her against the wall with passion burning so bright he was on fire with it. Except . . . he then released her. Was she wrong about the attraction between them? Perhaps she wasn't the one doing the seducing. She might have been the one seduced and tricked.

No. She refused to believe that. Kiril was different from a Dark Fae. He wouldn't demean himself with such tactics when he had other ways of getting what he wanted.

Doubt, however, lingered and grew in her mind.

"Leave," Kiril said in his deep voice, the desire banked and causing his face to be emotionless and cold as stone.

Leave? Was he insane? Where would she go? She couldn't go home and couldn't return to Balladyn. Ah, but he knew that.

And didn't care.

How could she have been so wrong about Kiril? She scooted along the wall away from him until she moved into the entryway. It wasn't until she took another step back that she saw his expression shift again.

His green eyes sparked once more, his gaze . . . ravenous.

"Doona do it, Shara. Doona run," he whispered.

She glanced down at his hands to see them fisted at his sides, his body practically vibrating as he fought to remain in place. Desire coiled deliciously through her.

With just a thought she could vanish before his eyes and reappear somewhere else thousands of miles away. But that wasn't what she wanted. She wanted Kiril—his hands, his mouth . . . his body.

She turned and ran through the house, around furniture and through doorways until she caught a glimpse of the pool through the windows.

It had stopped raining, leaving the night blanketed in almost complete darkness with the heavy layer of clouds. With the ruckus in town, Balladyn and Farrell both would have gathered their men.

Which meant no one was watching the manor.

Shara burst through the door, the humid night air sucking what little breath she had from her lungs. She started to go around the pool when strong arms wrapped around her middle and jerked her off her feet.

She had a split second to hold her breath before she hit the water. Beneath the water, Kiril unceremoniously turned her around and yanked her against him.

Her heart missed a beat when she felt his arousal against her stomach before his lips claimed hers. Shara wrapped her arms around his neck and floated beneath the cool water as she was kissed senseless by the only male who could turn her body molten with just a look.

A Dragon King.

They broke the surface, treading water, as he ended the kiss. She clung to him while he maneuvered them to the side of the pool where he trapped her between it and himself. Shara noticed that he had taken off his jacket and his shoes, leaving his white shirt to mold to his rock-hard body. She couldn't wait to run her hands over all that sinew, to feel the muscles move and bunch beneath her hands once more.

His hands roughly wrenched up her skirt as her hands fumbled with undoing his pants. He shoved them down his hips and was inside her in the next instant.

The breath left Shara in a rush. She sank her nails into his shoulders, shuddering at the feel of him filling her while she locked her ankles around his waist. How could she have even thought of allowing any other man to touch her?

As impossible as it seemed, she was Kiril's. He could play her body with masterful hands, honeyed words, and skillful lips. No one else could bring her to the edge of an orgasm with just a look.

Neither moved. He gazed at her, pleasure and ecstasy there for her to see. They were the same emotions filling her.

There were no words, because none were needed. The craving, the hunger to claim each other hung heavy between them. It spoke more clearly than words ever could.

He held onto the edge of the pool and used that for leverage as he rocked his hips. She slid a hand into his hair and buried her face in his neck. With every thrust the rhythm quickened, driving him deeper each time.

Water splashed around her. Their breaths were harsh and ragged, their bodies gliding easily against the other. Shara wanted to stop time and live in this moment for eternity.

She was so focused on remembering every second of Kiril and how he felt inside her, that the orgasm took her by surprise. She jerked, the scream locked in her throat it was so fierce.

A smile formed when she realized Kiril had climaxed with her, each feeding off the other, dragging the pleasure out until both were boneless and clinging to the other.

Perth, Scotland

Ulrik looked up from his paperwork at his desk when the Dark Fae appeared before him. He set aside his pen next to the six mobile phones, the accounting for the Silver Dragon forgotten as he focused on the Dark.

"What do you have for me?" he commanded.

The Dark smiled, his red eyes glittering with delight. "I just came from an . . . interesting . . . scene. The Dark female sent to seduce Kiril? It appears she has done just that."

Ulrik chuckled. "A Dragon King succumbing to a Dark Fae? Does he know what she is?"

"Yes."

"That is interesting, and possibly something I can use to my advantage."

The Dark clasped his hands behind his back. "There's more."

"More?" Ulrik asked with wide eyes.

The big male nodded, causing his long ruler-straight black and silver hair to move with him. "I followed the female yesterday as she visited Balladyn."

That caused Ulrik to raise a brow. The famous Light Fae warrior who had turned Dark. "And?"

"As I informed you earlier, he's the one who kidnapped Rhi."

"I know." Ulrik got to his feet and came around the front of the desk to lean his hips back against it as he crossed one ankle over the other. "Did he turn Rhi over to Taraeth as you suspected he might? Or did he keep her as I thought?"

"He's keeping her."

Ulrik took a deep breath and slowly released it. "Where is she?"

"Balladyn is holding her in his compound on the Fae realm."

"Draw every detail of this place."

The Dark Fae hesitated. "It's too late. Once a Light is taken by the Dark they're never the same."

Ulrik moved with lightning speed as he grabbed the Dark by the back of the neck and forced him to bend over the desk. "Draw!"

CHAPTER
TWENTY-ONE

Kiril stood staring out the windows of his bedroom without seeing the magnificent sunrise and the fusion of colors scattered across the sky. Any moment now he would hear Con in his mind. The question was, did he tell Constantine his plans? If he did, Con would likely come to Ireland just to ensure Kiril didn't carry them out.

He looked at the bed, still rumpled from the hours spent in it with Shara. It had been only a few minutes since she'd left, but he felt her absence keenly.

In between their bouts of toe-curling sex, he and Shara had come up with a plan. She'd be waiting for him at her family's house to let him in so he could reach the doorway to Balladyn's.

No longer did he doubt her. At least his heart didn't doubt her. His mind was another matter entirely.

Kiril sent a quick text to Phelan telling him he was headed back to Dreagan and that he should also return home. Hopefully Phelan would buy the lie, because Kiril didn't want to have Phelan's capture by the Dark on his conscience.

"Kiril?" Con's voice asked.

He sighed deeply and opened his mind to the King of Kings. "*I'm here.*"

"*Any news?*"

"*I know where Rhi is being held.*"

There was a pregnant pause before Con asked, "*Where?*"

"*In Balladyn's fortress somewhere on the Fae realm.*"

"*I feared as much,*" Con said wearily. "*It was too much to hope they had her in Ireland.*"

Kiril ran a hand over his jaw. "*Everything has gone to hell in a matter of hours. Balladyn discovered what Farrell had planned for me and stepped in.*"

"*Has Balladyn come for you?*"

"*He will soon.*"

"*Get home. Now.*"

Kiril hated lying to any of his brethren, but what he was going to do was better done alone. "*I'll be there soon.*"

"*If you're no' here by noon I'm coming for you,*" Con threatened.

"*The Dark female that was sent to seduce me? Her name is Shara. She is the one who found Rhi and told me where she's being held. If Shara comes to Dreagan, I want your word that you'll protect her.*"

"*A Dark? You want me to protect a Dark Fae?*" he asked incredulously.

"*Aye, Con, I'm asking that.*"

"*Do you love her?*"

"*I think I could love her.*"

Con blew out a harsh breath. "*Kiril, the Dark can no' be trusted.*"

"*You said the same about the Light at one time as well. And yet we've always trusted Rhi.*"

"*Rhi is different.*"

"*So is Shara. Your word, Con.*"

"*Dammit, Kiril. Please.*"

Kiril remained silent.

"*Fine,*" Con said despairingly. "*You have it.*"

"*Thank you.*"

"*You can thank me when your ugly arse gets home.*"

Kiril smiled despite himself. "*You better have that ninety-year-old bottle of Dreagan out when I do.*"

"*Consider it done. Now hurry home.*"

Kiril remained at his window long after the link between him and Con had been severed. He glanced down at the pool remembering the night. Never had a woman ever looked so good in the water.

He turned and exited his room and then descended the stairs. Soon, Dark would descend upon him. He could battle them, but they would eventually overwhelm him, and then he would find himself as their prisoner.

That couldn't happen, not if he was going to rescue Rhi.

It wasn't in Kiril's nature—or any Dragon King for that matter—to run, but he had to consider the options because more was at stake than his pride. Kiril looked around the house noting all the places the Dark would enter and surround him. There was nowhere for him to go that they wouldn't find him except for one place—the cellar.

Dragon magic kept the door hidden from everyone that wasn't a Dragon King. The Dark could search the entire house and never find him. No matter how much he wanted to battle the Dark, he was going to have to bide his time and wait until he had Rhi.

Then he would unleash hell.

Kiril walked to the hidden cellar door and entered. He put his hand on the door and infused it with more magic so that no Dark Fae magic would penetrate it. Kiril turned and descended six more steps and removed his clothes. He folded them and set them on the bottom stair before he walked to the middle of the cellar.

Any moment now the Dark would flood his home in an

attempt to find him. When they finally gave up, he would go to Shara who would lead him to the doorway to Balladyn's where he would locate and free Rhi.

It was a good, solid plan.

Why then did he have a sick feeling in the pit of his stomach that something was going to go wrong?

Shara was veiled for all of two seconds as she appeared in her bedroom. It was the longest she could remain veiled, although she knew there were a few special Fae who could stay veiled for long periods of time.

Fortunately for her, those two seconds were all she needed to know that no one was in her room. She yanked off the cold, and still damp, black dress from the night before and threw it in the corner.

She hurriedly dressed in black jeans and a sheer, billowy black shirt before she brushed out the knots in her hair. There wasn't time to put on makeup to look her absolute best, but if she was going to fool Balladyn, she had to make an attempt at looking decent.

It wasn't until she checked herself one last time in the full-length mirror that she heard the distant screams. She stilled, realizing they were coming from inside the house.

Shara slowly opened the door and stepped into the corridor. The screams were louder then. She followed the sound as she walked the hallway to the stairs leading to the first level. There were words spoken through the screams, but she couldn't make them out.

She paused when she reached the bottom. Usually the house was full of her family and extended family, but she hadn't seen a single one of them. Which meant they were all in her father's office.

Her head turned in that direction to hear another bout of agony-filled screams that came from his office. She started toward the double doors, unable to keep away. After what she had done by going to Balladyn, there was a chance they would lock her away again.

Or worse, kill her.

Still, she walked until she stood at the doors, her hand on the knob. From within she could hear a voice and recognized it as Farrell's as he begged for mercy.

A Dark Fae begging for mercy. Not even she had done that when she'd stood before her family awaiting justice.

She drew in a deep breath and flung open the doors. No longer would she try to slip anywhere unseen. She was strong and confident, and she didn't have to do evil to be either. It had taken only a few hours with Kiril for her to come to that understanding. Too bad she hadn't realized that six hundred years before.

Every head in the office swiveled to her, including Farrell's. He kneeled before their father, blood covering his face and clothes from various wounds.

She held her head high as she walked into the room. A path cleared for her leading to where her father stood with Farrell. She barely gave her father a look as she stopped beside her brother.

"How does it feel to be on trial before the family?" she asked.

He whimpered and tried to reach for her leg. Shara deftly moved aside, astounded by the crying, sniveling Dark before her.

"Please," he begged her. "Please, Shara. Tell Father what Balladyn said is a lie."

Shara laughed wryly. "You mean the part where you told others what I had done, what every Blackwood was supposed to never speak of to anyone outside of the family?"

"I didn't," Farrell wailed.

"Then how did Balladyn know of it? More importantly, why did you announce it in *an Doras* last night?

You wanted to kill me because I'm not good enough for this family. Now is your chance. *Brother.*"

"Shara," her father began.

She whipped her head around to him. "Stay out of this." She didn't wait for him to consent before she turned back to Farrell. "Well? Here's your chance. You've hit me enough times. Get to your feet and act like a real Dark."

Farrell bowed his head, his shoulders shaking as he cried harder.

"Now who's the one that doesn't belong?" she bent over and asked.

Shara was disgusted with the entire scene. She straightened and turned to walk out when her mother stepped in her path.

"Where are you going, dear?" her mother asked sweetly.

Sweet and her mother were never mixed in the same sentence. There wasn't an ounce of kindness in her mother, or forgiveness for that matter.

"None of your business," Shara stated and tried to go around her.

Her mother remained in her way. "We have a ceremony to prepare you for. Balladyn wants to claim you immediately."

Shara hid her frown. She'd expected to spend the day explaining her absence to Balladyn to cool his anger while Kiril rescued Rhi. It wasn't part of Kiril's plan, but someone had to occupy Balladyn. As soon as Kiril and Rhi were out of the compound, Shara planned to leave as well. Kiril wanted her to go to Dreagan, but she still had reservations about that. It wasn't something she was going to think about until their plans came to fruition.

"Balladyn came here last night," her mother continued in her silence. "He wants you as his immediately."

Shara just bet he did. It might have taken her awhile, but she had figured both Balladyn and her brother out.

For that matter, she had figured out her family as well. One more regret that she realized too late after having put herself in such a position.

She looked around, comprehending that it was a show everyone was playing. The "trial" Farrell was on was just for appearances. He would be dead within a few hours.

And he knew it.

Her mother's tight smile was an appearance of trying to become friendly with a daughter she had scorned now that Shara was set to be claimed by the second most powerful Dark and Taraeth's right hand.

The rest of the family was following her parents' lead.

Shara pivoted to look at her father. He watched her with eyes now filled with interest and a hint of respect. Of course he would. Balladyn wanted her, and in his mind she had to be something special to get a man such as Balladyn to stake his claim.

She wanted to roll her eyes. But she wouldn't. She would play the game with them. She had learned from the best, after all.

"The Claiming will have to wait. We have a Dragon King to find," she stated to the room at large.

Her father's eyes widened. "I thought Balladyn was going after Kiril?"

"Oh he is," Shara said with a grin. "I'll be joining him. I did all the work, after all."

Her mother's cold fingers wrapped around her wrist as she used to do when Shara was younger. It was her way of putting Shara in her place. "I don't think that's a good idea."

Shara looked down at her wrist before she lifted her gaze to her mother. She waited a heartbeat to see if her mother would release her before she purposefully, determinedly removed her mother's hand from her arm. "Don't touch me again."

Her mother took a step back, a look of fear flashing in her red eyes.

Shara turned her back on her mother and looked to her father once more. "Do you have anything else to say?"

"Will you return to us?" he asked.

She considered his words, drawing out the silence to stretch to an uncomfortable length. "I've not decided."

"We're your family, Shara," he said calmly. "It wouldn't look right if we're not with you at the Claiming. Besides, you're my only child out of nine left."

She glanced at Farrell who sat huddled in a ball. "You have other things to worry about. There were many who witnessed what Balladyn did to Farrell, and what is done to one of us is done to the family. The Blackwood family appears weak now. I'm not sure I want to be a part of such a family."

Her father frowned. "You would disown us?"

Shara turned and walked out of the room saying, "I'm considering it."

CHAPTER
TWENTY-TWO

Kiril dozed as he waited to hear the voices of the Dark above him. Hours went by with nothing, yet he lingered in the cellar. The house remained as silent as a tomb, and Kiril began to feel that it might very well end up that way for him. He closed his eyes and drifted back to his night with Shara.

Despite the wonderful hours spent holding her in his arms, nothing had changed. He knew she would never come to Dreagan with—or without—him. He knew it with the same certainty that his carefully thought-out plan was somehow going to go wrong.

He went over every detail of the plan and tried to determine where things could go wrong. The problem was there were too many places. Kiril limited Shara's involvement just in case she had a change of heart, or—even worse—Balladyn got ahold of her.

With nothing to do but wait, Kiril continued to doze while thinking of ways he wanted to take his anger out on Balladyn for what he had done to Rhi—and what he might do to Shara if Balladyn discovered she was helping him.

If Rhys were with him, Kiril knew his friend would caution him about trusting a Dark. He knew the chances, but if there was even the slightest chance that Shara really did want to help, then he had to take it.

Kiril wasn't senseless, and though his body yearned for her with a passion that couldn't be explained, he knew there was still the chance that Shara could be luring him into her well-crafted web.

It wasn't just the all-consuming desire that drew Kiril to her. It was her smile, her sharp mind, her soft touch. It was her eyes that gave away her every emotion, it was the strip of silver in her coal black hair.

It was the way she'd made him feel whole since his dragons were sent away.

Please doona let me be wrong about her.

Shara felt . . . free. It was the only word that came to mind as she stood outside of her family's home in the back garden. Never in her wildest dreams did she dare to talk to her parents as she had.

She wasn't sure what had come over her.

Yes, you do. Kiril.

There was no doubt. Kiril had changed her, and not just by the way her body reacted to him. He altered the way she thought and the way she saw things. He made her take stock of her life and how she saw her future, of how she wanted to live.

He was the one who accepted her for what she was and didn't demand anything from her or of her. He let her be herself, right or wrong. That had shown her what kind of person she could be—what kind she wanted to be.

The confidence she'd always had disappeared while locked away in her room, and somehow she had found it again in Kiril's arms. She remembered she was strong, smart, and resilient.

Shara breathed deeply, a smile on her face. Any moment now Kiril would arrive so she could take him to the doorway to Balladyn's fortress. He didn't know it yet, but she was coming with him. He would put up a fuss. In the end, however, she would get her way because he would realize he needed her.

A frisson of something cold and foreboding ran down her spine. Balladyn wasn't going to be as easy as her parents. He would have his entire army with him, but he had no idea what she had in store for him.

Like most powerful Dark, he would assume he could punish her for her so-called indiscretion. Shara wanted to laugh. As if she would allow that now. No one would ever again hold her prisoner.

Balladyn had enjoyed her spirit. She would wait for the right time and kill him. Dark like Balladyn would never think a female could hurt them. She didn't want anyone coming after her when it was all over—not Balladyn, not her family. No one.

She would be the one in control of her life. She would be the one to decide if she took a husband and who.

Shara could hardly contain her excitement for the dawning of a new era in her life, but before she was able to grasp it, she would have to put herself in peril. She was scared, but if Kiril was willing to risk his own life for Rhi, Shara would do the same to help Kiril.

It was frightening how much she was willing to do for Kiril. He had no idea the hold he had on her heart or how, without even trying, he made her see the true path she was destined to take.

"Just wait," she whispered.

"Wait for what?" asked a deep, menacing voice behind her.

Shara was frozen with shock. This wasn't the plan.

Thick fingers bit into her skin as Balladyn's hand

reached across her and clamped on her jaw. He slowly turned her until she faced him. The coldness she had glimpsed while he terrorized Farrell was now directed at her, and it iced her veins.

"I asked you a question. You will answer."

Fear kept her silent for a moment, then she remembered who she was. Shara narrowed her gaze on him. "I'm not yours yet, nor will I be if you continue this."

"According to your family, you're mine," he said and leaned close, squeezing her chin until tears burned her eyes.

Balladyn might be the right hand to Taraeth and a famed warrior. But he was just a male like every other Dark Fae who thought they could rule the females. How she loathed him. What made her ever think to use him? How stupid she'd been to think he was the answer to get out from beneath her family.

"I'm not yours until the Claiming," she said tightly, refusing to let the pain show.

He loosened his grip a fraction and pulled her against him so that his mouth was even with her ear. "You will be mine. Don't even think of fighting the inevitable."

Shara didn't think she could hate anyone as much as she hated Farrell. How wrong she had been. She envisioned lopping off Balladyn's head or cutting out his heart. Instead of telling him to go fuck himself, Shara held her tongue. One way or another she needed to buy Kiril time to get to Rhi.

Kiril was smart. He would figure out a way into Balladyn's fortress. Shara wouldn't be able to show him the doorway, but she would ensure Balladyn's attention was focused solely on her.

She jerked her head out of his grasp and raised her chin. "Convince me you're the male worthy enough for me."

"Oh, I'll convince you," he said and yanked her against him.

It was all Shara could do not to shrink away in revulsion as she felt Balladyn's arousal.

Dreagan

Lily dusted off her knees and stood from restocking the twelve-year-old Scotch, Dreagan's bestseller. She rotated her left wrist that still ached. It had been three months since the break had healed, but she feared it would always pain her.

The bones that had been snapped in half throbbed agonizingly a few hours before the rain came. It was like an early warning sign.

She glanced at the clock with the Dreagan logo of two dragons back-to-back, announcing it was well past time to end her shift. It was an early closing day for Dreagan, which meant she had the rest of the afternoon to herself. She grabbed the empty box and brought it behind the counter so Rhys or one of the others could take it to have it filled again.

There was very little wasted on Dreagan, and Lily found she liked the concept. It also helped that she could relax there. Relaxing hadn't been something she'd thought she would ever do again.

With all the tourists gone for the day, she filled a pail with water and headed through the open door outside to water the rosebushes set in huge clay pots on either side of the door.

Lily watered the first bush and leaned in to smell the fragrant creamy orange blossom. She turned to the second pot when she stilled as she caught sight of Rhys.

He was dressed in black jeans that looked light gray on the thigh as if they had been sanded. His button-down shirt was white and the sleeves were rolled up to his elbows. The back of the shirt had black wings embroidered and spread across his wide shoulders. The ensemble was completed with black boots, a black leather cuff at his right wrist, and a watch on his left.

Lily couldn't take her eyes off him. His dark brown hair was left loose, the long waves falling to brush his shoulders. From the distance she couldn't see his eyes, but she knew the color by heart—aqua ringed by navy.

He was smiling, his steps purposeful. Lily was about to call out a hello when he jerked to a stop and whipped his head around as someone said his name.

As soon as Lily saw Constantine she knew she should go back inside the shop, but she wanted just a few more minutes to gaze at Rhys with no one watching her. She lifted the pail to water the second bush when Con's voice reached her.

"Wanted to let you know that I heard from Kiril."

Rhys's smile widened. "I'm guessing it's good news, then?"

"Aye. He'll be home soon. I gave him until noon, but I suspect he's wanting a last farewell with his woman."

Rhys's smile vanished as he looked at his watch. "You spoke with him at dawn, aye?"

Con slapped him on the arm, his eyes crinkling in the corners from smiling. "Be happy, Rhys. Kiril is coming home. He's no' reckless as you are. If he says he's going to do something, he'll do it. Besides, I'm giving him another hour before I contact him again."

"You're right," Rhys said grudgingly.

Lily felt something wet hit her toe in her sandals. She looked down to discover she had overflowed the pot. "Oh, dang," she mumbled and quickly stepped back.

When she looked up, Rhys was no longer in the same

spot. She let her gaze quickly roam, but she didn't see him. With a sigh, she began to turn to enter the shop when she heard his voice filled with merriment.

"Ladies!" he shouted.

She gradually turned her head to find two women leaning on Rhys's red convertible Jaguar F-type. The women were drop-dead gorgeous, both tall, with long legs, slender bodies, and plump breasts. Both were blondes and had long, full hair. They stood, all smiles, as Rhys walked up.

Suddenly conscious of her dour, plain clothes that were several sizes too big, Lily glanced down at herself. She pulled on the oversized top and grimaced.

Rhys put an arm around the women before kissing each of them fully on the lips. He then walked them around to the passenger side of the car and opened the door. "Buckle up," he said with a grin as he closed the door and strode to the driver's side.

Lily swallowed hard as Cassie walked up beside her, her head shaking from side to side in displeasure. "That car only fits two. He can't have two women in one seat," she said in her American accent.

"He's gorgeous. It's no wonder he always has such beautiful women on his arms."

Cassie snorted derisively. "Puh-leeze, Lily. If you look up the word *skank*, you'll find a picture of those women beside it."

Lily found herself chuckling, but it didn't make her feel any better. Rhys was so far out of her league he wasn't even a speck on the horizon.

"He's charming. Always has been," Cassie continued. "But I wouldn't set my sights on him, if I were you."

"I wouldn't dream of it," Lily said and walked back into the shop.

She set down the pail behind the counter and grasped

her purse. When she straightened, there was a smile on her face. She had perfected it after years of learning to deftly hide the pain within her. "Good night."

"I'm only trying to help." Cassie stood in the doorway, blocking her exit. "I never meant to hurt you."

"You didn't," Lily answered honestly. She rubbed her wrist. "It's just been a long day."

Cassie nodded and moved to allow her to pass. She was walking past when Cassie sucked in a quick breath. Lily didn't have to look to know that she had seen the scar on her back.

"My God, Lily. What happened?"

She turned away quickly so that her back was no longer visible to Cassie. "It was an accident a long time ago."

"Of course. My apologies," Cassie said hastily.

Lily removed her purse from her shoulder and fixed her shirt to hide the scar. "I'll see you tomorrow."

"You bet."

Lily's legs felt as heavy as lead as she walked to her car. Would her lies never be finished? Would she never outrun her past?

She was so tired of reliving those years. If only she could have left the memories behind when she got away, but they were buried too deep in too much pain. It was why they revisited her every night in her dreams.

And it was one of a thousand reasons why she could only look at a man like Rhys and daydream of what could never—*would* never—be.

CHAPTER
TWENTY-THREE

Shara stood in the middle of Balladyn's chamber and waited for what was to come. He wanted her, but she wasn't sure if he would wait until the Claiming to take her or not. Shara hoped he waited, because she wouldn't be able to fake her enjoyment of him touching her. Not after she knew what true pleasure was in Kiril's arms.

"Strip," Balladyn demanded.

Shara raised a brow. "Why would I do that?"

"Because I want to see you."

The longer he stared at her, the more anxiety filled her. "After the Claiming."

"You wanted me, remember," he said as he lounged on the bed leaning on one elbow. "You sought me out. I know it wasn't for my charm. You wanted what my power could grant you—a chance to get away from your family."

Shara shrugged. "That's true. You're the only Dark that wouldn't worship every word my father spouted. You would make the rules."

"I do make the rules, Shara. For everyone."

"I thought that was Taraeth."

Balladyn smiled slowly. "Have you seen Taraeth since

the human lopped off his arm? He's not the same. It won't be long before I'm ruling."

"Everyone knows you'll take Taraeth's place."

"You have the cunning mind to be a perfect partner for me." He sat up and looked her up and down. "Yesterday I thought it was what you wanted, but that was before I knew you were sent to seduce the Dragon King."

Shara wisely kept silent. This made her all too aware of how little she knew of Balladyn. She had heard stories, but that was different than the man himself. For the first time, Shara wondered if she had gotten herself in too deep.

"Did you bed him?" Balladyn asked.

Shara held his gaze, refusing to talk.

Balladyn came off the bed in a blur of movement to put his face to hers. "Did you sully yourself as Rhi did with a Dragon King?" he yelled.

For a split second, Shara almost returned his yell with a "Yes!" But somehow she kept her wits about her. Balladyn might have been an impressive warrior for the Light, but his mind wasn't fully intact now. Whatever the Dark did to him to turn him had taken part of his mind.

Shara tried to teleport out, only to hear Balladyn's laughter as he walked slowly around her.

"Do you really think I would allow anyone other than myself to be able to appear or disappear in my chamber?" He shook his head, his eyes alight with malice. "You're not going anywhere, Shara. I told you, you are mine."

She tried to gather her magic, but nothing was happening. Shara turned and started running for the door when she was hit with a blast of magic from behind, slamming her into the door.

The wind was knocked out of her as she crumpled to the floor, leaving her powerless as Balladyn stood over her. With one twist of his hands, his magic divested her of her clothes.

Shara gasped in a breath and kicked out at him. If only she had managed to connect with his balls. She merely succeeded in angering him. She was beyond caring at that point. All she wanted was to get away, to get out of his chamber so she could teleport somewhere safe.

It became apparent a moment later how great Balladyn's magic was as he had her in the middle of the room with her arms held above her, hanging so that her toes only skimmed the floor.

Was this how a human felt? So helpless and powerless? She was filled with fury . . . and terror. Her magic wasn't anything to sneeze at, and yet she couldn't bring forth a pinkie full of it thanks to Balladyn.

He kept just out of sight except for his black boots as he walked around her. The humiliation of standing naked in the middle of his chamber was only the beginning. Shara knew he would do so much more to her.

She wondered if Kiril had come to her house yet. The fact Balladyn was with her meant that he wasn't looking for Kiril yet. And she had to wonder why. If it was so important to catch a Dragon King, why was he lingering?

"Why did you leave the pub?" Balladyn suddenly asked.

She swallowed and cut her eyes to the side when she glimpsed his boots. "As if I'd remain and get between two males fighting."

Balladyn cackled. "That wasn't a fight. That was my boot stomping on an ant." There was a pause before he touched her head, causing her to jump. His hand then slid through her hair. "If you hate Farrell as much as he despises you, then you should've wanted to see him put in his place. But you didn't watch it, which leads me to believe you used the time to go somewhere else. Your Dragon King, perhaps? What's his name?"

"Why would I want to be near a Dragon King?" Shara retorted, hoping the heat she added to her words would be enough to convince Balladyn.

He continued his caress down her back, pausing to fondle first one butt cheek and then the other. "I wanted to show you off, and I wanted you to see how I hurt Farrell. For you. I almost believed your lies, just as I believed Rhi's once."

Shara's heart pounded at his words. His meaning went deeper, but she wasn't sure how deep when it came to Rhi.

Her attention was diverted as he continued to stroke her skin. She wanted to cover herself and scream at him to never touch her again, but she couldn't. Not if she wanted to get out of this alive and be able to help Kiril. In the end, she knew her chances of living were on the slim side, but she would do it for Kiril.

No one had ever cared enough about her to risk such danger. Rhi had no idea how lucky she was, and Shara wished she could be the one to tell her.

"What's this?" Balladyn's voice had gone hard.

Shara's lungs locked when she realized he was tracing the spot on her shoulder that Kiril had nipped. Kiril had marked her. She hadn't comprehended it until then and it gave her hope. A man didn't mark his lover on a whim.

If there was a chance that he had feelings for her Shara would fight with everything she had to return to him.

She had to think of a story fast, or everything she had done to stay alive would vanish in an instant. "It was the Dragon King's response when I teased him to a state of desire and refused to finish him."

"Why would you do that?" Balladyn asked skeptically.

Shara tried to shrug, biting the inside of her mouth to

hide her wince when pain shot through her arm from hanging from invisible bonds. "My mission was to seduce him in order for my family to trap him."

"Is that what you do? Seduce?"

"I was released from my prison in order to carry out this mission. Do you really think I go about seducing males?" she asked sardonically.

He squeezed her butt painfully. "I think it comes easily for you. You set out to seduce me."

"Because I thought you might be worthy of me."

He lifted a black and silver brow. "And you no longer believe that?"

"No."

He smiled coolly. "It doesn't really matter what you think. By the time I'm finished with you, you'll be begging me to be mine."

Shara wondered if he would use magic to hurt her, or if he would force himself on her. So when the first lash fell across her bottom, she couldn't hold back the scream, she was so unprepared for the pain. Shara bit the inside of her cheek as she sat through five more lashes before Balladyn finished. Her ass was on fire, the skin crackling from the whip.

"I didn't break the skin this time," he warned. "The whip was made special for me. The wounds remain for days. No Fae magic or the naturally quick healing of our bodies will ease you."

As if that made it all better. Shara glared daggers at him. She was suddenly released. Her knees barely held her when she was back on her feet, and her arms felt as if millions of blades were piercing her when she was able to lower them and let the blood rush back to her fingers.

"Get dressed, Shara. You're coming with me to hunt the Dragon King. Since you were sent to seduce him and he knows you, you'll go in first so we can take him by surprise. You'll complete your mission. Only for me instead of your family."

She clenched her teeth when he tossed a dress on the bed and stood by the door waiting. Of course Balladyn would have a specially made whip, the bastard. Her skin was on fire, the stinging growing exponentially by the second.

Shara walked to the bed as carefully as she could while Balladyn watched her. The pain was excruciating, but she would survive it. She was glad to have something to cover her body from Balladyn's gaze, even if it was the horrid black dress that barely concealed her breasts or her ass.

When she turned to him, Balladyn held out a pair of black heels that dangled from his fingers. Shara put them on, never taking her eyes from him. She hadn't understood hatred and loathing until then. Now she realized she had only ever touched on the emotions.

Until Balladyn.

He gave a nod. "Perfect. Let's get us a Dragon King."

She walked out of the chamber beside him, animosity growing by leaps with each step they took.

Kiril came awake instantly when he caught Shara's scent. But she wasn't alone. Dark Fae were with her, though they hung back while she entered the house. He was hesitant to assume that she had betrayed him. Then again, she was a Dark.

Kiril wanted to unfurl his wings and spread them wide, to roar and take to the skies. Instead, he remained quietly laying in the cellar listening.

Shara's steps took her all over the house searching from one room to the next. She spent extra time in his bedroom, and he wished he could see what she was doing.

Eventually she came down the stairs and walked to the

front door that she threw wide. "He's not here," she shouted and turned to sit on the stairs.

It wasn't long before the footsteps of thirty Dark entered his house. It was everything Kiril could do not to burst through the floor and tear them to pieces.

"Are you sure this is where he lives?"

"Yes, Balladyn," Shara answered crossly.

Balladyn. Kiril should've known.

He scowled when Shara's tone penetrated his fury. She was angry, her tone clipped. So she wasn't here of her own volition.

"Ask Farrell's men if you don't believe me." Shara's voice was icy.

Kiril grinned. That was the spirit he knew, the passion he'd felt firsthand in his arms.

There were three seconds of silence before Balladyn told his men, "Search the house and the entire grounds. Leave nothing untouched. If the dragon is here, we'll find him."

When the footsteps of Balladyn's men faded, Kiril wasn't surprised when Balladyn remained behind. He wanted Shara. Kiril didn't need to see the Dark to know that. He could hear it in Balladyn's voice.

"Where is he, Shara?" Balladyn asked.

Kiril already hated Balladyn for taking Rhi, but now he wanted to personally do him harm for thinking Shara was his.

"Why would I know that?"

"You were sent to seduce him," Balladyn stated. "I assume you did your job well."

Shara made a sound at the back of her throat. "Do you think a Dragon King would reveal anything to anyone?"

"You're lying." The certainty in his voice spelled danger for Shara. "Perhaps you've already forgotten the feel of the whip."

Kiril saw red. Balladyn had hurt her. The Dark's fate was sealed. Kiril would be the one to personally kill him, and he would enjoy every minute of it.

"Cut me to pieces, and it still won't change what I don't know," Shara said, breaking into his thoughts.

"Nor will the fact change that I'm going to capture the Dragon King."

Shara thought she was going to gag on the words. Part of her had hoped Kiril was there so she could seek his help, but in the end she was ecstatic that he wasn't. Where he was, however, was the question. His Mercedes sat in the drive and the keys were on the entryway table where he had tossed them when he'd arrived the previous night.

Had it really been twenty-four hours since she had left Balladyn and waited for Kiril at the manor? What she wouldn't do to rewind time and have those hours with Kiril again. She would beg him to take her away and leave Ireland, the Dark, and her family far behind.

But she knew Kiril would never do that. He was an honorable man, a man who had come to rescue a friend. Only when he had Rhi would he return to Scotland.

"Did you hear me?"

Shara stopped short of rolling her eyes as she looked at Balladyn. He was out of place in Kiril's home, a foreign object in a residence of peace and pleasure. "Did you say something?"

His face mottled with rage. "Our Claiming will be talked about for centuries."

"I'm not going to be your wife. I've already told you that." She stood when her bottom began to hurt. The more she walked, the more she worked out the ache. Sitting or being still for a long period of time made the pain worse.

Shara leaned against a wall and sank her nails into her

palm when she heard the crashes upstairs begin. The Dark were literally tearing things apart. As if Kiril would be hiding under a bed or chest.

"You were practically begging yesterday," Balladyn said.

"I don't fear you. My family wanted me dead for centuries, and now I'm your captive. You can threaten and torture me all you want, but I won't be a part of the Claiming nor will I tell you anything about the Dragon King since I know nothing."

Balladyn folded his arms as he leaned against the front door. "Do you remember what Rhi looked like, Shara? I'm toying with her. Do you have any idea what I could do to anyone that I wanted to destroy?"

She lifted her chin despite the chill of foreboding that settled in her gut. Shara knew what Balladyn could do, and it terrified her. "I won't live in fear, nor will I live in chains, visible or not."

"You'll do whatever I tell you. You spurned your family, remember. Not to mention they would never dare to go against me. You have no one, Shara. No one but me. Remember that the next time you want to tell me what you will and won't do."

Across the entryway on the other wall was a mirror. Shara caught her image in the reflection and hated the red eyes. They had turned red the first time she kidnapped a human male. With the red eyes was a faint silver strip in her hair. It wasn't until she'd kidnapped the girls that the silver became more visible as it was now. She touched the strip of silver, despising it.

"You'll have more soon enough," Balladyn said, misinterpreting her actions.

Shara's eyes skated away. She stilled when she caught sight of a door that hadn't been there earlier, a door that stood less than twenty feet from the stairs.

A door she *knew* she had never seen in the times she had been in the house.

Her eyes jerked to Balladyn who walked to the stairs and placed a booted foot on the first step as he gazed upward. Two Dark appeared at the top of the stairs shaking their heads. Balladyn gave a sound of fury and turned to the other Dark searching the bottom.

"Anything?" he demanded.

"Nothing," one responded.

Balladyn pointed outside and told them, "Go help the others search."

Shara glanced at the new door. Suddenly she knew without a sliver of doubt that Kiril was through that doorway. She wanted in there with him, but she didn't dare draw attention to it. Even if she was the only one to see it, she refused to let Balladyn know.

"The moon is hidden again tonight," Shara said.

Balladyn looked at her and shrugged. "Your point?"

"His car is here, but he isn't. Where else would a Dragon King be but up in the sky?"

Shara didn't have to say more as Balladyn grabbed her. They appeared in his chamber where he deposited her before he vanished. She glanced around to see she was alone. That she was inside the chamber. He probably had others guarding her, and since she couldn't teleport out, she was going to have to think of something.

She pulled open the door, prepared to ask one of the guards a question, when she discovered the hallway empty. Finally, something was going her way.

Shara slipped out of the chamber and closed the door behind her. She walked with purposeful steps to the doorway that would lead to the Blackwood estate. Just before she stepped through, Shara veiled herself. The moment she was back on earth, she teleported to Kiril's estate.

She let the veil fall when she found herself alone.

Immediately, she walked to the door and paused. She still didn't know how she saw it, but it didn't matter if it led her to Kiril. Shara twisted the knob and pushed. The door opened easily. She was surprised it wasn't locked, but since she assumed it was supposed to remain hidden from view, there wasn't a need for it to be locked.

Once she walked through the doorway, she softly closed the door behind her. When she turned to look into the dimly lit room, she froze as she stared down at the most magnificent and frightening sight she had ever witnessed—a dragon.

CHAPTER
TWENTY-FOUR

Shara's knees buckled at the sight, and she fell back against the wall. The dragon lifted its massive head from its paws and regarded her silently with slanted, faceted royal blue eyes.

The burnt orange scales glistened with a metallic sheen in the light of the lamps hanging from the walls. His head was wide, his eyes unblinking. The dragon's nostrils flared as if scenting her. Then he drew in a huge breath, his body lighting up from within with a blue glow for several seconds. Her mouth dropped open in wonder and surprise.

"Kiril," Shara whispered.

In all her dreams, she had never imagined anything so spectacularly frightening. She wanted to go to him, to touch his scales, but trepidation kept her rooted to the spot. It was no wonder the Dark were panicky any time the Dragon Kings were mentioned.

Kiril shifted his shoulders, causing his wings to brush against the top of the cellar, triggering mortar dust to drift around him. It was wrong that he was hiding in such a small space when he should be soaring among the clouds.

"No one knows I'm here," she said and scooted to the first step. "I swear."

He blinked his huge blue dragon eyes.

Shara drew in a shaky breath. "Your original plan isn't going to work. We need a new one." When Kiril didn't respond, Shara urged, "Please. I want to help you. I *need* to help you. It won't right the wrongs I've done, but it's the only way I know to do something."

The shape of the dragon suddenly vanished, replaced by a very nude Kiril in human form. Still, Shara remained where she was.

"He dared to harm you." Kiril's words, harsh and rough, filled the cellar.

Shara gave an absent shake of her head. "Nothing I couldn't handle."

"He. Hurt. You."

His words were clipped and filled with rage. That's when Shara noticed that his hands were fisted by his sides. She rose to her feet, unmindful of her sore backside, and walked down the steps.

She didn't stop until she stood before him and placed her hands on his face. "I'm all right."

"How did you find me?"

"I saw the door. A door, mind you, that I've never seen before."

"You shouldna have seen it at all. I used dragon magic to hide it. Fae can no' see dragon magic."

Her arms fell to her sides as she shrugged. "I can't explain it. One minute it looked like a wall, and the next I saw a door. I let Balladyn believe you were somewhere else, and after he brought me to his fortress I came here."

"You were able to use your magic to leave the fortress?"

Shara twisted her lips in a rueful smile. "Not exactly. I tried, but apparently Balladyn has spelled it so no one can just appear in his home. I was able to use the doorway to my parents' home. I snuck through when a guard wasn't looking. Once I was back on this realm, I teleported here."

"You're risking a lot."

"I had to know if you were down here."

One side of his lips lifted in a grin. "Did you now? If you wanted to see me in dragon form, all you had to do was ask."

Shara rolled her eyes, even as she smiled in pleasure. "I can't believe you're teasing at a time like this."

"There's always going to be something going on." Kiril glanced at the door. "Good idea to tell him I was in dragon form, but it willna keep him away for long. Or keep him from returning to his fortress for you."

"I'll return there. With you." She melted against him when he drew her into his arms.

"I doona want you anywhere near him again."

She closed her eyes and savored being with him again. "I must return. If I don't, he'll come looking for me."

"No' if he's coming after me."

Shara leaned back and looked into his shamrock green eyes. She knew what he was about to ask. "I won't fit in at Dreagan."

"And you do here?" he asked, frustration clouding his face. "Shara, you may have been born into a Dark family, but you are no' a Dark Fae."

"Look at my eyes. Look at the silver in my hair. I'm a Dark Fae. Nothing is going to change that. We're the most hated beings on this realm."

"You'll be safe at Dreagan. They willna harm you."

"I wasn't harmed in my parents' home when I was locked away for hundreds of years either. Being ignored and scorned can be worse than any kind of torture."

Kiril released her and began to pace. Shara knew the situation was dire, but she couldn't stop looking at his splendid body. Her gaze stopped on his chest with his dragon tattoo, and she jerked because she would swear on her life that she had just seen the dragon move.

"You plan to remain here?" Kiril asked.

She pulled her eyes up from his chest and belatedly realized he had asked a question. "I've not thought about it."

"Unless we kill Taraeth and Balladyn and you rule the Dark, they'll relentlessly search for you."

Shara suddenly had a plan, one that she wouldn't share with Kiril. It wasn't to punish him, but to set him free—from her. He was honorable enough that he would continue to try to help her, which would only put him right back in the predicament he was in.

"Let's think of that once we have Rhi."

Kiril walked around her to the stairs where a set of clothes was neatly folded. He grabbed the pair of dark denim and slid first one leg and then the other on before he fastened them.

"You should go somewhere safe while I go into the fortress alone," he said as he pulled a solid black shirt over his head.

Shara was shaking her head before he even finished. "As I told you before, you'll never get past the guards at my house."

"Watch me," he said with a smile.

After all she had seen him do, Shara believed him. If only she could transport him from one location to another in a blink as she did herself, but she wasn't a powerful enough Fae to pull that off. "I believe you, but I also know that Balladyn will need distracting. Let me do that."

"Nay," he said, looking at her as if she had lost her mind.

And maybe she had. "It'll work. Besides, I got away from him just now. I can do it again. How else will you get around his compound?"

Kiril shook his head. "I doona like the idea of you going back to him."

"I can handle Balladyn. He doesn't scare me." At Kiril's knowing look, she rolled her eyes. "Okay, so he does scare me a bit, but I can get away from him, Kiril. Trust me. I had over a thousand years to myself going to many different realms and managing to stay out of any real trouble."

He finally sighed and gave a nod. "Doona make me regret agreeing to this."

"I won't," she said with a smile.

"We keep to the plan," Kiril said. "The difference is how I'll get into your house and to the doorway."

"You don't know which doorway it is."

"I will once you tell me," he said with a wink.

Kiril prayed she accepted all he was telling her, because if they didn't get moving soon, he was going to shift back into a dragon and fly her to Dreagan, regardless of whether she wanted to go or not.

Never mind the fact that she could return to Ireland with barely a thought.

"There are over a dozen doorways. You need to go to the . . ." She paused, her head cocked to the side. "Wait a minute. You can't see Fae doors."

Kiril sat on the stairs and tugged on his boots. "Let me worry about that."

"You're insane."

"Probably, but we can debate that later." He stood and held out his hand for her. They walked up the steps to the door. "Do what you have to do in order to keep Balladyn content. I doona want him hurting you again. Once I have Rhi, you can leave with us."

"Sure."

He wasn't fooled by her quick answer. It was the way her gaze flickered away right as she spoke that gave her away. Though no matter how hard he pushed, she wouldn't tell him more than she already had. He had to accept that. For the moment.

"Ready?" he asked.

"Not even close."

Kiril smiled and drew her against him to kiss her slowly, languidly. He would never grow tired of her sweet taste or the way she softened against him. As much as he wanted to continue the kiss, he pulled back and looked into her red eyes. He tugged on her strip of silver. "I want a promise from you."

"What is it?"

"If I'm caught, I want you to get as far from Balladyn as you can. He'll use you against me."

"You want me to leave you?" she asked incredulously.

"Aye, lass. I do."

She gave a firm shake of her head. "No."

"Aye. A Dark can no' kill a King, remember."

"They can do other things," she whispered.

"Other things that they will do to you to break me. They will bring you in to see if I give any response. I wouldna, but they will keep trying. I doona know how long I could hold back seeing you harmed. As soon as I do, they'll do whatever's needed to try and break me."

She looked at his chest. "Then don't go."

"Give me your word, Shara, that you'll go somewhere safe if I'm caught." When she didn't answer, he enfolded her in his arms and held her tight.

"I promise," she said.

Kiril kissed the top of her head. "Stay safe. No matter what. Say whatever you need, do whatever you need to do, but you stay alive."

She pulled back and looked up at him with red eyes swimming with tears. "Don't you dare get caught."

Without another word, she was gone, vanishing right

out of his arms. Kiril dropped his chin to his chest and reached for the doorknob before he stopped. He ran back down the stairs to the far wall. Using his magic, he wrote a message on the cellar wall that only a Dragon King would be able to see.

Kiril wished he could manage the rest of his plan on his own, but if he wanted to succeed, there was only one person who could help him. He pulled out his mobile and dialed the number. His call was answered on the second ring.

"I wondered how long it would take you to call me," Phelan said casually.

Kiril chuckled. "How is Aisley?"

"Sod off, Dragon. You're daft if you think I left Ireland. You didna fool me."

"What made you think I would call?" Kiril asked, intrigued.

"The fact you have no' left Ireland was the biggest clue, and then there's the female."

Shara. Kiril didn't want to think about how he was going to leave her behind. He couldn't force her to Dreagan, nor could he blithely leave her.

"Kiril?" Phelan said, worry pitching his voice lower.

He rubbed the back of his neck and quickly filled Phelan in on the past twenty-four hours.

"And this is why I didna leave," Phelan stated. "Damn, but I knew Balladyn or Farrell was going to screw something up. I'm here for whatever you need if it involves getting Rhi out."

"Shara described the layout of Balladyn's compound. He built it out of the ruins of some castle on their realm, but he incorporated many of the humans' tactics in their forts."

"In other words," Phelan said dryly, "this isna going to be a walk in the park?"

"No' even close. Still up for it?"

Phelan grunted through the phone. "As if you need to ask. Have you told Con?"

"Nay. It's better this way."

"If you say so. Where do I meet you?"

Kiril grinned despite himself. Phelan had proven himself many times. It was lucky the Kings had made an alliance with the Warriors and learned that Phelan was half-Fae. Without him, they would never find the doorways.

"On the outskirts of Cork. It's a prominent neighborhood, so leave any vehicles behind. We're going to be sneaking in undetected in all ways."

"I'll be there."

Kiril ended the call, a calm coming over him. Outside the cellar door were six Dark Ones. With a smile in place, he threw open the door, the force of his dragon magic filling him until he thought he would split apart.

And then he opened his mouth and let it loose, the blast of cold air freezing the Dark Ones instantaneously. Kiril saw himself in the mirror and the curls of cold air seeping from the corners of his mouth through his parted lips.

Damn, but it was good to be a Dragon King.

CHAPTER
TWENTY-FIVE

Dreagan

Constantine knew in his gut something had happened to Kiril. Whether Kiril remained behind of his own volition or someone had detained him, it all came down to the fact that he hadn't returned to Dreagan.

Con didn't bother to turn from his place at the window at the sound of the quick knock and the door opening. He wasn't surprised when four Dragon Kings filed into his office.

With the night as black as pitch, it made it easy for Con to see Guy, Tristan, Kellan, and Laith reflected in the window. Con finished off the last of his whisky and faced the group.

"What brings all of you here this late?" he asked.

Kellan's face twisted angrily. "Cut the shite, Con. You said Kiril was returning. That was hours ago."

"I know."

Guy ran a hand through his hair. "You know? Have you heard from him? Because he willna answer me."

"He's no' answering me either," Con admitted.

Tristan's dark eyes filled with confusion. "Then why are we just sitting here?"

"My question exactly," Laith said. "When Rhys finds out, he'll go to Ireland himself."

"Then he can no' find out," Con said as calmly as he could. They had no idea how close to the edge he was riding—nor would they.

It was Kellan who held his gaze before he snorted and shook his head. "You've no' told them."

"I didna tell you either," Con said. "You only know because you write the history."

Laith stepped away from the door. "What have you no' told us?"

Con could have cheerfully slammed Kellan through the window. He would have told everyone as soon as he formulated some kind of plan. "Kiril asked that I grant permission to offer safe harbor for a Dark Fae."

"That's no' what I meant," Kellan said. "Though if you tell them that part, then you need to tell them that she's the one helping him."

"A Dark Fae helping a Dragon King?" Guy asked.

Tristan exchanged looks with Guy. "Has that ever happened?"

"Nay," Kellan said. "No' once since the Fae ventured to this realm."

Laith tucked a long, wavy lock of blond hair behind his ear. "A female Dark? What is she to Kiril?"

"I'm no' sure exactly," Con answered.

Kellan walked around the set of chairs before Con's desk and sank into one of them. "Shara is her name. She found Rhi and told Kiril her location."

"I'll be damned," Tristan murmured.

Guy blew out a weary breath. "Kiril is going after Rhi, is he not?"

"I would in his place after what she did for me and Denae," Kellan said.

Tristan nodded. "Not to mention what she did for me and Sammi."

"Then why are we sitting here?" Laith asked. "We should be helping him."

Con shifted his eyes to Kellan. "We doona even know where to go."

The door to the office flew open. Every eye looked to see Rhys standing there, his face a mask of fury. "There is one who does. Phelan."

There was someone else he could contact, but she was only a last resort. It might very well come to that, but Con would hold off until that time arrived.

Constantine hit the speaker button on his desk phone and dialed Phelan's mobile.

"Make it quick," Phelan said in a low voice when he answered. "I doona have long."

Con pulled out his chair and sat, bracing his elbows on his desk. "Where is Kiril?"

"On his way to meet me."

"And where is that?"

Phelan sighed dramatically. "I really hate when I get put in the middle of King business. The fact is, he didna want to tell you. Something about you coming over here when Kiril knows that it would be the worst thing for you to do."

"And another Dragon King being taken by the Dark doesna warrant our action?" Kellan asked.

"Kellan?" Phelan asked. "Nay, that's no' what I meant. Balladyn is intent on catching Kiril. He's been hunting him all day. We have a narrow window in order to get to Balladyn's fortress on the Fae realm and find Rhi."

"Then Balladyn will be waiting for him," Tristan said.

"According to Kiril, aye. Balladyn has an entire army at his fortress waiting."

Rhys slammed his hand down on Con's desk. "Does he want to be taken?"

Phelan made a sound at the back of his throat. "Nay. Shara is going to help."

"So you think," Laith said.

There was a slight pause before Phelan said, "I remember my own brethren turning against me when they discovered Aisley was *drough*. Aisley was never evil. She did what had to be done to survive. Shara had no choice in things either. She was born into a Dark family. Think about that before you condemn her."

Con used his thumb and forefinger to squeeze the bridge of his nose. "Do you trust her?"

"I've no' meet her," Phelan said. "Kiril trusts her, and I trust Kiril."

"Is Kiril blinded by lust?"

"Well, you would be too if you got a look at her. I think he might have been in the beginning, but Kiril's smart. Shara found Kiril and didna lead the other Dark Ones to him."

Con lowered his arm to the desk. "Where is the doorway?"

"In the back garden of the Blackwood home."

"I need more than that, Phelan."

"Kiril will be here any moment. Look for the most ostentatious house in a neighborhood on the outskirts of Cork, and you'll find it. I see Kiril."

The call went dead.

Con pushed the chair back with his legs and stood. He looked at Guy. "Make sure the patrols are in place and the new sensors set for the Dark Fae. I want the mates in the mountain with the Silvers and guarded. Kellan, I want patrols in the air as well. Tristan, call the Warriors and let them know what's going on so they can be prepared."

"For what?" Tristan asked.

Laith braced his hands on the back of the vacant chair. "Because it could be a trap for us. They take Kiril, we go after Kiril, and they use our absence to attack Dreagan."

"It's just a precaution," Con said. "Laith, put some sensors around the Silvers as well. Another precaution."

Rhys lifted a dark brow when Con's gaze moved to him. "Your words to me better be to get ready to go to Ireland."

"I didna intend to say anything else," Con replied with a grin. "Though I'll be coming with you."

All five Kings stilled in various stages of leaving the office, their gazes locking on him.

"Are you going for Rhi?" Guy asked.

Con gave a single shake of his head. "Balladyn and I have some business that willna wait. Rhi will have Kiril, Rhys, and Phelan attempting to locate her. She doesna need my help."

They all filed out of his office except for Rhys. Rhys waited until everyone was gone before he approached Con's desk. "I think it should be more than just the two of us going in."

"I doona want them to know we're coming. We'll have to fly low."

"Low?" Rhys asked with a frown. "You want to chance the humans seeing us?"

"Lower."

Rhys rolled his eyes. "You think that will keep us hidden from the Dark?"

"It'll get us into Ireland, which is what I want."

"It'll take us longer, but it's the best way."

Con came around his desk. "We take the SUV to the coast."

Rhys turned on his heel and stalked from the office, Con on his heel. Con knew everything would be looked after on Dreagan. His concern was getting to Ireland, and then returning.

He got behind the wheel of the SUV and started the black Range Rover just as Rhys climbed in. The engine purred to life, and he threw it into drive. Con glanced in the rearview mirror at Dreagan. As long as things like this were going on, he couldn't concentrate on killing Ulrik, and yet the issues were all caused by Ulrik. Pretty soon Con was going to have to make a decision to leave missions to the other Kings and go after Ulrik himself.

"I'm going to kick Kiril's ass for this," Rhys muttered a half-hour into the drive.

Con glanced over at him. "Right after I have a go at him. He's never done anything this reckless."

"You mean he's never acted like me before," Rhys said with a wry grin.

"Aye. It's why I believed him when he said he was coming home. I should've known when he gave in so easily that something was up."

"He knows where Rhi is. I wouldna be able to leave her."

Con gripped the wheel tighter. "But I would?"

"Aye."

"You think you know me so well."

"You didna deny it," Rhys said.

Con veered off the road and parked the Range Rover behind a dense grove of trees. He turned off the engine and swiveled his head to Rhys. "You agreed with me when we killed Ulrik's female and bound his magic. Why is it you're against me every time now?"

"Someone has to irritate you or you'd think you could rule the world," he said with a smile as he opened the door and got out.

Con briefly closed his eyes before he exited the SUV

and removed his clothes, setting them on his seat. By the time he turned around Rhys was already in the water.

The sea was cool as Con stepped in. He dove beneath the gentle waves and swam out into deeper water. Con could see Rhys ahead of him, his yellow scales dimmed beneath the dark sea. The bottom suddenly dropped deeply. Con gladly shifted. He always missed being in his true form, but then all Dragon Kings did.

Living amongst the humans confined and restricted them. There were times Con had to fight to return to Dreagan after a night of flying in the clouds. None of his brethren knew that a few times he almost hadn't returned.

And none ever would.

He used his wings to swim through the water. It took significant time for them to traverse around the Isle of Skye and into the Irish Sea. Above them boats and ships maneuvered, unknowing of what was below them.

Rhys turned his head and motioned with his wing. *"Ireland is right here."*

"Aye, but we're miles from Cork. I want as close as we can get."

Con swam faster, and Rhys kept pace, swimming beside him until they finally reached St. George's Channel.

"Wait," Con said through their link.

When Rhys paused, Con slowly swam to the surface. He put just his eyes and nose above the water. As soon as he figured out where they were, he dove back down.

"Well?" Rhys asked.

"We're about twenty miles out."

They began to swim again, this time staying as close to land as possible. A few minutes later both shifted back into human form and swam to shore.

"We need to hurry," Rhys said.

"Aye. I have that same sense," Con said.

They ran out of the water, keeping to the shadows as they rushed toward their friend and fellow King. Yet the closer Con got, the more a sick feeling of dread filled him.

CHAPTER
TWENTY-SIX

Ulrik's gaze lazily drifted over the streets of Cork. Dark Fae walked the streets as if they owned it. The first of many mistakes Con had allowed.

"Where is the doorway?" he demanded of the Dark Fae with him.

The Dark dipped his head forward. "It's the next block over in an alley."

"Show me."

Ulrik followed the Dark across the street to the sidewalk around the buildings until he came to the alley. He continued down the narrow alley past several businesses, and stopped only when he reached the end of it.

The Dark had painted the back of a building red. He shook his head. It was easy to manipulate the Dark Fae and guess their motives, but they were also very vain and ridiculously idiotic at times.

Ulrik waited for the Dark to point out the exact location. When he didn't, Ulrik turned and gave him a glacial stare. "As I've told you—repeatedly—no one will know you showed me the doorway. Do you doubt my word?"

"Never. I've seen what you can do."

"So why are you hesitating? Again?"

The Dark swallowed and ran a hand through his short, spikey black and silver hair. "I . . ."

"Ah," Ulrik said, remembering. He pulled out a small leather pouch from his pocket and tossed it to the Dark, the sound of metal clinking together. "Payment as agreed."

The Dark's hand reached out and snatched the pouch from the air, his red eyes alight with satisfaction. "It's right in front of you."

"Halt," Ulrik said when the Dark attempted to walk away. "You're coming through the doorway with me."

"What?" the Dark asked in shock, his eyes widening in fear.

"If you just happen to have pointed to the wrong doorway, you'll be right beside me to correct your mistake. This way I willna have to hunt you down," Ulrik said, the last part spoken with enough menace to make the Dark Fae anxious.

The Dark cleared his throat. "You'll need to turn more to the right."

Just as Ulrik had suspected. The Dark feared Balladyn. Not Taraeth, but Balladyn. That was interesting enough, but not so much that it altered Ulrik's plans this time. There would come a time when he would need to have a chat with Balladyn. Until then, he would gather information that could be used against Balladyn until he could get the Dark warrior on his side.

"Lead the way," Ulrik said as he motioned with his hand.

The Dark walked on shaky legs through the doorway, and Ulrik was a step behind him. As soon as he entered, he was in another realm. It wasn't his first time leaving the realm of earth, and it wouldn't be the last.

Three steps in and Ulrik looked over his shoulder to

see several doorways. The one he entered through had a red haze around it that differentiated it from the others.

"This is Balladyn's," the Dark Fae said.

Ulrik saw him pointing to a large B etched into the wall. It was well known that Balladyn marked anything of his. Ulrik turned his head to tell his companion that he was finished with him, but the Dark was already running back through the doorway they had come through.

"Coward," Ulrik said.

The Dark Fae pretended to be the most evil, vile beings around, but Ulrik knew the truth. They were like petulant children trying to get back at their parents, the Light Fae. It was an ongoing family war that had lasted for countless eons and showed no signs of halting anytime soon.

Ulrik had watched the Fae Wars with interest from the sidelines. He really hadn't known which side he wanted to win—the Dragon Kings or the Fae. In the end, it really didn't matter. He was as he had been for thousands upon thousands of years.

All he had to go on were his memories of when he could shift into his dragon form and take to the skies, to hear his Silvers around him, to know that he was a part of something important.

Ulrik stepped into the shadows as a group of three Dark Ones came toward him. He watched as each of them went through a different doorway. He closed his eyes and pulled the drawing of the fortress that he had memorized into his mind's eye. With four routes already set, Ulrik's gaze snapped open.

"I'm coming, Rhi."

"Who were you talking to?" Kiril asked when he reached Phelan who squatted behind a hedge of bushes across the street from Shara's house.

Phelan's lips twisted regretfully. "I knew he'd call."

Kiril didn't need to ask who Phelan referred to. Con. "Damn. He'll be coming, which means we need to be in and out before he gets here."

"Con can help."

"Do you know what the Dark would do if they caught the King of Kings?"

Phelan let out a string of curses.

"Exactly. Now, how many are patrolling the Black-wood house?" Kiril asked.

"Six, but they're lazy, which means there are many more inside."

Kiril studied the house and the men who walked the perimeter. "Let's get them all out here."

"What do you want to do, shift into a dragon and roar?" Phelan asked sarcastically.

Kiril smiled at him.

"Of course you do," Phelan said with a roll of his eyes. "Are you sure the Dark willna see through my power?"

"Nay, but it's worth a try. They can no' see dragon magic so they might no' see yours."

"Your magic is much stronger than mine."

"You're part Fae, Phelan, and have a primeval god inside you. You're formidable. Now use those special powers of yours."

Phelan grinned before he unleashed his power. Kiril watched as an image of him as a dragon appeared in the street. It was odd seeing himself this way, and it made him want to shift immediately. The god inside Phelan gave him the ability to alter reality so that no one could know which reality was true and which wasn't. It had helped the Warriors many times in their battles with the *droughs*.

"Here they come," Phelan whispered.

More than a dozen Dark Fae rushed out of the house.

Phelan released a laugh as he sent the dragon into the air and flying over the neighborhood.

"Lucky for us you're able to alter reality that way," Kiril said.

"We're no' going to have much time. How do you want to go in?"

Kiril slowly stood as the Dark followed Phelan's dragon, spreading out through the neighborhood. "Over the fence, of course."

They both rushed across the street, and with one bound, leaped over the eight-foot wooden fence. Kiril glanced into the sky to see Phelan's dragon disappear into the clouds.

"What color did Shara say the doorway was?" Phelan asked as they crept through the garden.

"She didna. She said it was in the back to the right, separate from the others."

"Let's just hope we doona get it wrong then," Phelan said with a dour look.

Kiril stole through the garden as quick as a breeze. He slid against the house when he reached the other side and waited for Phelan who joined him a moment later.

"Do you see a doorway?"

"I see many fucking doorways in this awful place," he murmured crossly. Then he let out a breath and gave a single nod. "But aye. There's only one near us."

"Time's a wasting," Kiril said with a grin. "Tell me which way to go."

"How about you follow me?" Phelan said a second before he pushed away from the wall.

Kiril let out a curse and ran behind him. He hated going through Fae doorways, and hopefully this would be the last time for a long, long while.

As soon as they were through the doorway, Phelan skidded to a halt, causing Kiril to have to sidestep so as not to run into the back of him. Suddenly Phelan was thrown to the left, slamming viciously against the wall. Kiril rounded on a Dark Fae that turned his magic on him.

Kiril didn't want any alarms to sound, so he remained in human form and battled the Dark. He dodged blasts of magic and used his fists to punch the Fae. Kiril ducked another ball of magic and rolled, coming up with the push dagger in his palm.

He came up on his feet, ready to plunge it into the Dark's heart. Phelan got to him first, sinking his gold claws into the Dark's neck with a growl. A heartbeat later and Phelan took the Dark Fae's head.

Kiril watched the dead Fae fall at his feet. He looked back up at the Warrior with his god released—evident by his gold skin and eyes, claws, and his fangs. "Well, that's one way of doing it."

"He hit me," Phelan stated matter-of-factly.

Phelan tamped down his god, and together they moved the Dark into an empty room nearby.

"We stick out like a sore thumb," Phelan grumbled.

Kiril looked at him. "We do now, but with a little help from you, we willna."

Phelan's frown shifted as a bright smile took over. "I would've thought of that eventually."

"Is that before or after we have to fight more Dark?"

"Keep it up and I'll leave your dragon ass for all to see," he said with a smirk.

Kiril had never thought he could have the easy banter he did with Rhys with anyone else, but then he had met Phelan. It was no wonder Phelan and Rhys got along so well. They were alike in so many ways.

In the blink of an eye, Phelan used his power so that both would look like any other Dark Fae who walked the corridors of the fortress. They started through the compound walking side by side.

"Looking like one of these fuckers is one thing," Phelan said. "The tough part is going to be any confrontations we have."

"Already thought of that. We come from Taraeth."

Phelan turned his head to him and smiled. "Brilliant."

"I have to say, the red eyes just aren't a good look for you."

"Neither is your silver hair, but you doona hear me complaining," Phelan said.

Their conversation stopped when the corridor ended at the great hall that was filled to capacity with an army. Walking through them would be an issue since they were lined up, waiting for . . . Kiril.

Phelan nudged him with his elbow as he turned left. Kiril followed suit and soon spotted another group walking through the great hall. Phelan trailed them. Kiril glanced at Phelan to get his attention before he broke off and turned right down another hallway, Phelan on his heels. He didn't breathe easy until they were once more alone. They stopped and leaned against the wall.

"I've never seen a great hall that large," Phelan said with a frown. "That's four times the size of the hall at MacLeod Castle."

"The size of that army is nothing to sneeze at either."

"And to think they're waiting for you."

"Doona remind me. I've no' seen that many Dark Fae gathered in one place since the Fae Wars."

Phelan blew out a harsh breath. "Where to now?"

"It's no' that far ahead," Kiril said and started down the corridor.

It was a winding maze of hallways, but Shara had been specific in her description. Only once had they gone the wrong way, which Kiril quickly realized. As they walked he told Phelan the directions in case they became separated. No matter what, both agreed that Rhi had to be rescued.

"I'll kill them all if they've harmed her," Phelan muttered.

Kiril glanced at his friend. "The truth is she may no' be the same person you knew. The Dark have a way of torturing that gets quick results."

They turned another corner and instantly halted. Phelan hissed under his breath as Kiril focused on his new enemy—Balladyn—as they watched him enter a room.

CHAPTER
TWENTY-SEVEN

Shara paced the confines of Balladyn's chamber nervously. It had been too easy to get out and return. Way too easy. Or perhaps she was just overthinking things. She wrung her hands, her head pounding as thoughts—and panic—filled her.

The door was suddenly opened and Balladyn filled the entry. His gaze settled on her. Shara stared as he remained still, his eyes boring into her.

"Was your hunt successful?" she asked.

Balladyn walked into the room and softly closed the door behind him. Shara made herself remain still when all she wanted was to get as far from him as she could. Balladyn was dangerous, and she knew being so near to him meant that she might never leave the fortress again.

He leaned against the door and crossed his arms over his chest. "At first I believed you. I was ready to scour the skies for the Dragon King that you said must be flying."

Shara's heart knocked against her ribs.

"Then I realized you lied."

She tried to swallow only to discover her mouth was

dry as a desert. It was the coldness, the silent fury in Balladyn's gaze that hinted at very bad things to come.

"I was coming back here to get the truth out of you," Balladyn continued. "I stopped when one of my men received a report that a dragon was seen at your family's home."

Shara blinked. There was no way Kiril would have been that foolish. It had to be some sort of trick.

Balladyn tilted his head to the side. "Do you know what I did?"

"You went to see for yourself?" she asked.

"I went to see," he said with a nod. "By the time I arrived with my men, I was only able to witness the dragon disappearing into the clouds. What was odd was that the humans I saw about didn't even notice."

She shrugged absently. "They've no need to pay attention."

"Ah. My thoughts exactly. Until I saw the plane. It was on a direct course with the dragon, and yet it didn't detour. We saw the dragon because we were searching for it, but it wasn't real."

"I don't understand."

He dropped his hands to his sides. "I didn't either. It took a bit of digging. Did you know what the Light Fae can't stop talking about? It appears there is a half-human, half-Fae about with exceptional powers."

"I hadn't heard. I didn't think that was possible. We're not supposed to have offspring with the humans."

"I do believe the Dragon King has some help." Balladyn continued as if she hadn't spoken. "My question is why was he interested in Blackwood manor? Could it, perhaps, be because of you?"

Shara feigned outrage. "Me? He hates me. Why do you think he came to my house? He's out to kill me."

"That is one possibility." Balladyn pushed away from the door and walked to her. He lifted a strand of her hair in his hand and let it slide through his fingers. "However, I think it's because he wants you."

"Then he doesn't know me at all."

"You were sent to seduce him."

Shara faced Balladyn. "I've already admitted to that. Perhaps I got to him, but surely a Dragon King would realize he faced Dark Fae when he came to my family's home."

"It won't take long for me to mark you as mine. I mark everything as mine."

Shara lifted her chin. "And the Dragon King? While you're here talking to me, my family could well capture him and take your glory."

"They wouldn't dare." His words were casual, but the way his red eyes narrowed a fraction said he was considering it.

"Never underestimate a Blackwood. Isn't that what's always said about my family?" she asked with a smirk.

"I think I have underestimated everyone. You most of all."

Shara remained still. She wouldn't cower, but most of all, she wouldn't allow him to see how she trembled.

"I think the plan must have begun when you ventured into my fortress."

She couldn't draw air into her lungs. How did he know about her and Kiril? There was no way. No one knew, not even her family, so there was no way he should know anything.

He grunted. "Or was it after I showed interest? Is that when you and your family decided to trick me?"

A sigh of relief almost escaped her—until his words penetrated her mind. Her family. He thought she'd betrayed him with her family. She couldn't deny it either, because she *was* betraying him, only with Kiril.

"You're wrong," she stated as firmly as she could.

"Is that right? Why then did you leave my chamber after I deposited you here?"

"I went exploring."

His smile was tight, cold. "Where did you go, Shara?"

"I was here."

"With every lie you tell me, I'll give you ten lashes. And I did promise that if I had to use the whip again it wouldn't be welts I left."

Her bottom still ached from the lashes. "I was here."

"You really are a stubborn one. I'm going to hate to cut open that skin of yours, but you will learn your lesson. You see, the two guards hidden outside this chamber followed you to the doorway to your home and then back here when you returned."

There was no doubt about it now. She was royally screwed.

"I gather that's where Shara is?" Phelan asked with a nod to a door.

Kiril nodded. "How long is Balladyn going to stay in there?"

"Take a look around. Count the number of guards posted. That's his chamber."

"I know," Kiril said through clenched teeth.

"Are you sure she isna playing you?"

Nay. "Aye."

"I sincerely hope you're right, because I want to return to my wife," Phelan said.

Kiril glanced at him and grimaced. "We should find Rhi."

"Tell me something. How deep are your feelings for Shara?"

"Deep enough that I'm standing here trying to figure a way to get into that chamber and take her away from Balladyn."

Phelan whistled softly. "That deep."

"I'll come back after we have Rhi."

"Really? And you think I can keep your disguise up from that distance?"

Kiril scrubbed a hand down his face. Everything was falling to shit, just as he had suspected it would. His gut told him to call off everything and return to Dreagan immediately.

Then he thought of Shara.

And Rhi.

"Shara is smart. She'll keep up pretenses until she can get herself safe," he said and turned his head to Phelan. "Let's get Rhi while he's occupied."

They retraced their steps, and found the set of stairs that would take them to the lower floors that housed the dungeon. There were only two Dark guarding the entrance to the dungeon that paid them no heed.

"That was too easy," Phelan whispered as they walked down another short flight of steps.

"Who wants to get to the dungeon? It's the getting out that's going to be difficult." Kiril counted the metal doors on the right until he came to the twelfth one. He looked at the door, and then at Phelan. "There are no locks."

"Magic?"

"Perhaps." Kiril tentatively touched the door. When nothing happened, he placed his hand on the handle and pulled it open. The door swung open with ease, making only a slight grating noise as metal rubbed against metal.

He looked inside the gloomy cell through the darkness to a form that was chained to the wall. A thick mass of tangled black hair hung over her face, but Kiril knew it was Rhi.

"Dear God," Phelan mumbled. "What did they do to her?"

"You doona want to know."

Phelan's face was contorted with rage and helplessness. "Look at her! She's . . ."

"Chained," Kiril finished. "Shara didna say anything about chains."

"They're just chains. We should be able to break them."

Kiril shook his head. "Balladyn wouldna put simple chains on Rhi. She has verra powerful magic, and he knows that. Those chains must be special or she would've already busted out of them."

"I'm no' leaving her," Phelan stated emphatically.

Kiril swiveled his head to him. "Neither am I."

He opened his mouth to say more when voices reached them, coming closer and closer. Kiril shoved Phelan inside the cell and quickly closed the door behind them. Phelan flattened against the wall on one side of the door, and Kiril the other.

"I don't relish bringing you here, but it's for the best."

"Balladyn," Phelan mouthed.

Kiril nodded grimly. He wished there was a window or something so he could see who Balladyn was bringing to the dungeons.

"Forgive me if I don't believe your shite," stated a voice Kiril knew all too well.

He felt as if he'd been kicked in the stomach. Balladyn had Shara and was putting her in the dungeon. Kiril could get Shara and Rhi if he shifted into a dragon.

But getting back to earth from the Fae realm wouldn't be so easy. No one could see Fae doorways except the Fae because they didn't want anyone to know where their realm was—or how to get there.

Kiril fisted his hands and tried to control the wrath that was rapidly building inside him. He met Phelan's troubled gaze before he looked at Rhi.

"You shouldn't have betrayed me," Balladyn said to Shara. "I warned you what would happen."

"You mean you're a liar. Just like everyone else," Shara said saucily.

"You'll be in here until I can make sure every member of your family is wiped out. Only then will I know you aren't trying to betray me."

There was a loud bang as the metal door was slammed shut. Kiril squeezed his eyes closed at the sound. They had one chance to get out of the dungeon without being discovered. There wouldn't be two trips. All he could do now was pray that Shara could walk on her own, because Rhi couldn't.

Kiril opened his eyes to see Phelan next to Rhi. He walked over the rolling, rocky floor to them. He touched Rhi's hand to find it as cold as ice.

"That's no' good, is it?" Phelan asked worriedly.

"Nay," Kiril said.

"I tried to break the chains. I couldna even lift them."

Kiril took a closer look at the chains and scowled down at them. "We're fucked, my friend. Those are the Chains of Mordare thought lost. They were crafted by the Light Fae to hold the Dark. Once on, they can be removed only by the Fae who shackled her."

"Balladyn," Phelan ground out. "Rhi should've used her magic."

"Every time she does, a jolt gets sent through her body. Another perk of the chains. They're weighing her down, draining her of . . . herself."

"Nay." Phelan carefully moved Rhi's hair so he could see her face. Then he gently placed a hand on either cheek and tilted her face to him.

What stared back were eyes that were empty . . . soulless.

CHAPTER
TWENTY-EIGHT

"This isna Rhi," Phelan said.

"It's what's left of her." Kiril stood and walked away, unable to look at the shell of the vibrant Fae that had once been. "There might be a chance if we could get the chains off her, but that isna happening."

Phelan shot him a scathing look. "I'm no' leaving her."

"I doona want to either," Kiril said in exasperation. "Look around. You can no' even lift the chains. What does that tell you? If we can no' remove them, then we can no' take her out of this shit hole."

Phelan hung his head. "She wouldna leave me."

"I doona have an answer." Kiril put his hands on his hips and stared at the opposite wall. He wanted nothing more than to get Rhi as far from Balladyn as he could.

It had never entered his mind that Balladyn would have the Chains of Mordare. Had Kiril known that, he would have rethought his plan. As it was, he and Phelan were smack in the middle of an army that was on high alert.

"I should've never brought you here."

Phelan released Rhi and sat beside her. "You didna

bring me. I came of my own accord. This isna on your shoulders."

"And if you get caught? You, a prince of the Light? You've no idea what they would do to you. It would be a drop in the bucket compared to what they've done to Rhi."

Phelan bent his knees and placed his elbows on them as he dropped his head into his hands. "Rhi gave me a family I didna know I had. She searched me out and never gave up on me. How can I do any less for her?"

"You were fighting an evil Druid, Phelan, no' locked in a Dark prison. There's a difference."

His head lifted as he speared Kiril with his blue-gray eyes. "Would Rhi see a difference?"

"Probably no'," Kiril said and sighed. "Rhi has always been different from other Light Fae. She does her own thing, makes her own decisions, and risks her life without thought for those she cares about."

"Who was her Dragon King lover? I know it wasna you."

Kiril twisted his lips. "It wasna for my lack of trying. Hell, all of us wanted her. All of us. Fae are stunning creatures, but there was always a special light inside Rhi that set her apart, even from the queen. But Rhi had eyes for only one King."

"You willna tell me his name, will you?"

Kiril shook his head. "It's no' my story to tell. If Rhi wants you to know, she'll tell you."

"Why the big secret? It happened a long time ago."

"Because of the story itself. After . . . everything, we thought to never see Rhi again, and we didna until we began to interact with the Warriors."

"She was with me then."

"Exactly. Had it no' been for our alliance with you and

the other Warriors, I doona think Rhi would have ever helped us again. Which means, she wouldna be in this prison."

Phelan looked at her. "Balladyn wanted revenge. He would've found her one way or another."

"Aye." Just as it was inevitable that Ulrik and Con clash.

"What do we do now?"

Kiril dropped his arms and glanced at the door over his shoulder. "We get out and regroup. There has to be another way to break those damn chains, and we'll find it."

"Do you really think Con will risk Dragon Kings for Rhi? He hates her," Phelan stated, his gaze hard as he looked at Kiril.

"It willna be Con's decision. I'll return, and I know others will as well."

That mollified Phelan, because he gave a slight nod and rose to his feet. "It seems wrong to leave her, but we willna be doing her any good if we're caught."

"Wiser words were never spoken," Kiril said.

They walked side by side to the door, but as Phelan reached for the handle, Kiril thought about Shara. He put a hand on Phelan's arm to stop him.

Phelan compressed his lips for a moment. "I wondered when we'd get to her."

"You think it's all an act?"

"I doona know. You're the one who knows her best. Do you trust her?"

"Aye."

"That's enough for me."

Kiril prayed he wasn't wrong about Shara. If he was, he had just forfeited the life of a Fae prince. It was one thing when it was only his own life he had to worry about, but now he had to consider Phelan's as well.

"If you're caught, the Warriors will come looking for you," Kiril said. "As strong and powerful as all of you are, you've never fought the Dark Fae."

"The Dragon Kings have. Tell me, Kiril, if you're caught, will Con and the others leave you in here? Or will they come for you?"

Kiril grinned. "They'll come."

"Because that's what brothers do."

"All right. I get the point," Kiril said with a shake of his head. "I'll go for Shara. Stay close, but doona allow yourself to be seen."

Phelan's brow furrowed deeply. "I'm no' afraid of being caught by these fuckers."

"You should be." Kiril pointed to Rhi. "Look at her. That would be you. Do you want Aisley to find you like that?"

There was a pause as Phelan briefly closed his eyes. "Nay."

"Stay close," Kiril repeated, "but hidden. If I'm taken, get out of here and back to our realm. Go to Dreagan and tell them everything."

"If they capture you, Balladyn will be expecting more Kings."

Kiril slowly released a deep breath. "That's why you need to tell them no' to come."

"Have you lost your mind?" Phelan demanded angrily.

"Nay. I'm being practical. One of us caught is bad enough, but if they get their hands on more . . ." He let his voice trail off. There was no need to spell it all out.

"I want it noted that I loathe this plan, but I see your point. Just doona get captured."

"No' my intention," Kiril said as he dropped his hand and Phelan opened the door.

* * *

Rhys hadn't liked Cork the first time he visited, and he didn't like it any better now. "I feel as if I need to scrub my skin with acid to get this dirty feeling off," he mumbled as he walked down the streets beside Con.

"Aye," Con mumbled as his gaze swept the area.

He glanced at Con to see his gaze taking in the sheer number of Dark Fae mingling with the humans. "I tried to tell you it was this bad."

"We're supposed to protect the humans, Rhys. We've kept to Scotland for too long if this is happening so close to us."

"The problem was us not eradicating the Fae during the war."

"That was impossible, and you know it."

"Aye, but we could've made them leave for good."

Con shifted his shoulders to the side to make room for a group of college-aged girls. "We were all weary of fighting. The treaty was the only option, or we'd still be in the middle of a war with them."

"I know."

"You question my decisions again?"

Rhys shrugged and tugged on the too-small shirt that he'd stolen. "I think we've become lax and kept to ourselves too long."

"I do believe you're correct."

Rhys nearly tripped over his feet. His head whipped around to Con. "Of course you'd say that when none of the others were around to hear it."

Con chuckled briefly.

Rhys flexed his hands in anticipation of killing Dark Fae. "I'm going to rip Kiril a new one if he's been taken."

"You willna be the only one. I doona like being lied to."

"It's no' as if he could've told you the truth."

Con cut his black eyes at him as they crossed one of

the many bridges out of town. "You try controlling a group of Dragon Kings and tell me how it goes."

Rhys remained quiet until they reached the end of the bridge. "You know Balladyn will be expecting us."

"You're assuming we find the correct doorway."

"Then there's that. Kiril has Phelan for help. We doona have that advantage."

"Oh, really?"

Rhys looked at Con and saw him smiling at someone. Rhys slid his gaze to where Con was staring. He didn't need to be told the gorgeous woman with coal black hair and eyes the color of molten silver was a Light Fae.

The woman was smiling, a look of aloofness about her that could only come from a Fae. She stood in the middle of the sidewalk so that others had to go around her. Rhys thought she looked familiar, as if he should recognize her face.

And then he did.

Her eyes shifted to him and her smile grew. "Hello, Rhys."

"I didna think you'd come," Con said before Rhys could reply.

She shrugged a slim shoulder clad in a tight denim jacket with a lacy pale pink tank beneath. Skintight denim encased her legs while slinky heels in the same pink as her tank covered her feet.

Her smile vanished, and she pierced Con with a dark look. "As if I would ignore any information when it comes to Rhi."

Rhys glanced at Con, but either the King of Kings had no idea that the Light Fae was known as one of the most famous actors in the world, or he didn't care.

"Will you help us?" Con asked.

She regarded him silently for a moment. "No Light has

ever gone into the part of our realm the Dark rule for one of our own."

"Why?" Rhys asked.

Her gaze returned to him, as did a slight grin. "Because as sad as it is to say, a Light can become Dark, but a Dark can't become Light."

"Have you tried it?"

She frowned, as if never considering his words before. "No, we haven't."

"So the Dark take the Light, but the Light never thought to take the Dark?" Rhys asked with a dry laugh. "Fabulous."

"You don't know them as we do," she replied quickly.

Con said, "We know them well enough. We also know the Light. I honestly didna think you'd come."

"Rhi is important to us, to me," she said.

Rhys frowned as he realized Con had actually gotten in touch with the Light Fae. He had a sneaking suspicion of who the Light was, but he needed it confirmed. "And just who are you?"

Her smile was blinding as she said, "Usaeil, Queen of the Light."

CHAPTER
TWENTY-NINE

Shara stood in the middle of the small prison cell and tried not to fall apart. This was so much worse than being locked in her room. This was hell.

How could she have ever imagined Balladyn being the answer to her problems? Just like the rest of the fortress, there was no way she could use her magic to teleport out of the cell to somewhere safe.

No, she was well and truly stuck. The worst part was not knowing what Balladyn would do to her. After what she saw when looking in on Rhi, she feared Balladyn wouldn't hold back his cruelty with her.

Would she be able to withstand what he had in store for her? And afterward he expected to go through with the Claiming. As if she wouldn't fight that with all she had.

It hit her then that she would be doing it alone. She had turned her back on her family, so they wouldn't come to her aid. Kiril, wherever he was, would have no idea she was being kept against her will.

She walked to a wall and leaned back against it before she slowly slid to the ground. Shara hugged her knees to her chest and rested her forehead on her knees. The anticipation of what was to come was most likely worse than what would actually happen. Or at least that's what she tried to tell herself.

The darkness was something all Dark Fae sought, and yet Shara wished to see the moon. Ever since she'd found Kiril in dragon form, she wanted to see him flying through the night sky, the moon silhouetting him. What a magnificent sight he would be.

Whereas her people were among the humans, the dragons were gone from the realm. Sent away so the humans could live. Shara didn't think either of the Fae would have allowed such a thing to happen. All the while, the humans thrived as the Dragon Kings remained concealed.

If that wasn't enough, the Dark wanted to find something they had hidden. Shara lifted her head as she considered this. The Dragon Kings were completely immortal. There was nothing that could be done to them by any being that they wouldn't survive.

It took a King turning on a King to kill one, and that happened on such rare occasions that the Dark couldn't wait for that to happen.

The Kings protected themselves to the point that they would do anything for one of their own. So different from how she was raised, and yet the Fae might feel the same if their race was threatened.

Whatever the Dark searched for couldn't be to kill a King. But it could be used against them.

It was like a lightbulb went off in her head. The only way a Dark could beat a Dragon King was with whatever they searched for. She hoped the Kings hid it well enough that the Dark never found it, because if they did, the realm of earth would be forever altered.

The idea of it left her numb. Odd how so much of her way of thinking had changed since she had come to know Kiril.

Her gaze snapped to the door when it suddenly opened. She quickly stood when she spotted a Dark Fae enter. Shara blinked and abruptly he was Kiril.

"What are you doing?" she demanded of the Dark.

Kiril smiled and took a step toward her. "It's me, Shara. The Dark Fae is a disguise to allow me to move around this place."

"I'm supposed to believe you?"

"Shall I prove it then?"

She merely looked at him, neither agreeing nor disagreeing in case this was some trick by Balladyn so he could punish her more.

"You found me in the cellar," he said. "By a door hidden with my magic. You saw me in my true form—that of a burnt orange dragon."

There was no way anyone else knew that. She ran to him and flung her arms around his neck as she held him close. "I didn't think I'd ever see you again."

"I'm here now," he said and smoothed his hands over her back.

She leaned away. "How did you find me?"

"I saw Balladyn enter his chamber, and I knew you were in there. I waited for a while before I came down to get Rhi. That's when I heard him toss you in here."

"So you have Rhi?" she asked excitedly.

His face was bleak. "Nay."

Shara's hands slid down his shoulders to his arms. "Then let's get her now."

"We can no'. She's being held with the Chains of Mordare."

Shara jerked away, surprise making her heart pound faster. "That's impossible. They've been missing for eons."

"Balladyn found them. He's using them on Rhi."

Shara felt as if all the wind had been taken out of her sails. "He's the only one who can unlock those chains."

"Let's get you out. I'll return once we figure out another way to get those chains off Rhi."

Shara knew it wasn't right that she was being rescued when Rhi was being left behind. Kiril had come for Rhi, not her.

"I'm coming back for her," Kiril whispered as he led her out of the cell.

As soon as they stepped out of the cell, Kiril's face disappeared, once more replaced with that of a Dark Fae. "How are you doing that?" she asked.

"I'll tell you when we're out of here."

He didn't trust her, and she didn't blame him. Kiril was surrounded by enemies. He was just being cautious. It was a lesson she needed to learn after all the mistakes she had made with her family and Balladyn.

She remained beside him with his hand on her arm as if she were his prisoner. As long as they didn't encounter Balladyn, they should make it out fine. They made it up the first short set of stairs without incident. It wasn't until they reached the top of the second flight that things went from bad to worse.

"Hello, Shara," Balladyn said as he leaned a shoulder against the wall and examined a small dagger in his hand. "I knew you would manage to find your way back up. Who's your new friend?"

She swallowed, and kept her gaze locked on Balladyn. "How am I supposed to know? I thought you sent him to fetch me."

"It seems my warnings to you about lying need a better lesson."

Shara began to shake. Kiril's fingers tightened around her arm, giving her strength.

Balladyn looked up from the dagger to Kiril. "I sent no one. So that begs the question of just who you are."

"I got orders," Kiril said.

"From who?"

Kiril shrugged. "It was a Dark from Taraeth's guard."

Balladyn's eyes narrowed dangerously. "Taraeth isn't here."

"His guard is."

Shara was glad Kiril was quicker with answers than she was, because he just might get them through this.

Balladyn suddenly threw back his head and laughed as he pushed away from the wall. "Ah, Shara, what a performer you are. I never had any doubt that you would deliver the Dragon King."

Her knees threatened to buckle as realization sank in. And she knew by the way Kiril's hand relaxed on her arm that if she fell, he wouldn't catch her.

"I don't know what you're talking about," she said, her voice wobbly with outrage and anxiety.

Balladyn grabbed her and pulled her next to him. She stumbled, her eyes darting to Kiril in the hopes that he would know she'd had nothing to do with whatever was going on. The warmth in his eyes was gone. Possibly forever this time.

"Show me your true self," Balladyn demanded.

Kiril's smile was as frosty as the Arctic. "If that's what you want."

The next instant, his true face appeared once more. "No," Shara said, but it was drowned out by the Dark who quickly surrounded him.

She watched as he was hauled back down to the dungeon without putting up so much as an ounce of fight. It wasn't right, none of it was. Shara cried out as something sharp pierced her neck behind her ear. She stilled instantly when she comprehended that Balladyn held the dagger.

"No more lies," he ground out in her ear. "You'll forget about the Dragon King, because even if he gets free, he'll think you betrayed him. My guess is that if he sees you, he'll kill you before you have time to utter a single syllable."

Shara sagged against Balladyn, the truth of his words slamming into her with the force of a tidal wave.

"You're mine, sweetheart. The sooner you realize that, the better off you'll be."

"But I don't want you," she said. It no longer mattered what happened to her. Balladyn was right. Kiril would never listen to her try to explain, much less believe her.

If she didn't have him, she had nothing.

Balladyn snorted. "I don't care what you want."

To prove his point he kissed her brutally, painfully while keeping her tight against him. Shara desperately tried to pull free, but the more she fought, the more he hurt her.

He ended the kiss, pressing the point of the blade deeper until she felt something warm and wet slide down her neck. "I wanted you beside me ruling this fortress, but I'm just as content keeping you as my slave, chained naked in my room waiting for me anytime I want you."

"Do what you want, but I'll never go through the Claiming with you."

"Sure you will." His eyes were filled with a strange light that bordered on insanity. "Unless you want to watch as I torture Kiril."

There wasn't a need to ask if he meant it, because Shara knew he did. She turned her gaze away from him. "You make me ill."

"I don't need your mind as I'm fucking your body."

As he pushed her into the arms of two of his Dark Fae soldiers who dragged her away, all Shara could think about was Kiril.

Phelan stood not five feet from Balladyn, but the bastard never saw him. Phelan made sure of it by using his power and concealing himself so that when Balladyn looked at the wall, all he saw was gray stone.

The hard part had been remaining still as Kiril was taken. Phelan vowed in that instant to kill Shara for her treachery. He almost left then to try to get to Kiril, but something held him back. It was a good thing he did, because he learned how Balladyn had tricked them all. The ass had only suspected the Dark leading Shara was Kiril, and he had counted on Kiril's worry over whether Shara would deceive him or not.

Phelan's beloved, Aisley, had once been forced by a *drough* to do horrible things. The same was happening to Shara except the horrible things would be done to her.

Phelan glanced down the stairs to the dungeon. He had given his word to Kiril to leave if he was taken and let the other Dragon Kings know what happened. Kiril would be guarded at all times, and since Phelan couldn't get inside the cell to talk to Kiril, his only choice was to find the other Dragon Kings.

Phelan turned his gaze to Shara as she was half-dragged, half-led down the hall. Whatever awaited her wouldn't be good, if the smug light in Balladyn's gaze was any indication.

Now it wasn't just Rhi who needed to be saved. There was Kiril and Shara as well.

Phelan followed the guards to make sure he knew where Shara was being held before he made his way back to the doorway. He stepped through the doorway back into the garden at the Blackwoods' and stopped dead in his tracks when he came face-to-face with Con, Rhys, and Usaeil.

CHAPTER
THIRTY

Kiril let his rage build and fester until it was as feral and uncontrollable as Ulrik's Silvers had been when they killed humans.

Shara's betrayal cut deeper than anything Kiril had ever experienced. He'd trusted her with not just his life but Rhi's. And even though Shara didn't know about Phelan, her betrayal affected him as well.

At least Phelan would be able to get out of Balladyn's fortress and back to Scotland. It was small comfort, but anything was better than nothing.

"Wait until Balladyn gets ahold of you, Dragon," a Dark Fae sneered, contempt contorting his face as they chained him to the wall of his prison.

Kiril looked at him calmly, hiding his fury completely. "Enjoy your reign, Dark, because it willna last forever."

The solider looked at his comrade and they both laughed before exiting. The sound of the door closing reverberated in the silent, eerie dungeon.

Kiril took a deep breath and pulled on his chains. He wasn't able to break them. Then he tried to shift, which would shatter anything that dared to try to hold a King. But for the first time, he wasn't able to.

Just as he had guessed, they were spelled to hold a Dragon King—in all ways. The same kind of chains that had held Kellan—except Kellan had gotten loose with his mate's help. Kiril didn't have a mate.

His gut churned with the treachery Shara had dealt him. How could he have been so wrong about her? Her duplicity had given the advantage to the Dark Fae.

He fisted his hands. When he got free—because he *would* get free—he was going to hunt Shara down. He'd wrap his hands around her neck as before, except he wouldn't release her or stop squeezing.

To think he had felt sorry for her, been lured in by her sad tales in regards to how her family treated her. Kiril had never thought himself able to be duped in such a manner.

Ulrik probably hadn't either.

Kiril didn't know what made him think of his Dragon King brother, but once he had, he couldn't stop the comparisons. The anger rushing through him was great, as was the need for retribution.

That was only after a few minutes. What would he feel like thousands of years from now? The answer to that was simple: much, much worse.

They should have embraced Ulrik to help him past his rage instead of sending him out on his own in a world he despised with every fiber of his being.

The door to his prison opened slowly, and a shape took form as it stepped inside. Kiril blinked, unsure whether his eyes were being tricked.

"It's been awhile," Ulrik said as he looked him up and down.

Kiril tried to take a step toward him, but the rattle of

the chains followed by a jerk as he reached the short leash stopped him. He looked over the jeans, black button-down, and boots to the golden eyes he knew well and long black hair that hung loose. "Ulrik? Is that really you?"

"Aye. Of all the Kings, I wouldna have expected to find you here. Rhys, aye, because he has always been the rash one, but no' you."

Kiril didn't bother to respond since there was nothing to say.

"Odd," Ulrik continued, "how females no matter what species they are have a way of deceit. I think it's part of them, just like breathing."

Kiril had to agree with him. "How much did you hear?"

"Enough. I wonder though, how much did you hear?"

"Excuse me?" He was taken aback by Ulrik's words. Kiril searched his mind for what had happened when Balladyn came upon them. He'd heard and seen everything.

Ulrik shrugged nonchalantly. "It's none of my business. I'm no longer one of you."

"You've always been one of us."

"Really?" He chuckled softly . . . coldly. "Is that why Con has spied on me all these years? Is that why I'm welcome anytime at Dreagan? Is that why my brothers visit me?"

Kiril glanced at the ground feeling as low as a slug. "There have been many wrongs done by us through the years."

"Always the diplomat, aye, Kiril? Sometimes I think you should've been King of Kings."

He shook his head. "I had enough trouble being King to my dragons. I never wanted Con's troubles."

"The men who make the best leaders are the ones who doona want the position."

Kiril cocked his head to the side. He remembered all too well that there was only one other who could have bested Con and taken the crown—Ulrik. But he hadn't wanted to be King of Kings. He had shunned the idea, stepping aside to let Con have it unchallenged.

"You matched Con in strength and power," Kiril pointed out. "You didna want the position."

Ulrik smiled, though it didn't reach his gold eyes. "A mistake I see now."

"Why are you here? I doona believe it's to help me."

"It's no'," he replied in a matter-of-fact tone. "I couldna release you if I wanted to."

"And you doona want to."

"When did any of you help me in the thousands of millennia I walked this wretched realm never able to see my Silvers held within Dreagan? When did any of you come to me through the long years as I suffered staring at the sky but unable to shift?"

As he spoke, his voice grew harsher, the hatred stronger. Kiril took a deep breath. "We thought we were doing the right thing. You were killing humans."

"Who killed dragons," Ulrik hissed.

Kiril looked down at the chains around his wrists and ankles that held him so securely that not even his dragon magic could get him loose. "Is this why you've come? To moan about your problems?"

"Nay. I'm here for another matter."

Kiril's head jerked up, but it was too late. Ulrik was already gone, the door closing softly behind him.

"What the fuck?" Phelan asked as he stumbled to the side after almost colliding with Usaeil.

"Watch that mouth of yours," she said with a haughty tone. "You may be a prince of our people, but that doesna mean you can speak so . . . crudely."

His gaze shifted to Constantine who had a smirk upon his lips. "Bite me," he told the King of Kings.

Rhys held out his hand as they clasped forearms. "It's good to see you, Warrior."

Phelan nodded and returned the grip before releasing him. "No' half as glad as I am to see you three. I was just about to contact Fallon so he could take me to Dreagan."

Con's smirk disappeared. "I gather you doona have good news?"

"The worst." Phelan ran a hand through his hair and sighed. "Kiril has been taken."

"The Dark female betrayed him."

Phelan narrowed his gaze on Con. "Why would you say that? Because she's a Dark? You who sided with me against the other Warriors when Aisley was still *drough*."

Usaeil's silver eyes shifted to Con as she lifted her eyebrows. "And don't dare say a Druid who gives their soul to Satan in order to have black magic is any different than a Dark Fae."

"What happened?" Rhys asked before Con could respond.

Phelan moved away from the doorway and relayed the entire ordeal in quick order. "Balladyn didna know it was Kiril. He guessed, and he was counting on Kiril believing Shara deceived him."

"Which she didn't," Usaeil murmured, her arms crossed over her chest.

Phelan shook his head. "Balladyn has her as well. I didna wait around to see what he would do to any of them."

"Good choice," Con said, his black eyes troubled.

Rhys rubbed his hands together. "I say we go in guns blazing, so to speak."

"You would," Con said with a shake of his head. "Nay.

We need to be subtler. Kiril and Rhi are being held close together, which will make freeing them easier."

Phelan licked his lips as he glanced at the Queen of the Fae. "You did hear the part where I said Rhi was being held by the Chains of Mordare?"

"Don't even say those words," Usaeil ordered, her skin going pale.

Con didn't even give Usaeil a glance as he said, "I heard you. It doesna change the fact we need to get her free."

"That isn't possible," Usaeil said. Her eyes met Phelan's, and they were filled with sadness.

"Regardless of how heavy those chains are, they can no' be too heavy for a dragon," Rhys said. "If we can no' get them off her, we take her—and the chains—to Dreagan."

Usaeil was shaking her head of black hair before he finished. "You don't want to do that. Those chains . . . just trust me. You don't want them anywhere near Dreagan."

"I'm no' leaving her in there," Phelan stated emphatically.

Rhys's forehead creased in a frown. "How bad is she?"

"Terrible."

It was all Phelan could say. There were no words to state how he had found Rhi. In the short time he had known her, she had always been bright and filled with laughter and a sarcastic reply at the ready.

He used to laugh at how often she changed the color of her nails and how they always matched what she was wearing. She was loyal to the Light Fae and to him to a degree that often put her life in danger. And despite a sordid history with the Dragon Kings, she had come to their aid several times recently.

"I can't lose her," Usaeil said softly.

That drew the eyes of all three males. It was Con who nodded and said, "We need a plan that will get us all in and out with our friends."

"I'll get Shara," Phelan stated. "I know where's she's kept, and I know Kiril will want her freed."

Rhys slapped him on the back. "Aye. You're right. I'll go with Usaeil and get Rhi."

Phelan didn't miss the frown upon the Light Queen's brow. He didn't have a chance to question it since Usaeil herself cleared her throat to get everyone's attention.

"I've got someone else I must see inside the fortress," she declared.

Con glanced around. "If you've no' noticed, Usaeil, we're standing in the middle of a Dark Fae lawn. I'm no' going to argue with you over this."

"That's right," she said ardently. "We don't have time. You get Kiril, Rhys will get Rhi, and Phelan will find Shara."

Phelan understood then. "While you confront Balladyn."

The Queen of Light smiled as she tossed back a lock of midnight hair over her shoulder. "He was once my greatest warrior."

"What was he to Rhi?" Con asked.

Usaeil hesitated a moment. "They were like siblings. Balladyn was there after . . ."

There was no need for her to finish. All of them understood she was referring to when Rhi and her Dragon King lover ended their relationship.

Phelan looked at Rhys and Con. It could be either of them. Yet, Phelan had seen Rhys with her. She interacted with Rhys like an old friend, not a lover.

Con, on the other hand, Rhi hated with a passion. And he returned the sentiment. There was too much hate for there to have been anything more, no matter how long ago it might have been.

"What's the plan then?" Phelan asked.

Con looked at Usaeil, and the two of them smiled cruelly. It was Con who said, "First, Usaeil will draw out Balladyn . . ."

CHAPTER
THIRTY-ONE

Shara couldn't stop shaking. She was cold all the way to her soul—cold because she knew whatever slim chance she might have had with Kiril had evaporated like a puff of smoke.

"Whatever made you think you could walk away from me?" Balladyn asked.

"It was all a ruse, just like you said." She cut her eyes to him. "I'm a very good liar."

His gaze grew hard. "That you are, but I think you truly did consider me."

"Maybe for an instant, before I realized what I'd be getting into."

"It doesn't matter. I've decided no one else but you will do."

She turned her head away from him. She knew it would infuriate him, so it was no surprise when his fingers clamped painfully on her jaw and jerked her head back around.

"I do love your spirit," he said, his red eyes alight with madness.

"Why not choose from one of hundreds of females who

crave to be your mate?" Shara asked after she wrenched her head out of his grip.

"Because they aren't you. You are my match in every way. Once you realize you were made to be mine, you'll come to accept that your place is ruling beside me. We have eternity for you to come to that understanding."

"That won't happen." At least she prayed it didn't.

"It will." He gave a firm nod. "I suspect it'll take only one or two tasks before we get more silver in your hair. That's all it will take to get that Dragon King out of your head once and for all."

She blew a piece of hair out of her eyes. "Ah. So that's what this has to do with. It's not me. It's the fact that I interacted with Kiril. Just as Rhi had a King lover."

"Rhi should've never gotten caught up in that world!" he bellowed, his chest heaving. "I told her it was wrong. I told her it would end badly."

"Let me guess. You were there when your predictions came true."

"I was," he stated with a small smile.

Shara wanted to wrap her arms around herself and try to get back some heat, but she refused to show Balladyn that tiny degree of fear. "Rhi needed you then. You did something good."

"I vowed to her family to protect her always." Balladyn looked at the ground, anger radiating from him. "I failed by letting her become involved with the Dragon King. She deserved better than him. Rhi was precious, important."

That's when it hit Shara. "You were in love with her."

His gaze slid to hers as he peeled back his lips is a sneer. "A mistake that was rectified when the Dark took me."

"No," she said with a shake of her head. "You still love her. That's why you've held onto your revenge. It's why you want to turn her Dark. Then you can have her."

His face slackened into a smile. "If that's true, why would I go through with the Claiming with you?"

She swallowed hard as her future came to her in crystal clarity. "To gain advancement through my family connections. To be with a female who was born Dark and not turned. Even if I do become the woman you want and rule beside you, the moment Rhi turns Dark, you'll kill me. Then claim her as your own."

One black and silver brow lifted. "You're much smarter than I gave you credit for, Shara. You'll make a fine match for me during our time together."

He walked away, his boot heels sounding on the stones. Shara barked with laughter that stopped him in his tracks. He slowly turned to her. "You find something amusing?"

Shara shifted her eyes to him, her smile still in place. "You assume that Rhi will remain here for you to turn her Dark."

"The Light never come for their own," he declared, the malice and hate dripping from his words.

"Those aren't the only friends she has."

It took a moment for Balladyn to catch on, but when he did, he spun and rushed out of the room. Shara couldn't stop her laughter. It grew louder with each moment as she pictured Balladyn rushing to Rhi.

No matter what punishment Balladyn had in store for her, the look of hatred and concern on his face was priceless. He'd underestimated the Dragon Kings, just as her brother had done. It was a lesson she herself had learned the hard way.

The laughter died instantly as melancholy consumed her.

"Oh, Kiril," she murmured.

She could accept her fate and remain with Balladyn, or she could make a run for it. She had no idea where she would go, and the chance that she would be killed was great. But it was better than living as Balladyn's mate.

Shara wouldn't wait around for Balladyn to return. The perfect time for her to do something was while he was occupied. She stood and walked to the door. There she paused for a brief moment to gather her courage before she threw open the door. Two Dark soldiers stood guard on either side of the door. She smiled at one as she leaned forward and grasped his sword.

They were so surprised by her tactic that Shara had time enough to hit the second guard with her elbow before plunging the sword into the first. Shara withdrew the blade and spun around, sinking the sword into the gut of the second guard.

If she was caught, she had sealed her death by killing two of Balladyn's men, but she didn't care. Shara had to get to Kiril and break him free of the dungeon.

What if Balladyn is in the dungeon?

She stumbled as the thought went through her mind, but she kept running. Her only thought was to get to Kiril who could hopefully find a way to free Rhi as well.

Shara rounded a corner and met another of Balladyn's men. His eyes widened as he recognized her. With no other choice, she thrust the blade through his heart. He crumpled at her feet, his red eyes staring lifelessly up at her. She looked down at her hands to see the blood spray on them. It turned her stomach. She wanted to curl up in a little ball and cover her ears while she closed her eyes and pretended none of this had happened.

That was something a little girl would do. She was no longer a little girl. She was a grown woman, a Fae.

And it was time she proved it.

Shara set her shoulders and pulled the sword from the dead Fae's body. She wiped the blade on his clothes before she continued onward. She managed to get down two more floors without incident. Most of the Dark didn't know who she was, and they left her alone. She was one floor away from the dungeons when she heard her name.

"Sharaaaaaaa!"

Her blood froze in her veins. It was Balladyn. And he would be looking for her now.

Phelan walked the halls of Balladyn's fortress once more in the disguise of a Dark Fae. He strode decisively toward the chamber where Shara was being held, only to pause when he heard Shara's name yelled by Balladyn through the corridors. He grinned, because it meant Shara had managed to free herself from Balladyn briefly. He had little time to find her before Balladyn did. Phelan raced toward the dungeon, because he knew that was where Shara would be headed.

A few Dark gave him weird looks as he sprinted down the corridors. Phelan could see the stairway up ahead that led to the dungeon. It was the only way down to the lower level. He caught sight of Shara as she turned the corner and began to race ahead of him. He started to call out to her, but stopped when he heard shouts ahead of them.

He let out a string of curses when Shara slid to a halt and lifted the sword in her hand to defend herself against six Dark Ones that came at her. Phelan dropped the Dark façade he wore and called to the god within him. Immediately claws sprang from his fingers and fangs filled his mouth. He saw a Dark come at her from behind and used his speed to reach her.

Phelan's arm came out in time to knock the Dark Fae away before it could hit her. Shara's gaze met his for an instant before they were fighting back-to-back against the Dark.

When the last Dark hit the ground, Phelan turned to Shara only to feel the press of the blade against his neck.

He held his hands up, noting how she looked at his gold skin and claws. "We doona have time for this."

"Who are you?"

"A friend of Kiril's."

"You're not a Dragon King," she murmured, her gaze on his hands.

Phelan grinned and wiggled his gold claws. "That's because I'm no'. I'll explain who I am later. Right now we need to get you out of here before Balladyn finds us."

"I'm—"

"Others are helping Kiril," he interrupted.

She lowered the blade so that it rested against her leg. "Oh."

"I know you didna betray him. There will be time to tell him everything once we're all safe."

"What's your name?"

"Phelan," he said and glanced around. He reached for her arm, but she moved back. "What are you doing, lass?"

"As long as Balladyn is after me there is time for you to get Rhi as well."

"Wait," Phelan said when she took another step away from him, half-turning as she did.

But it was too late. Shara was already running down the hall. Phelan started to follow her when he spied a group of Dark coming at him led by none other than Balladyn. He quickly altered reality again so to them he was part of the wall. He stood silently against the stones as Balladyn knelt beside the fallen Dark One.

"I'm going to kill her," Balladyn stated angrily.

Balladyn rose and stormed off with his men behind him. Phelan waited until they were gone before he appeared and once more looked like a Dark Fae. Phelan looked to where Shara had ran off to and knew he had to go after her. She was putting herself in danger to help them. The least he could do was make sure she didn't die.

Phelan followed Balladyn and his men as they tracked Shara through the labyrinth of hallways. He slowed, and then halted altogether when he approached the great hall and saw the multitude of Dark soldiers lying upon the floor unmoving.

Balladyn stood in the middle of the hall looking at the devastation of his men in confusion. "Shara!"

"Shara didn't do this," said an ethereal voice Phelan recognized.

"Usaeil," Phelan whispered. A smile formed when the Light Queen appeared next to Balladyn with a bright light around her. She floated a few inches off the floor, her inky hair billowing around her in slow motion.

Balladyn's face contorted with rage when he saw Usaeil. He turned his head and spit. "You dirtied yourself to visit me finally."

"No. I came for Rhi."

Balladyn shifted his feet, his hands clenched in fists at his sides. Behind him, his men were fanning out around them. Phelan crept closer in order to help in any capacity that he could. Not that the queen needed it.

"Your precious Rhi. I should've known. I was that important to you at one time," Balladyn said.

Usaeil never dropped her gaze. "Had I known you were being kept by Taraeth, I'd have come for you myself. Rhi would've as well."

"I don't believe you!" Balladyn shouted.

"And I no longer care what you think," she replied calmly.

"I'll never let you have Rhi."

"You'll have no say in the matter once I'm finished with you."

Balladyn smiled confidently. "It'll never happen."

Phelan had witnessed the Dark Fae fighting, but he hadn't seen the queen. Balladyn's men began to close in on the duo, their intentions clear. Phelan's claws lengthened and his fangs filled his mouth. No one was going to lay a hand on his queen.

He readied to leap out and attack when the light surrounding Usaeil grew, becoming larger and brighter until even Phelan couldn't see. He raised his hand to shield his eyes while trying to squint and still see Usaeil. There were shouts around him that soon turned to screams of pain.

Then there was nothing.

Phelan opened his eyes to see the Dark who had been about to attack Usaeil lying upon the ground at odd angles, obviously dead. All except for one—Balladyn. He was missing.

Phelan straightened and lifted his gaze to his queen who turned to him.

"Find Balladyn," she ordered and then disappeared.

CHAPTER
THIRTY-TWO

Kiril ignored the blood running down his arm from the cuts on his wrists as he continued to yank on the chain from the wall. As soon as a cut opened, his body began to heal it. One of many perks of being a Dragon King.

"You won't be getting free."

His head jerked around to Balladyn who stood in the center of his cell. A look behind the Dark revealed that the door was still closed, which meant Balladyn had teleported in. "Always so confident. You'll be knocked down a peg or two soon."

"I doubt it," Balladyn said with a smirk.

Kiril grinned as he realized there could be only one reason Balladyn would use his magic instead of walking through the door. His friends were there. "I doona."

"Tell me, Dragon King, why did you ever trust the lovely Shara? She's Dark."

Balladyn's words struck their mark, just as he'd intended. Kiril didn't want to ever hear her name again or even think about her. And he never wanted to speak of her again. It hurt too much. But he couldn't let Balladyn know that.

"Who says I trusted her?" Kiril taunted. "Did it never

cross your tiny mind that I might've been using her to get you to do exactly what you've done?"

Kiril's grin grew as he saw Balladyn's expression shift from confident to a glint of uncertainty. That flicker would soon turn into a full-blown tide of doubt. He might not be able to help his brethren fight the Dark Fae, but Kiril would do all he could with what he had. Words were a sharp weapon.

"Lies," Balladyn stated, one side of his lips lifted in a sneer.

"Are you so sure?"

"I have you, don't I?"

Kiril held up his hands, the chains rattling as he did. "It appears that way. You went to a lot of trouble to get me here. Why no' tell me what it is you want?"

"I want what the Kings have hidden."

"We've hidden a lot of things. Treasures greater than anyone could imagine, the recipe for our whisky, the—"

"Stop!" Balladyn's bellow bounced off the stone walls. "You know what it is I seek."

"Keep believing that."

Balladyn took a step closer. "Are you telling me you doona know where it's hidden?"

"Perhaps if I knew what you were looking for?" Kiril knew Con kept it secret for a reason, but it was past time for those kinds of secrets. Especially when it put every Dragon King on the radar of the Dark Fae.

Balladyn chuckled. "Pretending won't stop what I have planned for you."

"It's you who should stop pretending. You doona even know what you search for."

Balladyn was suddenly before Kiril, nose to nose, his eyes flashing. "I know it's a—"

His words were cut off by a loud bang at Kiril's door.

Kiril wanted to shout his frustration as Balladyn smiled coldly and vanished.

"Dammit," Kiril said and slammed his fists back against the stones.

The door flew open on the third hit, and Con filled the doorway with a smile. "Doona look so happy to see me."

"What are you hiding from everyone?" Kiril demanded.

Con's face closed off, his smile wiped away in a blink. "None of your concern, and before you ask again, it's that way for a reason."

Kiril wasn't surprised by the answer, and had in fact expected those exact words. "The Dark willna give up so easily."

"Nay," Con said as he walked to Kiril. "For now, let's concentrate on getting you free."

"Balladyn was just here, Con. He teleported in and out."

Con's hands stilled on the chains. "Where did he go?"

"I doona know. Tell me you didna come alone."

"Of course no'." His smile was full of retribution.

So Phelan had found them. Kiril dropped his head back against the wall and sighed while Con grabbed the chain in both hands and tried to wrench the links apart. Kiril found his mind turning to Shara. He was going to miss holding her in his arms, miss having her near. In the back of his mind, he had always known she could betray him.

"Will it ease your mind to know she didna deceive you?" Con asked as he gritted his teeth and yanked on the chains.

Kiril lifted his head and frowned. "What are you talking about?"

"Shara." Con's gaze was on the chains, his muscles flexed as he pulled. His voice was strained, the words coming through clenched teeth as he said, "Balladyn tricked you."

Kiril thought back to their encounter and how Shara had vehemently denied Balladyn's words. Her red eyes had beseeched him, but Kiril had been all too ready to believe Balladyn. Just what the bastard had expected him to do. Kiril should've known it was a trick.

"What has he done to her?"

Con relaxed his grip and shrugged. "Phelan went after her. He's the one who heard their exchange after you were taken and knew what Balladyn was really about. Phelan will find her. Doona worry."

"I've been such a fool."

Con caught his gaze and held it. "So you do care about her?"

"I would no' have asked you to offer her sanctuary if I didna."

"Aye, but that's no' what I'm asking, now, is it?"

Kiril turned his head away. "You're asking if I have feelings for her."

"Do you love her, Kiril?"

"Maybe. I doona know," he said with a shake of his head.

"There'll be time enough to figure that out once we've left this place behind." Con lifted the chain again and pulled.

Kiril looked at the links, but despite Con's strength, they weren't coming apart. He was about to tell Con to go find Rhi when he saw something out of the corner of his eye. His head swiveled at the same time as Con's. Kiril could only stare at Balladyn who had a satisfied smirk upon his face and a blade to Shara's throat.

She was breathing heavily, her hair stuck to the side of her face with sweat. Kiril saw a drop of blood roll down her throat as the blade sank into her skin a fraction.

"Stop," Kiril demanded, more afraid than he had ever been in his very long life.

Balladyn moved his gaze to Con. "You can pull on that chain for all of eternity, and you won't ever get it off him."

"You should know no' to ever say never to a Dragon King," Con stated casually.

"For years, I listened to how wonderful you Kings were, but I know the truth. I know just how dishonorable, immoral, and untrustworthy you really are. I know your secrets."

Kiril kept his gaze on Balladyn. He didn't dare look at Shara, because if he did and saw her fear, he would lose his precarious hold over his control. "You're referring to Rhi."

"You all had her fooled," Balladyn said with a laugh. "But soon she'll see the Dragon Kings for what you really are."

"He loves her," Shara said.

Balladyn pushed the blade deeper, and the blood ran faster down her neck. It was only Con's hand on Kiril's arm that kept him still.

"So you want to hurt us," Con said with a shrug. "Or do you want to find something we've hidden? I'm confused."

"I'm going to do both," Balladyn stated. His gaze slid to Kiril. "First, you're going to feel what I felt. You're going to watch someone else destroy your woman, as you Kings destroyed Rhi."

"Rhi wasna destroyed," Kiril said quickly to stop whatever it was he had planned for Shara.

Balladyn made a sound at the back of his throat. "If you believe that, then you don't know her as you think you do. Nor do you realize how deeply she loves. She loves with everything she has, holding nothing back. She gave all of herself, and what did she get in return?"

A dark mass seeped up through the stones in the floor and surrounded Shara. She jerked helplessly the moment the mass touched her. Balladyn released her and stepped back. Kiril watched in horror as the black mass suspended her above the floor.

Her eyes were wild with terror. Their gazes met, and he saw the regret in her red depths just before she was thrown against the far wall, her screams filling his head.

"Nay!" Kiril bellowed as he tried to go to her, only to be held in check by the damn chains.

Con rushed to Shara, but before he reached her, she was tossed against the ceiling. Kiril looked at Balladyn to see his homicidal grin just before he disappeared.

Kiril lost what little control he had as fury and trepidation filled him, sending him into a fit of despair to get free and get to Shara.

Rhi lay on her back basking in the sunlight, her hand twirling leisurely in the brilliant rays. How she had missed the sun. Never again would she descend into anything to do with the Dark. It didn't matter who asked for her help.

Even if it was *him*.

A large hand smoothed down her hair, a hand she knew well. Rhi turned her head and looked at her lover. He smiled down at her as he covered her body with his own. No one had ever loved her as he had. And no one ever would.

She wanted to ask him where he had been. She wanted to know why he had turned away from her, but none of that mattered right now. Not when he was in her arms again.

Her fingers delved into his long hair. Normally he kept it trimmed much shorter, but he had grown it out for her.

How sexy he looked with his long hair. Whether he wore it in a queue or let the silky locks graze his shoulders, he was by far the most gorgeous male to ever walk the earth.

She gazed into his eyes the color of—

"Hello, pet."

She jerked at the hated voice that had entered her dream. Rhi tried to turn away from Balladyn, to get back to the place with her lover, but it was gone, vanished. The pain from the jagged floor dug into her legs and ass. Rhi searched for the light that was inside her, the light that made her Fae. It was what had kept her going, but she feared it was dead now.

"Look at me," Balladyn demanded.

She kept her head down, though not by choice. It was too hard for her to lift it to glare at him. The Chains of Mordare were sapping her of every ounce of strength the longer they were on her.

"What? No sarcasm?" Balladyn taunted. "Is the light gone, pet? I thought you would've held out longer. Perhaps you aren't as strong as I thought you were."

Rhi wanted to remember her hatred of Balladyn even after she became Dark. He would be the first one she killed. No longer did she deny what would be her fate. She accepted what was to come, but there would be consequences.

Dimly, she could hear screams from somewhere else in the dungeon. It was a woman, and by the fear and pain in the cries, Rhi knew exactly what was attacking her. It was the same thing that had attacked her.

A male shout joined the female's screams. Rhi wanted to feel sorry for them, but she couldn't bring herself to feel much of anything.

Balladyn leaned close. "You're weak, pet."

She couldn't even bring herself to come up with a

response. He was right. Balladyn had always been right about her, about everything. Hadn't he been the one to tell her it wouldn't work between her and her lover?

"Give yourself to the dark," he whispered seductively. "Let go of the pain and the past. Become who you were meant to be."

Meant to be. She was meant to be guarding her queen. She was meant to be doing everything she could to annoy the Dragon Kings.

She was meant to be in the sun.

"No," she said, though it came out more like a mumble instead of the shout she'd intended.

"No one wants you. Not like I do," Balladyn continued. "I had to hurt you to break you and make you into the Dark that will bring the others to their knees. Just say yes, and I can free you from those chains."

Rhi wanted the chains off desperately, but not enough to give up the last of her light.

"No one will come for you," Balladyn said, a note of glee in his voice. "Especially not your Dragon King. He turned you away, remember? He released you, forsaking your love. He cast you aside like a piece of filth he couldn't get rid of fast enough."

No!

The shout echoed in her mind even as Rhi began to shake with rage.

CHAPTER
THIRTY-THREE

Con burst through door after door in the dungeon looking for Balladyn. He hadn't been able to free Kiril or stop whatever was attacking Shara, but he could kill the bastard who'd instigated it all.

Rhys was on the opposite side of the hall searching for Rhi with no luck. It would be just like Balladyn to move Rhi at the last minute before they could reach her.

Con kicked through the next door and stilled when his gaze landed on Balladyn squatting beside someone. Con barely recognized the figure as Rhi, and he probably wouldn't have realized it was her except for the fact she began to glow.

Whatever Balladyn was whispering in her ear wasn't working as he'd expected, if his face was any indication. Balladyn got to his feet and took a couple of hasty steps back.

Rhys rushed through the door and skidded to a stop beside Con. "Oh shit."

"There's no escaping what comes next," Con said to Balladyn.

Balladyn's head snapped to him. "There is for me."

In the next second, Balladyn was gone. Con shouted to Rhys to warn Kiril. Rhys rushed back out as Con started toward Rhi to try and calm her before she destroyed the fortress. Only once before had Con witnessed the explosive power of her fury. When the dust had settled, there had been nothing left of the realm.

"Rhi!" he shouted as he neared. "Rhi, you need to focus. Think of creating, not destroying!"

His words weren't penetrating her mind as the glowing increased. Con stopped before her and touched her, only to jerk his hands back when her skin burned him. Her head lifted, the strange glow shooting from her eyes as well. She opened her mouth and screamed as the glow burst from her lips.

Suddenly her arms were outstretched, the clinking of the chains drowned out by her shout. Con looked on worriedly as something lifted her upward until she hung in midair and the glow grew blinding.

There was half a second of silence before the explosion from Rhi shook the very foundation of the compound. Con flew backward from the shock wave. He slammed into the far wall, the impact knocking the air from his lungs just as the walls crumbled around him, trapping his arm.

Con covered his head with his unpinned arm as chunks of stone rained down on him from the ceiling. It took several minutes before the collapse stopped. Once it did, he lifted his head and shook off the dirt and debris. His gaze searched the rubble looking for a glimpse of Rhi. He found her lying, unmoving, atop a pile of stone, no longer glowing.

Con tried to rise, but his right arm was well and truly trapped. With his free hand, he shoved off the stone nearest him, but it did nothing to help. He continued to push stones away as rapidly as he could. Rhi was vulnerable right now, and it was also the perfect time to get her somewhere safe before she woke and repeated the process.

He had to see to Rhi, Rhys, Kiril, and Shara so they could get out before any Dark found them. Con grunted as he rolled off a large stone that allowed him to almost get free. A movement caught his eye. He looked up to see a shape standing in the large hole in the wall near Rhi. The shape became that of a man who turned to him.

Anger spiked through Con when he recognized him. "Ulrik," he said through clenched teeth.

His nemesis smiled slyly. "Did you think I wouldna hear she was taken?"

"Leave her."

"Or what?" Ulrik asked. "Shall we finally battle, *brother*?"

Con jerked his pinned arm against the stone, and managed only to scrape a large portion of skin from his arm in his bid to get free. He ground his teeth together as he watched Ulrik walk to Rhi and squat beside her.

Ulrik chuckled softly before he lifted Rhi in his arms. She hung limply, the broken Chains of Mordare dangling from her wrists.

"This is the first of my many wins over you," Ulrik said with a smile before he stood and walked away.

Con let his rage free. It erupted from him as he bellowed furiously and busted through the last of the stones. Blood ran down his arm from the rapidly healing wound as he raced after Ulrik, but it didn't matter where he searched because Ulrik—along with Rhi—was gone.

Kiril opened his eyes to see nothing but wreckage around him. He was lying on his stomach, stones pinning his legs and back. By the pain shooting from his back, he knew it was crushed. The fact he couldn't feel his legs meant that he had to get the stones off quickly so he could heal and look for Shara.

He pushed against the ground with his arms to try and dislodge the stone from his back, but it wouldn't budge. Kiril tried again, but managed only to rock the large stone, sending more pain along his spine.

"Wait," came a faint voice Kiril recognized.

"Rhys?"

"Aye," his friend replied. Rocks began to move around him as Rhys's face came into view. Rhys was covered in dust and blood, but his smile was bright.

"About damn time," Kiril said.

Rhys grunted. "Never satisfied, jerk. Just like a woman."

Kiril smiled at his teasing. It was a moment later that Rhys moved the stones from his back and legs. He held up his arms to see the chains dangling from them, but no longer attached to the wall. Only one leg was still chained to the wall.

Rhys quickly smashed the rock, breaking Kiril free completely. Kiril didn't want to wait for the healing as he pulled himself into a sitting position and searched for a glimpse of Shara.

"I'll look," Rhys said grimly. "I doona know what caused the collapse, but I doona think it was Balladyn."

As soon as Kiril could move his legs, he began to shove aside stones while calling Shara's name. The longer they went without finding her, the more worried he became.

"She was here," Kiril said as he stood against the left wall and pulled the dangling chains close so they wouldn't get caught beneath any of the stones. "Balladyn had sent something to torture her. She was here. I saw her. She was right here when the walls began to come down."

"It must've been Rhi who blew up everything," Rhys said as he straightened from rolling away a large stone.

"What about her? And Con?"

Rhys cursed and rushed away, only to return a moment later, his face bleak. "They're both gone."

"Maybe Con got her out," Kiril said, though his mind was on Shara.

"There's a chance Shara got out as well."

"Nay," Kiril said. He began to move the stones quicker.

Rhys grabbed his arm. "We need to get out before the Dark come."

Kiril glared at him. "I'm no' leaving without her. Or Phelan."

"Shit. Phelan," Rhys mumbled.

"Someone call my name?" Phelan asked as he walked into what remained of the cell.

Kiril saw him holding his arm. The Warriors healed, just not as quickly as a Dragon King. The fact Phelan was part Fae meant he mended almost as quickly as a King.

"I gather this was caused by Rhi?" Phelan asked as he looked around grimly.

Rhys nodded. "Where is Usaeil?"

"I doona know. She leveled a group of Dark Fae with some magic after talking to Balladyn. She told me to find the bastard, and I've been searching ever since."

"Did you see Shara?" Kiril asked.

Phelan exchanged a look with Rhys before he nodded. "Aye. She led Balladyn away to give us time to get to you and Rhi."

"Balladyn brought her here," Rhys said.

Kiril inhaled deeply before slowly releasing it. "He tortured her in front of me, knowing I couldn't help her."

"I'm so ready for that asshole to die," Phelan stated.

Rhys nodded. "I second that."

Con stalked into the cell then, his face a mask of fury unlike anything Kiril had seen since Ulrik attacked the humans.

"What is it?" Rhys asked.

Con's nostrils flared. "Ulrik."

Kiril grimaced. "I didna get a chance to tell you. Everything happened so quickly."

"He was with you?" Con asked incredulously.

"Aye. He didna have much to say, and he refused to help me."

Con dusted the dirt from his shoulders. "He took Rhi."

"What?" Phelan bellowed.

Rhys ran a hand down his face. "Ah, damn."

"Where do you think he took her?" Kiril asked.

Con glanced around. "Something I plan on asking Usaeil. Where is she?"

"No one knows," Rhys said. "She sent Phelan after Balladyn before she disappeared."

Con turned on his heel. "It's time for us to leave."

"Nay," Kiril said. "I'm no' leaving without Shara."

Con paused and slowly turned to look at him. "You've no' found her?"

Rhys kicked a small rock. "Nay."

"There is a lot of rubble," Kiril said. "She could be beneath any of it."

"Is there a chance she got away?" Con asked.

Kiril put his hands on his hips and dropped his chin to his chest. "You saw what Balladyn was doing to her. There was no time for her to get away."

"Let's hurry and look then," Phelan said.

Con gave a nod. "First, Phelan, you're Fae, so see if you can get those chains off Kiril while Rhys and I start looking."

Kiril waited impatiently for Phelan to remove the shackles from his wrists and ankles. Then the four began to quickly and efficiently look through the piles of rock. With every piece of rubble they moved, Kiril held out hope that he would find Shara, and yet there was nothing.

"There's no' a trace of her anywhere," Rhys said gloomily.

Kiril had to face the fact that she was gone. But where? How?

"Balladyn left before Rhi's magic exploded," Con said.

Phelan met Kiril's gaze and said, "So there's a chance he could've taken her."

"Then I'll find him," Kiril vowed. His gut twisted with anxiety at what Balladyn could be doing to her.

"Nay," Con said as he stepped in front of him. "*We* find him."

Balladyn surveyed what was left of his fortress and let his anger seethe and grow until it consumed him. To make matters worse, both Rhi and Shara were gone.

He didn't know who had them, but he would hunt down and kill whoever had taken them. Then he would bring both females back. Rhi was close to becoming Dark, and Shara he would punish for several years for what she'd dared to do to him.

As for the Dragon Kings, he wasn't finished with them either.

"This didn't exactly turn out as you wanted, did it?" asked a cultured English accent.

Balladyn whirled around, ready to take his head off when he recognized the man. Taraeth had aligned with him years ago, and it was because of him that they knew the Dragon Kings were hiding a powerful weapon.

"What do you want?" Balladyn demanded, looking into his gold eyes.

He smiled. "I want only to help you."

"Then where were you when I had the Dragon King?"

"Kiril?" He waved his hands at the name. "He's not who you need to concern yourself with. It's true that having any

Dragon King is a coup, but there is another King you need to focus on."

Balladyn rolled his eyes, because the answer was obvious. "Constantine."

"No. If you want to win, you need to divide and conquer the Kings. First, division. I've already begun it with Tristan. I'll have him soon enough."

"Then who?" Balladyn demanded. "And why aren't you telling Taraeth?"

The man smiled, his gold eyes twinkling with glee. "I already have. He's in agreement regarding who we target next."

"Who?" Balladyn asked again.

"One who challenges Con daily. None other than Rhys."

CHAPTER
THIRTY-FOUR

"Our time is running out here," Rhys said as he met the others in the great hall.

Kiril blew out a breath. "I agree. We've searched this entire fortress for Shara and Balladyn."

Phelan cracked his knuckles while he looked around at all the dead Dark. "I doona like this place."

"I know Shara's scent. I could find her in dragon form," Kiril stated.

Con crossed his arms over his chest and raised a blond brow. "And draw every Dark in this wretched realm? Your feelings for her are making you careless."

"You mean, he's acting like me," Rhys said, contempt lacing his voice.

Kiril stepped between them and placed a hand on Rhys's chest. He waited for Rhys to give a nod acknowledging he was calm, and then Kiril turned his head to Con. "No' all of us can sever our emotions as you have."

"I made sure all of you did for thousands of centuries."

"That all changed for the Kings," Phelan pointed out. "Con, no' even you can stop someone's feelings once those feelings have begun."

Kiril grew perplexed by the way Con didn't bat an eye at Phelan's words. It made Kiril suspicious of just what Con would do if he was pushed.

"I hate to agree with Con, Kiril," Rhys said grudgingly. "But we're no' in a castle hidden in Ireland as we were with Kellan and Tristan. We're on the Fae realm. Shifting into a dragon wouldna be wise."

Kiril swallowed and turned away from everyone. "I know. Remaining here any longer is dangerous. We need to return to our realm."

"Scotland," Con corrected.

Phelan snorted. "First, we need to get the hell off this realm through the one doorway I know that leads back to Earth."

Kiril fell into step behind Rhys, who followed Phelan as they exited the great hall down a corridor. He glanced over his shoulder at Con whose black eyes were as cold and blank as always. Something more was going on that Constantine wasn't telling them. The fact Ulrik had been there was bad enough, but he had also left with Rhi. Nothing good could come of that.

"Was Rhi awake when Ulrik took her?" Phelan asked Con.

"Nay."

Rhys shot Con a glare over his shoulder. "Really? One-word answers?"

"I doona know if she'll wake, to answer your next question, Phelan," Con said.

Phelan cleared his throat twice before he asked, "Has she ever . . . done anything like that before?"

"You mean blow up a place?" Rhys asked with a wry smile. "Once."

"And she was all right," Phelan said in relief and threw a smile over his shoulder.

Kiril had only to look at Con to know that everything was far from all right. "What are you keeping from us?"

Phelan halted and faced them. "Answer him, Con, or we doona leave."

With Phelan being the only one to see the Fae doorways, he could keep them there as long as he wanted. Kiril's gaze moved to Con while he waited for him to answer.

"There's a verra good chance Rhi is gone from us."

Phelan's gaze slid away to stare off at nothing. "You think Balladyn turned her."

"I didna say that," Con said in a kinder voice. "I'm merely stating that she was held for a while."

Rhys briefly squeezed Phelan's shoulder. "We willna know anything until we see her again."

"*If* we see her, you mean." Phelan's blue-gray eyes were filled with apprehension.

Kiril looked at Con, waiting for him to reply. When he didn't, Kiril said, "It might take some time, but if she'll return for anyone, it'll be you, Phelan."

"And if she returns, but isna the same?" Phelan asked. "If she's Dark?"

Rhys shook his head. "She willna be. No' Rhi."

The fact Con didn't utter a word was deafening. Kiril knew Con wouldn't say anything else as long as Phelan was around. Then again, he might try to keep it from the rest of them as well.

Phelan turned his back to them. "Let's go home."

He took two steps and was gone. Rhys glanced at Kiril before he followed Phelan, but Kiril held back.

"What did Ulrik say to you?" he asked.

Con stared at him with hard eyes. "Nothing worth mentioning. He was running his mouth."

"And Rhi?"

"Doona count on her help in the future."

Kiril squeezed his eyes closed for a moment. "You think she's now Dark?"

"I think she willna be the same. It doesna help that Ulrik has her."

"You mean there's a chance she'll stay with him."

Con gave a small shake of his head. "I'm merely saying it's a possibility."

Kiril pivoted and walked through the doorway with Con on his heels. As soon as they returned to Earth and the gardens at Blackwood Manor they encountered a full-on battle. Both pulled up short.

"Where the fuck have you been?" Phelan asked angrily as he growled, showing his fangs and using his claws to slash a Dark Fae's head off.

Con let out a rumbling growl and glanced at the gathering rain clouds that didn't quite block the sun. "Phelan, keep this contained."

"Already done," the Warrior stated.

There was a loud roar as Rhys dove from the sky in the form of a yellow dragon. Kiril took off running toward a group of Dark who were gathering their magic to direct at Rhys.

Kiril jumped into the air, shifting as he did, and slammed his left wing into the group, severing their heads. He spread his wings and sailed straight to the sky, only to turn and glide as he surveyed the battle.

A flash of light glinted off the metallic gold scales as Con roared loudly and swept through a group of Dark. Kiril drew in a deep breath and let loose a volley of icy breaths with Rhys blowing fire next to him.

Soon flames engulfed the house while Dark were frozen in place before being shattered into a million pieces by Phelan. The Dark scattered as they tried to decide to fight or save the house. Con didn't give them a choice as he caught several in his grip and crushed them.

Phelan was doing his part on the ground as he dodged their magic and killed any Dark who was stupid enough to get close to him.

Kiril spotted more Dark coming toward the house. *"We need to leave. Now."*

Rhys swooped down and grabbed Phelan before he flew into the swollen rain clouds. Kiril made a pass over the house as he searched for any sign of Shara. Lightning forked through the sky, followed closely by a loud rumble of thunder that rolled on for several seconds. Con soared past him, his tail hitting Kiril on his wing.

"It's time we returned to Dreagan," Con said.

Kiril spotted Shara's father, who stood still, his gaze on the dragons, amid the Dark scrambling around him. Kiril titled his wings and turned to follow Con and Rhys.

"Well, that was fun," Rhys said, sarcasm dripping from his words.

Con said, *"We should've remembered where we would return to."*

"We got away and made a dent in them." Rhys laughed. *"I didna like being surprised with it, but I did enjoy killing those ass wipes."*

Kiril didn't join in the laughter. *"We were lucky. If more Dark had been there, things could've gotten bad."*

"But it didna," Rhys said.

Kiril glanced over at his friend and saw a part of his hind leg was charred. *"You didna say you were injured."*

"I'm fine."

"Fine?" Con asked angrily. *"If everything is fine, they why are you no' healing?"*

None of them mentioned that there was only one being who could kill—or seriously injure—a King.

"You three are doing that mental-talking thing, aye?" Phelan asked in a shout as he looked up at them.

In response, Rhys tucked his wings and rolled several times through the air. When he stopped, Phelan's lips were pulled back in a big smile. Kiril looked over at Constantine to see a worried frown upon his face.

Something was wrong if Rhys wasn't healing. They healed almost instantly, and though a Dark Fae's magic could hurt them, it had never done anything like that before. The only Dragon Kings that had been there were the three of them, and neither he nor Con had sent any magic close to Rhys. Who then was responsible?

Kiril didn't like the apprehension and anxiety that nestled uncomfortably in his gut. He kept glancing at Rhys's injury, but not once did it heal.

They flew high in the clouds dodging planes. A couple of times Rhys wasn't able to hide his discomfort, causing Kiril and Con to fly on either side of him. They let him set the pace, keeping him a little ahead of them at all times so they could keep watch. Kiril's worry grew with each flap of his wings.

By the time they reached Dreagan, Rhys could no longer hide the fact that he was in tremendous pain. He struggled to remain in the air, dropping several feet at a time, only to fight to continue to stay with them.

Kiril had never been so glad to see the familiar mountains of Dreagan. They glided lower so that they could touch the top of the mountains if they wanted. He hung back behind Rhys while Con stayed beside him. Kiril grew more worried for his friend as Rhys's breathing became labored, his sides heaving.

When the manor came into view, Rhys stopped trying to remain in the air. He flew low, dropping Phelan in the field behind the large opening in the mountain.

Con tucked his wings and flew inside the entrance

first. Kiril flapped his wings to hover in the air as he watched Rhys try to make it to the mountain. Rhys's left wing scraped the ground and crumpled, sending him crashing into the ground where he lay still as stone.

Kiril dove toward him, spreading his wings to land just before he hit the ground. As soon as he touched down, Kiril shifted into human form and knelt beside his friend.

"*Rhys?*" he asked.

"What happened?" Phelan asked breathlessly as he raced up.

Con handed Kiril a pair of jeans as he walked out of the mountain and inspected Rhys's wound. "Just as I thought. This was done with dragon magic."

Kiril finished putting on his jeans, the news hitting him with the force of a dragon wing. He hadn't wanted to believe it, had refused to even consider it on their flight from Ireland. But the truth was staring him in the face. "How is that possible? I didna use my magic, only my power, only ice."

"I also didna use magic," Con said softly.

"What the hell?" came a shout behind them.

Kiril turned to see Laith and Kellan come running toward them. They skidded to a halt as a wide shadow passed over them. Kiril looked up to see an amber dragon circling them. A moment later and the dragon descended, shifting into human form before he touched the ground and rolled to a stop. Tristan stood and rushed to them.

"I didna know he was injured," Phelan said and wiped a hand down his face lined with concern.

Tristan stood beside Rhys inspecting the injury. "There's no doubt it was dragon magic."

"If it wasna us, then who?" Kiril asked.

Con's face mottled red as he lifted his gaze to the horizon. "Ulrik."

Tristan turned to Kellan. "Such events come to you so you can record them as Historian. Who did this to Rhys?"

"It's no' that simple," Kellan said and scratched his jaw. "I doona see your everyday lives. I see battles, meetings involving our future."

"The important stuff," Laith grumbled. "This is important. This was a battle."

Kellan shrugged. "I wish I could help. But right or no', that's the way of it. I doona have a choice of what I get to see or doona see."

"Only dragons can use dragon magic," Kiril pointed out.

Tristan laid a comforting hand on Rhys. "Kellan, what if you try to discover what happened?"

Everyone turned to Kellan as he closed his eyes. Several seconds passed before he took a deep breath. "I see the battle," Kellan said. "I see the Dark Fae and the house. I see the four of you fighting—Phelan in Warrior form, and the rest as dragons."

Kiril held his breath, both wanting to know if it was Ulrik so they would have an answer, and hoping it wasn't him.

"I see Kiril laying ice and Rhys laying flames along the Dark. I see Rhys grabbing Phelan before being hit with the dragon magic. Then you all are returning home." Kellan opened his eyes and looked at Con. "I can no' see who directed the magic at Rhys, only the impact."

"Which tells us nothing," Laith said into the silence that followed.

Con faced Kellan. "Only a dragon can use our magic. The only other King is Ulrik."

"Aye, but we bound his magic," Kiril said.

Con's black gaze cut to him. "He's figured out a way. Maybe Druids are helping him, or even the Fae. I doona care the reasoning. What this tells me is that it's time I killed Ulrik."

CHAPTER
THIRTY-FIVE

One minute Shara was fighting for her life against the black smoke, and the next she was surrounded by light so intense she couldn't open her eyes. She sat huddled, her eyes squeezed tightly shut as she waited for death to find her.

Except nothing happened.

Seconds stretched to moments. She dared to peek and see if the light was still there. It was, but not nearly as blinding. Just bright enough to chase off all of the darkness.

A gentle hand touched her shoulder as a woman's voice, kind and soft, said, "You can open your eyes now, Shara."

It wasn't a voice she recognized. More importantly, not a single Dark Fae would ever sound so . . . pleasant. Shara was used to the taste of fear, but there was courage added to her arsenal now as well.

She lifted her head at the same time she opened her eyes, only to have her lungs lock as she looked at the room. It was filled with flowers—some tall, some short— but each petal drenched with color from bright to pastel.

The floor and ceiling were white as were the tall columns that held up the roof. There were no walls, just open air showing nothing but brilliant blue skies and rich, green grass.

Shara stood, her legs shaky and her heart pounding against her ribs. She knew where she was, but she couldn't believe it was possible.

"I gather I've surprised you."

Shara turned at the sound of the voice. Her gaze locked on a woman of unspeakable beauty with long, flowing locks of coal black hair and eyes that sparkled silver. Her smile was kind, and her eyes knowing.

She was suddenly very conscious of her red eyes and silver lock of hair. Shara glanced around to see if anyone else was in the room even as she noted the very human attire on the Light Fae.

"You know where you are, but do you know who I am?" she asked.

Shara shook her head. "Did you bring me here?"

"I did, Shara. As for who I am, I'm Usaeil."

The Queen of the Light. Shara felt her knees weaken. She was standing before the ruler of the Light, and still had no idea why.

Usaeil smiled and swept her hand to a set of chairs. "Why don't we sit? You've had a bit of a shock."

Shara's legs felt wooden as she followed Usaeil to the delicate-looking chairs of soft green. She sank down on one and waited for the queen to continue.

Usaeil regarded her for a long moment as she relaxed in the chair. "Tell me about Kiril."

"Kiril?" Just thinking of him brought a pain to the center of Shara's chest. "He's a good man. An honorable Dragon King."

"Yes, he is both of those things. However, I want to know your thoughts on him."

Shara rested her hands on her thighs as her mind drifted back to the short time she'd had with him. Her stomach clenched when she thought about his kisses, just as desire unfurled at the thought of being in his arms.

She blinked away the tears that gathered. "He trusted me when my own family didn't. He offered me sanctuary at Dreagan if I wanted it. He's unlike any male I've ever known. Or ever will know. I care about him deeply."

Love. It was love she felt, but she dared not say it, not to anyone. She was a Dark Fae. The only ones who would ever accept her were her own kind. At least they used to. They wouldn't now.

"You risked your life to help him even though he believed you'd betrayed him," the queen said.

Shara swallowed as she focused on the Light Fae. "I knew he wouldn't listen to my explanations, and they didn't matter anyway. He came for Rhi, and his friends came for both of them. I wanted to help."

"Do you know Balladyn was once a highly regarded member of my court and army?"

"He told me as much."

"Taraeth broke him as Taraeth has done to so many of my people," the queen said sadly. "Rhi was lost without Balladyn. He was like a brother to her."

"And yet he coveted her for his own."

Usaeil's lips compressed. "Yes, I know. Everyone knew but Rhi. I thought Rhi might come to see him as her future husband, but then she met . . ."

She trailed off, but Shara knew who she meant. "Her Dragon King."

"Aye. Their love was instant and powerful. It, like their desires, wouldn't be denied."

"Did you approve?"

Usaeil grinned slightly. "It wouldn't have mattered one

way or another. There was no stopping the two of them. Until . . . he ended it."

"Do you know why?"

She shook her head. "Only the two of them know the truth, and I doubt either will ever tell anyone. Rhi returned to us broken. It was Balladyn who helped to heal her. Or so we thought. Rhi, in her mindless state, ventured into the wrong doorway. A doorway, mind you, that not even I dare go into."

"Her lover did, didn't he?" Shara guessed.

"Aye. As soon as he learned where she went, he followed. No Dragon King had ever entered a Fae doorway before."

"How did he find it? Only the Fae can see our doorways."

Usaeil crossed one long leg over the other. "He asked me to take him to it, and I did. I honestly didn't expect him to go through it, but not only did he, he also returned Rhi to us. To this day thousands of years later, she doesn't know what he did for her."

"Why not tell her?" Shara didn't think she could keep such a thing to herself.

"Because he asked me not to."

"And you complied? I didn't think the Kings and the Fae liked each other."

She shrugged nonchalantly. "The Light get along all right with them, though we tend to keep our distance. I agreed to his demand because it was the right thing to do. If Rhi knew what he did for her, she would go to him, and he made it clear there could never be anything between them again."

"What a sad story." Then it hit Shara that there might be a reason the queen had shared it with her. "Is this your way of telling me that there can never be anything between me and Kiril?"

"Not at all. I don't know why I told you about Rhi and him."

"Who was her lover?"

Usaeil merely smiled. "That you won't get from me."

"No one will tell me."

"There's a reason for that."

Shara found that she had relaxed during their chat. She leaned over and smelled a bright yellow flower. "The Dark Fae don't come to the side of Light."

"We share a realm, Shara. The invisible line that divides our realm doesn't keep the Dark from taking the Light or the Light from venturing into the Dark."

She met the queen's silver gaze. "Why am I here?"

"I've watched you, you know. I've seen you with Kiril, and I've seen the decisions you made. He changed you."

"Yes," she admitted in a mumble as she looked at the floor. "I can't be the Fae my family expected me to be, but I can't be anything else. I'm Dark."

"Are you?" Usaeil asked casually. "I don't believe so."

Shara's gaze snapped up. She lifted the lock of silver hair. "Look at my hair. Look at my eyes. I'm Dark."

"I see one thick strand of silver in your hair, yes."

Shara could feel her heart pounding against her ribs. The one glance she had spared around the large room hadn't shown a mirror. She wondered if there was one nearby.

"Ask me," Usaeil urged.

The courage Shara had found earlier evaporated as if it had never been. The thought of looking into the mirror and seeing her red eyes again would be too much. Instead, she said, "Tell me why you really brought me here."

"Should I have left you with the Dark for them to kill you? Or perhaps I should've returned you to your family and let them torture you for a few thousand years," Usaeil stated icily.

"I meant no offense."

"You didn't. Unlike the Dark, we Light don't punish for such things." The queen sighed dramatically. Then she grinned. "If we did, I'd forever be punishing Rhi."

Shara felt as if she would never have her feet beneath her again. She had no idea what was going on or how she should feel about any of it. She dared not to hope for anything. That had happened once already, and she'd watched Kiril slip through her fingers like grains of sand.

It was too painful to go through again. Hope might strengthen, but loss destroyed.

"I can bring you to Dreagan," Usaeil offered, her voice soft once more. "You can explain everything to Kiril."

"So he did get out of Balladyn's fortress?" she asked, one knot in her stomach unwinding.

Usaeil nodded. "That he did. As did the other Dragon Kings and Phelan, who you met."

"And Rhi?"

Usaeil quickly looked away. "She's no longer in Balladyn's grasp, but she's not with us."

"Is she with her lover once more?"

Usaeil's gaze turned back to her with a smile. "Ah, what a romantic you are."

It was true. She was a romantic. She hadn't realized it until she met Kiril. Shara looked down at her lap and licked her lips. "Thank you for the offer, but I can't go to Dreagan."

"Kiril scoured Balladyn's compound for you."

Shara smiled and felt the tears threaten again. Somehow she wasn't surprised Kiril had done that. He was that type of man. "That is the reason I can't go to him."

"Because he's looking for you?" the queen asked.

"Because I don't deserve him." She lifted her gaze to the queen and wiped away the tears that had fallen. "If I hadn't been born Dark, I would fight for him."

Usaeil raised a black brow and cocked her head to the side. "You come from one of the strongest Dark families. Are you going to let something like your birth, which you had no control over, stop you from taking what you want?"

Shara parted her lips to answer, but found she couldn't put a voice to them.

"You saw Kiril in his true form," Usaeil continued. "Did you find him difficult to gaze upon?"

"Far from it. I couldn't stop looking at him. He was awe-inspiring, beautiful, and spectacular."

Usaeil's lips lifted in a grin. "Those were almost the exact words Rhi used to describe her lover."

Shara couldn't sit any longer. She rose and paced, her mind racing with questions she couldn't begin to answer. It was all too much, and yet not enough.

"What is it?" the queen asked.

Shara halted while wringing her hands. "Fear has ahold of me. Fear to dare to dream of something I don't deserve."

"And?"

"Fear that if I don't try for that dream then I'll be filled with misery the rest of my days."

Usaeil came to stand beside her. "In the end, we only regret the chances we don't take."

"What if he doesn't want me?"

"You can't know the answer until you speak to him."

Shara faced the queen. "And if I don't? Can I remain here?"

"This is where you belong. You'll always be welcome here."

"Even though I'm Dark?"

Usaeil's smile was mysterious. "Are you sure?"

"Pretty damn positive."

The queen turned to walk away, and as she did, she waved her hand. Shara stepped back as a large square mirror appeared in front of her, hanging at eye level. Her gaze locked on that thick stripe of silver that fell by her cheek. She could use glamour to hide it, but she wouldn't be able to conceal it from Kiril.

She was about to turn away when she looked into her own eyes—eyes that were no longer red but . . . silver.

CHAPTER
THIRTY-SIX

Shara quickly turned away from the mirror. She was breathing hard as confusion swarmed her. Her gaze latched on Usaeil with a fierce glower.

"I know I'm a Dark, but it doesn't give you the right to trick me like this. Do you think it's funny to give me something I desperately want, and then watch as I learn it isn't real?"

"Whoever said it wasn't real?" the queen asked in a calm voice. She bent over and smiled down at a bright pink flower, her fingers reverently touching the petals. "There are many things that separate the Light from the Dark. Trickery is one of them."

Shara refused to believe what she saw in the mirror. It hurt too much. "This could all be a trick played by Balladyn."

The queen's cool façade vanished as she whirled around, her silver eyes shooting daggers. "When have you ever seen a Dark attempt to re-create the Light?"

"Never, but then I was born into a Dark family."

Usaeil folded her arms across her chest as she stared

hard at her. "I deal in truths, Shara. You can either accept that or you can't. Make your decision now."

She wanted to turn away from Usaeil and demand to see the truth, but there was the tiniest thread of doubt that what she saw was reality.

"Hope is one of the most powerful weapons to have. Love is the other," Usaeil said evenly.

Instead of turning away, Shara took a deep breath. "How are my red eyes gone?"

"It's true the Dark tell their own that once a Fae turns to the Dark there is no turning back. The fact is, it's a lie. Not everyone knows that, and most times I tell others that it can't happen. Before you ask, I've my own reasons for that."

Shara grabbed her stomach as if someone had just punched her. Was everything she had been led to believe a lie? Her world was spiraling out of control, and she needed something to hold onto. She needed Kiril.

"Doubt undermines the truth your heart senses."

Shara fell to her knees. She grasped for breath, to steady the world that was rapidly falling away. Truth. What was the truth? Could she recognize it after a lifetime of lies?

Usaeil knelt beside her, her arms going around Shara as she did. "Search your heart," she whispered. "The answers are there, waiting. You have to be brave enough to see them."

Shara squeezed her eyes closed and rested her forehead on the cool white tiles of the floor. If Kiril were beside her she could do it. If Kiril were there, she could face anything.

He is here, within you.

She stilled. The realization that Kiril had left a part of himself with her was like stepping into the sun and being surrounded by warmth and light. Shara grabbed Usaeil's hand, and with the part of her that Kiril had changed irrevocably, she searched her heart. She was hesitant at first, afraid of what she might find.

Then the truth fell over her one drop at a time until it was raining down upon her in a shower that cleansed her, graced her.

She sucked in a mouthful of air as she sat up. Her eyes opened and she saw the magnificent room with new eyes, eyes not blinded by lies and deceptions. The flowers were richer, the light warmer. Everything felt right, as if she had finally found somewhere she belonged. She turned her head to Usaeil to see the queen smiling brightly.

"I knew you could do it, Shara. You're special."

"What just happened?"

The queen helped her to her feet and guided her back to the chairs. Once Shara was sitting, Usaeil resumed her own seat. "I could've brought you here anytime I wanted, and you could've left at any time. I watched you as a child. I watched as you decided to end the suffering of the humans you kidnapped for your family, but you weren't ready yet. Then I saw you with Kiril. I saw how you looked at him, how you touched him. I saw your love."

Shara folded her hands together. "How do you know it's love? I'm not even certain."

"Yes, you are," she said with a wink. "Otherwise, why would you have been ready to give your own life for him? That's what changed your eyes, Shara."

She touched the corner of one eye timidly. "Because I loved him?"

Usaeil gave a little wave of her hand. "That was part of it. Anyone can love. You loved your parents, your family, and yet that didn't alter you. Your love for Kiril opened your heart and your world. Your willingness to give your life for his is what ultimately changed you."

"I did . . . awful things before. How can all of it be wiped away so simply?"

"It isn't simple. I don't think you understand how love can heal. And forgive."

Shara rose and walked to the mirror once more. She stared into her reflection, trying to recognize herself. "So this is me now?"

"This is you. If you want it to be you."

Shara smiled, giddiness making her want to dance. "Oh, yes."

"Good. Now. Let's talk Kiril."

It had taken Kiril and the others in dragon form to move Rhys into the mountain so he would be hidden. With every minute that ticked by and he didn't heal, Kiril could see more and more of the Kings blame Ulrik.

The blame couldn't lay at another's feet. The Dragon Kings that were awake had all been accounted for, and the ones still sleeping in the mountains had remained asleep. And yet it didn't make sense. Why would Ulrik attack Rhys? His hatred was focused on one individual—Constantine.

"He'll heal," Kellan said from beside him as they gazed at Rhys. "Con had a similar wound once."

Kiril turned his head to him. "When? I don't remember that."

"Few know of it. He's had two such wounds. One when he fought the King of Kings for the throne. The second was when he and Ulrik fought before Ulrik was banished."

Kiril shook his head in confusion and took a step back. "I might be old and my memories many, but I would recall if Con had been injured."

"Nay, you wouldna," Kellan said cryptically.

Kiril grabbed Kellan's shoulder and spun him around. "What are you saying?"

"I'm saying that Ulrik and Con had a confrontation before Ulrik's magic was taken from him. They fought. Both were injured severely."

"How did I no' know of this?"

Kellan shrugged. "Con didna want anyone to know. Neither of them did. It's why they fought well away from any one of us seeing them."

"Why tell me now?"

"I probably would've shared it sooner had I no' been sleeping for thirteen hundred years."

"There were millennia before that you could've told us."

Kellan looked away, a muscle jumping in his jaw. "I was dealing with other things."

His revelation was so perplexing that Kiril almost forgot the first part of it. "You said Con was injured like this twice."

"Did you ever want to be King of Kings?"

Kiril scrunched up his face. "Never. I had enough to deal with with my dragons."

"Most Kings have felt the same, but a few coveted that crown. A select few have it in their destiny."

Kiril thought back to Con's predecessors. "In all our time, we've only had five take the throne."

"Aye."

"What are you no' telling me?"

Kellan clamped a hand on his shoulder and changed the subject. "Have you heard anything about Shara's whereabouts?"

"Nothing, and it's driving me insane." Kiril knew he had changed the subject on purpose, and he would allow it for now because his mind was full of her.

"There is someone who can help."

"Broc." The Warrior could use the god inside him to find anyone, anywhere.

Kellan nodded and dropped his hand to his side. "It's a thought."

"What's a thought?" Tristan asked as he walked up and peered at Rhys's wound. "I do believe it's gotten a little better."

Kellan grinned at Kiril and strode away. Kiril watched him walk to his mate, Denae, and the two of them disappeared deep into the mountain, arm in arm.

"He's more mysterious at times than Con," Tristan grumbled.

Kiril chuckled and faced the newest Dragon King. Tristan had once been a Warrior with his twin, Ian. All the Warriors thought Tristan had died, but he had been reborn as a Dragon King.

"He mentioned I could ask Broc to find Shara," Kiril explained.

Tristan stuffed his hands in the front pockets of his jeans. "Aye, you could. Broc would be willing to help, I'm sure of it. Shall I contact him?"

Kiril shook his head, his gaze on Rhys. "Shara is a survivor. I'll search for her once Rhys is once more himself."

"And if Balladyn has her?"

"He doesna." At least Kiril prayed he didn't. "If he did, Balladyn would've let me know to rub it in."

Rhys moved, a rumble of a moan coming from him. Kiril looked at his scales to see the yellow wasn't as bright as before.

"It's been hours," Tristan said. "He should've healed by now."

"You've no' had to fight other Dragon Kings so you doona know how deadly one blast of our magic can be. We're powerful creatures, and it's why only another Dragon King can kill us."

"And it takes longer to heal from such a wound?"

Kiril placed a hand on Rhys's shoulder near his large dragon head. "Aye."

He removed his hand and began to turn away when Tristan stopped him with a firm grip on his arm.

"Look," Tristan said as his gaze focused on Rhys.

Kiril followed his gaze to Rhys's wound. He frowned as he saw it heal a fraction. Kiril touched Rhys again, and to his surprise, the wound healed once more.

He dropped his hand and told Tristan, "You try it."

Tristan put his hand on Rhys, and a moment later the injury shrank.

"I'll be damned," Kiril mumbled. He looked at Tristan. "Find as many of us as you can."

Tristan ran off as Kiril put his hand on Rhys. "Come on, old friend. It's time you woke."

"What's going on?" Con asked as he entered with the others.

Tristan returned to Kiril's side and put his hands on Rhys. Hal, Guy, Kellan, Banan, and Laith did the same.

Con stopped on Kiril's other side. "Kiril?"

"We touched Rhys and he healed," he explained.

Kellan's forehead creased. "We've never had to heal one of our own, but if it works, who are we to complain?"

"Since when can we heal our own?" Hal asked.

Kiril looked at each of them. "What does it matter? The past is the past. We're dealing with enemies on every side. Let's look to the future."

"All right," Con said and put his hand on Rhys. He leaned close to Kiril and whispered, "That was some speech."

"Whatever works, aye?"

Kiril looked up and found Kellan staring at him from the other side of Rhys's dragon form. Kellan's celadon eyes were watchful, vigilant, but he had a feeling he wasn't the one Kellan was watching. That it was Con.

"It's working!" Guy yelled with a whoop.

Kiril forgot about Kellan and Con as he turned his focus to Rhys's injury as they all watched it shrink and then disappear entirely. It was a heartbeat later that Rhys opened his orange dragon eyes and then shifted into human form. He braced one arm on the ground as he reclined and frowned up at all of them. "What the hell is everyone looking at?"

The cheer was deafening. Kiril held out his hand and helped Rhys to his feet as they slapped each other on the back.

"I was dying, Kiril," Rhys whispered in his ear before he turned away with a too-bright smile for the others.

Kiril's smile faded. It seemed their list of enemies just gotten longer and even more mysterious.

CHAPTER
THIRTY-SEVEN

Two days later Shara was standing beside Usaeil on the edge of Dreagan land. The previous days had been spent at Usaeil's side talking of Kiril, but also of the role she would have with the Light.

"The treaty says we can't go onto Dreagan land," Shara said anxiously.

Usaeil gave her a gentle push over the invisible boundary. "They offered you sanctuary and protection, Shara. They don't go back on their word."

"What if Kiril doesn't want to see me?" she asked as she looked over her shoulder at the queen.

Usaeil's smile made her eyes twinkle with merriment. "You won't know that until you go to him. His room is on the second floor at the west corner of the manor. Good luck."

Shara glanced away, and when she looked back, Usaeil was gone. "Wonderful. I get to do this alone."

She rolled her eyes as she talked to herself. Not a good way to start things. Then again, was there a good way to approach a lover who thought you'd betrayed him? Shara could face her family and even Balladyn, but she didn't think she would ever be ready for Kiril to turn away from her.

You don't know that he will.

It was true, she didn't, but there was a very good chance he would. She went over the speech she'd prepared the day before and repeated it countless times. It wasn't really a speech so much as a detailed explanation.

Shara watched the sun sink farther and farther into the horizon until it disappeared behind the mountains, and still she remained where she was. A distant sound had her looking to the sky where she caught the shape of a dragon amid the darkening sky and clouds. The darkness hid the color of the scales, so she didn't know if it was Kiril, but she suspected it was.

Shara used her magic to teleport to the top of a mountain deeper onto Dreagan so she could get a better look at the dragon. When she looked up, she realized the dragon wasn't alone. She counted at least six of them as they glided effortlessly between the clouds, their massive wings spread wide.

She sat and simply watched them, recalling how Kiril had spoken of a time when they had filled the skies. Shara would have loved to have seen that. The fact that the Dragon Kings remained secret made her sad.

They protected the realm and the humans, and yet they couldn't be who they really were. They couldn't take to the skies when they wanted or announce their true forms. They were prisoners of a realm that would likely try to annihilate them if given the chance.

It made her forlorn, just as watching them gave her an odd peace she hadn't expected. She had seen Kiril in dragon form, but she hadn't seen him fly, she hadn't witnessed him spreading his beautiful burnt-orange wings.

She wrapped her arms around her legs as she brought her knees to her chest and rested her chin on her knees.

The breeze was cool, the night silent except for the flap of dragon wings. The sky had enough clouds to keep them hidden, but also to allow her to see them.

One dragon branched off from the others and dove lower over the mountains. He disappeared behind one mountain only to reappear a moment later. It wasn't until he tucked his wings and dove into the valley next to the mountain she was on that she realized he was flying in the valleys, twisting and turning in an aerial show that left her gasping for breath and silently begging for more.

Kiril's mind was filled with Shara, and had been since the last time he'd seen her. He had a call in to Broc to see if the Warrior could locate her. He had yet to decide whether he would go after her when he discovered where she was. He had promised her safety, and the first time Balladyn confronted them, Kiril had turned his back on her.

With his mind so filled, he had taken to the skies. All it did was remind him of how Shara had reacted when she had found him in dragon form. That in itself still boggled his mind. She had seen his dragon magic. That was impossible. Then again, so much of the impossible and improbable didn't seem to apply to Shara. She broke all the rules without even seeming to realize there were any.

He tilted his wings and changed course. He flew low over the mountains and into the valleys. It felt wonderful to be free to fly to his heart's content.

And yet he felt . . . fragmented.

As if a part of him were missing.

He knew without even having to guess what was missing—Shara. She was so much a part of him that he thought he detected her scent. Kiril's mind snapped to attention. He swooped up from the valley and then turned to glide over the mountain. As he neared the peak, the scent grew stronger.

Then he saw her.

He turned and flew over her once more just to be sure it wasn't his mind playing tricks on him. He wanted to shout for joy when he saw her watching him. Kiril flew to the peak and landed. He folded his wings as she jumped to her feet and faced him. His gaze drank in the sight of her as he inhaled her beautiful scent.

"Kiril," she whispered.

Was that fear he saw in her eyes? He blinked and looked into her eyes again. They were no longer red. Was it some new glamour she was using? She took a step toward him at the same instant that he shifted into human form. He wrapped his hand around her neck and backed her into a boulder.

"I told you no glamour," he ground out.

Her smile was sad as she wrapped her hands around his forearm. "It isn't glamour."

"Your eyes are no longer red."

She swallowed hard, but held his gaze. "I didn't betray you. Balladyn lied."

"I know. Phelan told me."

"You're not happy to see me." Her voice was particularly desolate as she looked away. "I shouldn't have come."

There was no way he was allowing her to go anywhere. He held her firmly without squeezing her throat. "Why did you come?"

"To explain everything."

Kiril thought she might care for him if she had returned. The emptiness that had threatened these last few days grew. "As I said, Phelan told me. Now tell me why your eyes are different?"

"I'm no longer Dark."

He frowned. "That's impossible."

"I thought so as well," she said with a wry twist of her lips. "But it's true."

"Was it magic?"

"Of a sort."

He lowered his gaze to her lips, which was a mistake because then he wanted to taste her, to kiss her until she was breathless, until she forgot everything but him.

"It all worked out," Shara said into the silence.

Kiril knew he should release her, but he feared she would vanish on him. "I suppose it did. What will you do now?"

"I'm with the Light. Usaeil has asked me to join her guard."

"A high honor."

He looked back into her eyes. There were no more words as they stared at each other. He rubbed his thumb against her skin. Her eyes dilated and her breath quickened.

"I should go," she said.

"Why did you really come?"

"I told you. I wanted to explain myself."

"Then explain," he urged. Anything to keep her with him until he could come up with a reason for her to stay.

Her throat moved as she licked her lips. "I'm sorry for everything. I should've listened to you from the very beginning."

"They were your family. You should've been able to trust your family."

"It was you," she said and lowered her eyes to his chest. "You made me see there was so much more out there. I came to realize the only one responsible for my life was me, and I had to make the decisions, not my family."

"Good for you."

Shara shivered. His voice was deep and rich, almost a whisper against her skin he was so close. He moved nearer until their bodies touched. She was having a hard time putting thoughts into words with him so near. All she wanted to do was lift her face and place her lips on his.

"I . . ." She trailed off as a gust of wind moved over them and blew his long hair out of his face.

He was naked, the heat of him making her weak. And hungry. Her hands were on his arm, but she wanted to caress his chest with the dragon tat, his shoulders, his back. All of him.

"Aye?" he urged as his face lowered until their lips were breaths apart.

She rested her head back against the boulder and fought for breath to fill her lungs. "I was Dark. I knew you wouldn't believe anything I said after what Balladyn did, and I wanted to help."

"So you put yourself in danger?"

He had such a sexy voice, and that brogue. It sent chills over her skin and made desire pool low in her belly. She nodded, unable to form words.

"You could've died."

Shara met his gaze. "For you. I would have for you."

A low growl rumbled from his chest as he pushed his body against her, his arousal pressing into her stomach. "Doona ever do anything so foolish again."

She opened her mouth to respond, only to have him kiss her. It was violent, ravenous and yet sensual and alluring. His hand released her neck to slide around to cup her head.

Kiril couldn't get enough of her. He wanted to strip her right there and fill her. What stopped him were his brethren flying around and watching them. He kissed down her throat as she dragged in lungfuls of air. Her arms wound around his neck as her fingers delved into his hair.

"That was part of what changed me," she said between breaths.

Kiril lifted his head to look down at her. "And what was the other part?"

Silence stretched as she debated whether to tell him. Kiril wasn't going to let her off that easily. He kissed her again, slowly and thoroughly until she was limp in his arms.

"Tell me," he pleaded.

"Love."

His heart missed a beat. Could it be possible? Did he dare to hope?

"Say something," she whispered.

He cupped her face, holding the long strands of her black hair back. His gaze snagged on the silver lock of hair that he wound around his finger. "You stole my heart, Shara. Whether you're Dark or Light, I must have you."

"Many will still consider me Dark."

"I doona care. I marked you as mine."

She ran a finger along his jaw. "Yes, you did. Do you really want me?"

"I made a call to a friend who is able to locate anyone, anywhere. He was coming in the morn so I could find you. Aye, you silly Fae, I want you. Now. Forever."

Tears spilled from her eyes as she threw her arms around him and held him close. "I didn't dare believe."

"Believe," he said and kissed her shoulder.

"I love you, Kiril."

He pulled back and looked into her silver eyes. "And I love you."

CHAPTER
THIRTY-EIGHT

Shara looked out over the scenery while she rested her head on Kiril's chest, his fingers idly running over her back. The night had gone by entirely too fast as they made love again and again atop the mountain. The difference was that this time, she didn't have to say farewell.

"You do know they saw us," Kiril said, laughter in his voice.

Shara smiled as she heard the flap of dragon wings somewhere behind them. "Yep."

"They better no' have looked too closely at you."

She bit back a smile when she heard the possessiveness in his voice that caused a thrill to run through her. Shara rose up on her elbow to look at him. She trailed a finger along his strong jaw to his chin. "I fear this is all a dream, and I'll wake at any moment. Or worse, a trick by Balladyn who has gotten into my head."

In a heartbeat, Kiril rolled her onto her back and covered her body with his. "It's no' a dream, nor is Balladyn in your head. You're here with me. It's where I want you to remain always."

"A Fae and a Dragon King. That didn't work the first

time around." She didn't want to bring up Rhi's involvement with the Kings, but she had to for her own peace of mind.

"You're no' Rhi, and I'm no' . . ." His voice trailed off as he briefly looked past her. "We're no' them."

"Even now you won't tell me who her lover was?"

"It'll be the only thing I keep from you from here on out."

"Why is it so important that Rhi's lover be kept secret?"

He kissed her leisurely, carnally. "I'd rather talk about us."

"What about?" She let him change the subject. There was a reason the Kings felt the need to hide the name of whoever Rhi's lover was, and though she was intrigued, Shara respected that privacy.

"I want to show you every inch of Dreagan." His shamrock green eyes held hers. "I want you beside me. Eternally."

Shara's heart jumped in her throat. She was afraid to talk, afraid to even hope. It was enough that he loved her. She didn't expect more, though she wanted it with every fiber of her being.

And yet, she was a Fae.

"You were meant to be mine," Kiril continued. "And I was meant to be yours. I doona care what you are or what you were. You hold my heart, and that's enough for me."

"Even the one King who dared to take a Fae as his lover didn't remain with her. I'd rather know that this can't go anywhere than to get my hopes up for more."

Kiril jumped to his feet and held out his hand. "Come."

"Where?" she asked, gathering her clothes before grabbing his hand.

He pulled her to her feet. "Dawn is here."

She looked at the sky to see the clouds drenched in deep red and the same burnt orange as Kiril's scales.

Shara finished dressing and turned to him, only to find a dragon before her once more.

"Oh, you did that on purpose," she said with her hands on her hips. "You can't tell me anything now. We're going to have to discuss some rules, you know."

She could've sworn he smiled. Even then she couldn't stay irritated at him. Dragons began to fly closer to them, as if dawn signaled the end to their freedom.

Shara gazed at the huge hand with glossy talons that Kiril held out palm down. She understood what he was asking and didn't hesitate to go to him. Her hands slid along his shiny scales to find them warm to the touch.

She glanced at his head to find his dragon eyes watching her. Shara hurried up his arm and shoulder to settle at the end of his neck where it met his back. He rose, causing her to laugh as she quickly grabbed onto his scales. A moment later he leapt into the air, his enormous wings spreading wide to catch the air current.

Her smile was wide, her laughter loud as the wind whipped around her. Shara wasn't afraid of falling, because she knew Kiril would keep her safe. He soared among the clouds, sailed over the land showing her a world she would never have been able to imagine.

She spread her arms wide and threw back her head with her eyes closed. This was heaven, nirvana. How she wished she could've seen the world when the dragons still ruled.

Kiril dove down, causing Shara to grab hold of him once more. She saw he was headed toward a mountain that had an opening large enough to fit a jumbo jet inside it. One by one the dragons disappeared into the mountain the higher the sun rose. Kiril circled the mountain twice, gliding lower and lower each time.

Shara spotted a man standing at the entrance. He wore

a pair of faded jeans and nothing else. His gaze was locked on her as Kiril flew straight at the opening.

The euphoria vanished when Kiril flew through the mountain entrance and alighted softly upon the ground. The dragons she had admired in the sky were once more in human form and staring at her.

"He willna shift until you've gotten down," said a voice to her left.

Shara looked down to find a man with a dragon tattoo on his chest and long, wavy, dark brown hair and aqua eyes. His smile was kind, if not a little reserved, as he held out his hand for her.

"I'm Rhys, by the way," he said, waiting for her to accept his help.

Kiril turned his head to look at her over his shoulder and gave a single nod. Shara knew Kiril, but she also knew the stories of Dragon Kings and their power. With a healthy dose of respect, she threw a leg over Kiril's neck and took Rhys's hand. He helped her slide to the ground.

"You looked to be enjoying yourself," Rhys said.

Was that approval she saw in his eyes? "I did, though I enjoyed watching all the dragons fly as well."

"She more than enjoyed herself," Kiril said as he came to stand beside her.

Shara had been so worried about the other Dragon Kings that she hadn't even seen Kiril shift to human form. Relief eased her tight muscles when he reached her side.

"Were you concerned?" he asked with a frown.

She licked her lips, her eyes briefly meeting Rhys's gaze before skating away. "They're all looking at me."

Rhys chuckled and held out his hands to another male who threw something across the way. Rhys caught it and then tossed the bundle to Kiril who unfolded the material to reveal jeans as Rhys said, "That's because we all want to see the woman who has taken Kiril."

"It's not because of who I am?" she asked.

Kiril finished fastening the jeans and then looped an arm around her shoulders. "Oh, they want to know, but that will come later."

"Doona make us wait too long," Rhys said with a wink.

Kiril guided her to an arched opening that led into a maze of tunnels. Shara was so intent on looking at all the drawings and etchings of dragons along the walls that she would've run into things had Kiril not steered her along.

"This place is amazing," she whispered in awe.

"It's our home."

Her head swung around to him. "Why are you showing me this? There's a reason Fae aren't allowed on Dreagan."

"No' all Fae are prohibited. Rhi comes. Or she used to."

All the happiness faded from Shara at the mention of the Light Fae. "Still no word on her?"

Kiril shook his head as he took her hand and led her out of the mountain and into a house. Shara blinked as she looked around at the splendor that surrounded her.

"Welcome to Dreagan Manor," said a deep voice.

Shara's eyes locked on a tall, blond male in a navy suit with a pale pink dress shirt opened at the neck. He didn't wear a tie, but a flash of metal drew her gaze to his wrists where she spotted gold cuff links in the shape of a dragon head. There was no doubt in her mind this was the infamous King of Kings—Constantine.

"Con, this is Shara," Kiril said.

The King of Kings smiled, though it didn't quite reach his eyes. "A Dark who became Light. An impossibility that has now become possible."

Kiril cleared his throat and gave a hard look at Con. "Shara, this is Constantine."

"I've heard a great many things about you," she said to Con. "It's said among the Dark that you're the cause of the Kings still being so powerful."

Con's black eyes narrowed ever so slightly. "The Dragon Kings are powerful because we are united."

"Exactly." She ignored Kiril who squeezed her hand. After all she had been through, she wasn't afraid of anyone, not even the King of Kings. "United. You've managed to keep all the Dragon Kings here, and I guess there is a good reason for it other than this place being so beautiful."

Kiril frowned. "Shara?"

She looked at him and smiled, silently asking him to trust her. His slight nod was all the confirmation she needed that he did just that.

"What's your point, Fae?" Con demanded.

Shara didn't know if anyone at Dreagan would ever welcome her, but as long as Kiril wanted her there, she would remain. Even if she hadn't ever been allowed on Dreagan, she knew she must tell them what she knew.

"Taraeth is still in power, but Balladyn has his sights set on eventually taking it from him. There were a few things Balladyn said that made me think he wasn't working alone."

"Another Dark?" Kiril asked. "Someone powerful like your father?"

She shook her head. "Someone else."

"Someone outside of the Fae," Con guessed.

Shara looked from Con to Kiril. "It's just a guess."

"A good one, however," Kiril said, his lips twisted with regret.

Con looked away as he sighed. "If our greatest strength is our unity, then it's only reasonable that they'll try to destroy that."

"Bloody hell," Kiril mumbled.

Shara moved closer to Kiril. "It'll take something great in order to do that."

Constantine focused his gaze on her once more. "Do you know what the Dark searches for from us?"

"That was never divulged to me. All is I know is that they want it badly."

Kiril ran a hand down his face. "What is it they want, Con? Why is it something we doona know?"

"Because."

"That's all I get?"

Con put his hands in the pockets of his slacks and raised a blond brow. "It is. What is hidden must remain hidden. We should be more concerned with the person helping Balladyn."

"You know who it is, don't you?" Shara asked.

Kiril blew out a long breath as he realized he too knew who it was. "Ulrik."

"The banished Dragon King?" Shara said in shock. Why hadn't she put that together herself? It all made sense now. "Of course."

"You know of him?" Con asked.

"Didn't you discover all you could about your enemy before a war?"

Con smiled, this time it reached his eyes. "Naturally."

"So did the Dark. What they learned has been shared through the years. There's been much speculation about what Ulrik did to be banished."

Kiril's brow furrowed. "So you know of Ulrik, but no' what he did?"

"Yes."

"How did the Dark learn of him?" Kiril asked.

Shara shrugged, noting that both men's eyes were riveted on her. "Some say Taraeth sought him out, but the story that's the most popular states that it was Ulrik who came to Taraeth and made a deal to work together."

"To bring us down," Con finished with a curse.

CHAPTER
THIRTY-NINE

Rhys ducked into the barn and checked his side where the injury had been yet again. He could still feel it eating through him, though he was healed. The agony had been unimaginable, the torment inconceivable.

The fact he had been dying slowly, painfully was mind-boggling.

Dragon magic. There was no denying that's what had hit him. He knew because he had been struck with dragon magic before during the brief period when the Kings were split on whether to kill or protect the humans. Those faithful to Ulrik had rallied to help him annihilate the humans. Thankfully, the battle between the Kings had been fleeting, but even then many of them had died needlessly.

There was no doubt in his mind that the magic hadn't been used by Kiril. Con, though an arrogant ass most of the time, wouldn't be so underhanded. If Con had a problem with you, he dealt with you face-to-face.

Which begged the question of who had tried to kill him. There were no other Dragon Kings in Ireland at the time. Nor could a Dark Fae use dragon magic. Ulrik, though he had been in Ireland was unable to use his magic. Con had seen to that ages ago. The mystery was eating Rhys up inside.

His mobile dinged with a text. He pulled it from his back pocket to see it was from Banan's mate, Jane, who was manning the gift shop.

A WOMAN IS WAITING FOR YOU. SAYS SHE'S EXPECTED, the text read.

Rhys had completely forgotten about his date. Normally he dropped everything to spend his nights with a beautiful woman, but he wanted to be alone. To think and . . . to forget the horrors almost dying had brought him.

He typed, TELL HER I'M UNWELL AND WILL CALL HER SOON.

Rhys hit the send button and set aside his phone face-down before he braced his hands on the table and hung his head. None of the others could know his concern. Already the Kings were being hit from too many sides by their enemies.

His eyes closed and the face of every Dragon King scrolled through his mind's eye while he discerned if they held a grudge against him. There were many Kings who had returned to their sleep after the battle alongside the Warriors and Druids.

Any of them could have slipped out unnoticed from their caves and found him, but why would they? Rhys had yet to come up with a reason why he would be targeted by his brethren.

The barest of pops sounded from the hinges on the door, alerting him that he was no longer alone. Rhys quickly straightened and grabbed the electrical sheep shearers near him. He was cleaning the blades when he spotted Con out of the corner of his eye.

"Everything all right?" Con asked nonchalantly.

He glanced at Con and forced a smile. There was nothing casual about his visit. "Never better."

"I saw your date leaving without you. What's going on?"

Rhys stilled for a moment before he grabbed a rag and wiped the blades. "It's no' exactly a good time to be having fun, now, is it?"

"That's never bothered you before."

"It does now." Rhys prayed Con would leave things and walk away. He should've known better.

Con strode farther into the room. "I suspect Kiril will want Shara as his mate."

"Most likely. He loves her," Rhys said with a shrug.

"Who do you think would be a likely candidate to tear us apart?"

Con's question, posed in a soft tone, sent warning bells ringing in Rhys's mind. He slowly set aside the shears and turned his head to Con. "You think Shara is here for that?"

"She was a candidate for all of a heartbeat. She's true to her word and Kiril."

Rhys shifted to face Con and leaned his hip against the table. "There is the Dark Fae, MI5 or any other human organization who have aligned with the Dark, and then there is Ulrik."

"So you do think he could be a part of this," Con said with a small smile.

"It's a possibility, but why do I get the feeling you've got an individual in mind?"

One of Con's shoulders lifted in a shrug, his black eyes revealing nothing. "I asked for your opinion."

"I doona have one." He turned back to the table and oiled the shears.

Con leisurely walked around the room as silence grew. Rhys's side burned where his wound had been, causing him to grit his teeth. However, he refused to allow Con to know anything was wrong. He didn't want anyone worrying over him, and if Con thought something was amiss, he was just as likely to try to keep Rhys confined while he figured out what was wrong as to let Rhys discover it on his own.

One could never determine which way Con's decision would fall.

"You never told me what you think of Shara," Con said.

Rhys set down the shears with a frustrated sigh. "I like her. Now, if that's all, leave me to my work."

"It's no' all." Con stopped beside him. "Did you see another Dragon King in Ireland while we were battling the Dark?"

Rhys gave a shake of his head. "Did anyone leave Dreagan?"

"Nay," Con stated angrily. "Everyone has been accounted for."

That left only Ulrik. Rhys squeezed the bridge of his nose with his thumb and forefinger. "It can no' be Ulrik. We took all of his magic. You and I both know if his magic were returned he'd be back here in an instant for his Silvers."

Con leaned back against the table and rested his hands on the wood near his hips. "The simple fact is that he was in the Fae realm. He talked to Kiril, and he took Rhi."

"Of course he took her," Rhys said with a small shake of his head. "You expected anything different?"

"It doesna matter what I expected," Con said with a wave of his hand. "Shara told me of a tale spread among the Dark that Ulrik came to Taraeth and struck a deal."

Rhys's head swiveled to him. "What kind of deal?"

"I'd like to know." Con's nostrils flared. "A Dark's magic can no' trump ours. There is nothing a Dark Fae could do to reverse what our dragon magic did to Ulrik."

"Are you trying to convince me or yourself?" Rhys asked, his brows raised.

Con pushed away from the table and walked to Rhys's other side. Rhys remained as he was and turned his head to track Con's movements.

Something else was bothering Con, but Rhys learned long ago it was better not to ask questions. Con had a way of turning things around in short order, and Rhys didn't want to be party to anything at the moment.

"How bad is it?" Con asked offhandedly.

Rhys glanced at the shears and pretended not to know what he meant. "Only two blades are bent. I'll repair it."

"I was referring to your wound."

Rhys briefly closed his eyes before he stepped away from the table. "I doona know what you're talking about," he said and looked into Con's eyes.

"You're usually a better liar than that. I can see how you favor your right side. It's minimal, pain that comes and goes, but it's enough for me to notice."

"I'm fine."

"Another lie. If you were 'fine,' as you put it, you'd have taken that striking blonde out to dinner and then given her a good fuck as you usually do your women. The fact you're out here in the barn raises some flags. Now, are you going to tell me or no'?"

Rhys ran a hand down his face and considered Con for a moment. "Swear to me this goes no further than the two of us."

Con bowed his head, his black eyes holding Rhys's. "I give you my vow."

"It was dragon magic that struck me, but there was something else added to it. I can still feel the wound. The pain is at times nonexistent and at others immense. Whatever happened is no' through with me yet."

* * *

It was well into the afternoon before Kiril was able to abscond with Shara after Con had taken them into his office and grilled her for hours.

"I'm fine," she said, devouring the tacos on her plate.

Kiril reclined in the chair opposite her at the table in his room and watched her. The lines of strain around her eyes and mouth said she was anything but.

She swallowed a bite and playfully kicked his foot beneath the table. "Stop it. Con had questions, and I'm happy that I could give him answers. I want to help."

"Aye, and I'm happy you are, but I refuse to allow him to interrogate you as if you're a prisoner."

Shara shrugged after she took another bite. Her look said it was worth it. Kiril, however, thought differently. The longer she was with him, the more protective he became.

There was a soft knock on his door, and then Denae's voice came through the wood. "Kiril? Is Shara rested now? We'd love to chat with her."

"No' yet," he answered before Shara could.

Shara gave him a droll look and set down the last of the six tacos. "Why are you keeping me from them? Are you embarrassed of me?"

"Embarrassed?" The word shot from him with a blast as he jerked upright. "Never. I keep you here because I want you all to myself. The entire time we were in Ireland I longed for any glimpse of you I could get. The moments we were able to snatch were altogether too short."

"I'm not going anywhere. I told you that."

So she had, but it still wasn't enough. "I wasna jesting earlier. I want you with me always."

"I know," she said with a smile. "I wasn't teasing when I agreed."

"I doona think you realized my intent. When I say always, Shara, I mean as my mate."

"Need I remind you that it didn't work between a Fae and King before?"

Kiril rose and walked behind his chair, leaning his hands upon the back. "The same could be said of the dozens of relationships the Kings have had with humans. Please doona use that as a guide. I love you. I let you down in Balladyn's fortress by no' believing you. I'm prepared to spend eternity making that up to you."

"You're serious," she said softly, her silver eyes hopeful.

"I doona ask this of you lightly. No King does. I'm no' whole without you. I didna realize what was missing until I found you, and then the awareness became so obvious it was difficult to get through each day."

Her gaze dropped from his to the table. She stared at her food.

Apprehension turned his blood to ice. He had worried it would be asking too much of her, but he couldn't not ask her. If it took forever before she consented he would remain with her and keep asking.

He swallowed past the lump of emotion in his throat. "If that's too much, I understand. You've been under your family's rule. You probably need some time to yourself. Just promise you'll return to me as often as you can."

His heart was in his throat as he waited for some kind of response. Finally her eyes lifted to his. She set aside her napkin and stood. Kiril straightened, his hands fisted at his sides so he wouldn't pull her against him.

"You want me?" she asked in such a soft voice he had to strain to hear her.

"More than anything in all the universe."

She dropped her face into her hands. Kiril glanced around, unsure of what to do. He had no idea what to do or if he should do anything. Was she happy? Distraught? Angry? Did she want his touch? Should he leave?

Every question ran through his mind in rapid succession without a single answer to help him. He decided to remain where he was. Kiril couldn't imagine her turning away from him, but he didn't want to chance it. It would destroy him as nothing else could.

When her head lifted, her cheeks were streaked with tears. "I didn't dare hope for such words."

Kiril's shoulders sagged with relief as he closed the distance between them and pulled her against him. Her face was in his neck as fresh tears soaked his shirt.

"Is that a yes?" he asked hopefully.

At her nod, he held her tighter. He didn't know how he had gotten such a woman to be his, but Kiril was determined to ensure that she was always happy. No matter what he had to do, she was his priority.

EPILOGUE

Three weeks later...

Rhys stood back with a glass of whisky in hand as he watched Kiril and Shara leave the cavern after their mating ceremony.

Kiril's smile was a mile wide as he gazed adoringly down at Shara who only had eyes for him. She was beautiful in a deep-orange floor-length strapless gown. Her long black hair was down with the silver strip pulled back with a clip. Around her wrist was a bracelet of emerald-cut rare padparadscha sapphires from Sri Lanka—a gift from Con as a welcoming to their world.

On Shara's left upper arm was the new dragon eye tattoo that signaled her as a mate of a Dragon King. In the few weeks Shara had been at Dreagan, she had imparted things about the Dark Fae.

Henry, the Kings' human friend in MI5, was keeping track of Dark Fae movements around the world. In the short time they had been watching, it was clear the Dark were up to something.

Rhys's gaze shifted to Con who was the last to leave

the cavern. He had been quietly watching Ulrik for days through the video feed from Perth, waiting for him to make a wrong move, but so far Ulrik had done nothing. Rhys wondered how much longer Con would wait before he went after Ulrik.

"Another mated," Con said as he stopped beside him.

Rhys lifted his glass in salute when Kiril looked at him. With a smile on his face directed at Kiril, Rhys told Con, "It's unstoppable now. We went through thousands of millennia without mating. Perhaps it's time."

"Are you next then?"

His smile disappeared as he jerked his gaze to Con. "Doona even jest. It's no' for me."

"Nor me," Con agreed. "Yet the others seem happy."

"Let's hope they remain that way." Rhys downed the whisky in one swallow. He glared at Con when he found him staring. "The pain is minimal tonight."

"We willna be able to keep it from everyone for much longer."

"We have to," Rhys said urgently. "I doona want anyone to find out. At least no' until we know what's going on."

Con's lips flattened into a line. "I'm working on it, though it would be easier if I could have others looking into it as well."

"It's bad enough you mentioned it to Phelan."

Con faced the festivities as music began to blare. Kiril and Shara were in each other's arms dancing in slow circles beneath the moonlight. "He willna say a word to anyone. He's trustworthy."

"I'm finding it hard to trust anyone," Rhys admitted. "A King did this to me, Con. I want to know who."

Con grimly watched him disappear into the night. "I do too, my friend."

* * *

Rhi opened her eyes only to be blinded by bright, beautiful sunlight. She squinted against it, her fingers moving in the warm rays. She rolled over onto her back and realized she was in her cabin. Her private place. A place no one else was supposed to know about—not even her queen.

Rhi sat up and looked down to find herself covered only by a coral-colored blanket spun of the softest cashmere. Her skin was clean and there were no manacles around her wrists. Yet she knew without a doubt she had been in Balladyn's prison. It hadn't been a dream.

And neither was this.

She had experienced those "dreams" while chained, and during that awful time she had been deluded into believing the dreams were real, but now that she was free of the Chains of Mordare, she could tell the difference.

Which begged the question: who brought her to her cabin?

Rhi stood, carefully keeping the blanket wrapped around her, and walked out of her bedroom expecting to find someone sitting on her sofa. But there was nobody there or in the kitchen.

Her gaze went to the door. She walked silently to it and threw it open before she walked onto the porch and found him sitting in the rocker.

"It's about time you woke up. I was getting concerned," Ulrik said, looking up at her with his golden gaze from the small piece of wood he had been carving.

She drew in a shaky breath. "What are you doing here?"

Ulrik folded his knife and tucked it into his pocket before he got to his feet and faced her with a smile. His black hair was long and loose, giving him a dangerous look that was accentuated by the black shirt with a large silver fleur-de-lis on the front and dark denim on his legs. "The correct response is to thank me."

"For what?"

His smile slipped and a frown emerged. "You doona remember?"

"I suppose you got me out of Balladyn's?"

"Interesting," he said, more to himself than to her. He took a deep breath and flipped the piece of wood in the air before catching it again. "You blew up his fortress."

Rhi closed her eyes. Not again. "I see."

"You broke the Chains of Mordare with that little show. They'll never be used on anyone again."

She opened her eyes and looked anywhere but at him. It was too difficult. "So what do I thank you for?"

"I pulled you out of the rubble and brought you here."

"You?" she asked with a snort. "You want me to believe you found your way into a Fae doorway and just happened upon me?"

"I went looking for you."

She kept her face averted. "You should've left me there."

"Because that's what the Light Fae do?" He made a sound at the back of his throat. "I doona do that." He moved in front of her and she turned her head the other way. "You think ignoring me will work?"

"What do you want?"

"To help," he said in a soft voice.

Rhi pulled the blanket tighter. "How did you know of this place?"

"I've always known, Rhi."

"Thank you for what you've done, but I don't need your help." She turned on her heel and walked back into the cabin where she slammed the door behind her.

She stopped, waiting to hear him leave. Minutes ticked by before she heard him expel a loud breath. Then, his voice came through the door. "You've been asleep for a few weeks. Everyone's been looking for you since I brought you back."

The sound of footsteps told her he was walking away, and then they paused.

"By the way," Ulrik said. "Con saw me take you."

"Wonderful," she whispered to herself.

She waited until Ulrik was gone before she released a pent-up sigh. She looked around at the frilly, ridiculous things she had accumulated through the years and anger seized her.

Rhi didn't stop it, didn't restrain it. She let it free as she went from room to room destroying everything. Not even the bottles of nail polish she had meticulously ordered by color were spared.

By the time she finished, she was breathing hard as she stood in the middle of the cabin. She no longer knew who she was. Balladyn had gotten into her mind and obliterated the person she had been.

She was wrecked, damaged.

Shattered.

The Fae she had been was gone.

Who she was now . . . well, she'd have to find out.

Con leaned his arms on the stone wall and stared off at the Chinese landscape beneath the night sky. He was on a portion of the Great Wall of China not open to visitors, as if that would stop him.

But he hadn't come for the sights. He'd come for a meeting.

The click of heels on the stones made him smile. "Do you go anywhere without those damn high heels?"

Usaeil leaned on the wall beside him and grinned. "Never."

She was in a good mood, and he hated to disappoint her, but there was no use putting it off. "I've no' heard anything of Rhi or from her."

"Us either." Usaeil linked her fingers together as if she

were praying and looked at the land. "How many more weeks will we have to worry?"

"Perhaps no' long at all."

She turned her head to him. "Ah. You want to ask the Warrior Broc."

"Only if you agree."

Her silver Fae eyes regarded him silently for a moment. "You have concerns about involving Broc?"

"I do. If Rhi wants to be found, she will. She may need some time."

"And the fact she's with . . . Ulrik . . . doesn't bother you?"

"I didna say that. I'm merely pointing out that we doona know what torture Rhi withstood. The Chains of Mordare are enough to bring most Fae to their knees."

"And Balladyn messed with her mind," Usaeil said with a grim nod. "I just want to know she's safe."

Con couldn't give her that, because he wasn't sure himself. Not one of the cameras he had watching The Silver Dragon, Ulrik's place of business in Perth, had shown him bringing Rhi there.

But where had he taken her?

"I'm not the patient sort," the Queen of the Light said.

Con chuckled. "That I know."

She straightened from the wall and dusted off her hands. "I did always find those tattoos stunning," she said and ran her finger down his dragon tat on his back. "You flew here."

"How else did you expect me to come?" he asked and turned to face her.

Her smile was slow and deliberate. "I certainly don't mind seeing it in the buff."

Con chuckled but didn't take the silent offer.

Usaeil licked her lips and slid her gaze to the countryside again. "If Rhi joins Ulrik, we could have a problem."

"She willna."

"You're so sure of her," the queen said with a shake of her head. "I wish I had your confidence."

Con opened his mouth to reassure her, but she disappeared before he could. He drew in a deep breath and slowly released it. Ulrik and Rhi were just one of many problems he had. The most pressing one was Rhys.

He jumped onto the side of the wall and leapt into the air, shifting into dragon form and heading back to Dreagan and the mountain of enemies that continued to grow.

Read on for an excerpt from the next book by
DONNA GRANT

HOT BLOODED

Now Available from St. Martin's Paperbacks!

Laith set Keith's ale in front of him and caught a glimpse of someone out of the corner of his eye. He turned with a smile, ready to pour them a drink, and then stopped cold.

Her lips, wide and tempting, were quirked in a half-smile giving her an air of mystery. Her shoulder-length wavy blond hair was wind-blown, as if she had been walking among the heather.

She was tall and slender, her white shirt just tight enough to cling to her breasts. There was a smudge of dirt on her elbow as if she had been lying upon the ground recently.

His gaze returned to her face as she claimed a stool at the bar. She tucked her hair behind an ear and glanced down at the bar before returning her coffee-colored eyes to him. Her skin held a golden glow, denoting that she was often in the sun.

Laith took a step closer to her, noting the sprinkle of freckles over her nose. "Welcome to The Fox and The Hound. What can I get you?"

"Your best ale," she said, her lips curving into a deeper smile.

Laith was powerless not to respond. He returned her

smile and turned to get her ale. Surely it was a trick of the light or something to cause him to react in such a way. Once he looked at her again, he would see she was like every other female who walked into his pub.

He finished filling the glass and hesitated for a moment. Laith twisted to the newcomer, and was hit once again by her earthy appeal. If someone had asked him, he would have called her a child of the forests.

Her smile fell a bit as he stared. Laith shook himself and set the ale in front of her. Their eyes met again, held. He felt an uncontrollable, undeniable pull to this woman. It was more than just lust. This . . . feeling . . . was on another plane all together.

"Thank you," she said and reached for the ale.

Their fingers touched briefly, but that was all it took for a current of pure, utter desire to heat his blood. She jerked her hand away, proving she felt it as well. Her eyes darted to the left before skating back to him.

"You're new here," he said, even as he put together who she was in his mind. Iona Campbell.

She nodded and took a sip of the ale when he released the glass. "Yes. I'm Iona Campbell."

"My condolences about your father. I liked John a lot."

"It seems everyone did," she murmured with a hint of confusion.

Laith knew he should walk away, and yet he found himself asking, "Do you intend to remain in town long?"

"Actually, no. Once everything is taken care of I'll be back to work."

"And where is that?" Laith couldn't begin to understand why he kept asking questions. He told himself it was information for everyone at Dreagan, but in reality, he was more than curious about her.

She laughed softly, the sound shooting straight to his

cock. He glanced around and noted that he wasn't the only one who couldn't take their eyes from her. The rest of the patrons were staring with interest.

"I'm a photographer. I travel the world taking photos of people and events."

"I'm impressed." And he truly was. It couldn't be an easy life, but she obviously loved what she did. "The arts run in your family."

It was the wrong thing to say because a small frown formed on her brow and the smile disappeared. She ran her fingers along the condensation of the glass. "I guess it does."

Laith gave a nod and returned to his other customers. Several times he caught her staring at him through the mirrors behind the bar.

A little later he saw her with a camera as she scrolled through photos. Somehow he managed to keep his distance until her ale was almost finished.

"Would you like another?" he asked.

She glanced up and smiled. "Please."

He poured her another ale and placed it before her. Just as he turned to leave, she caught his eye. "What is it?"

"How well did you know my father?"

Laith shrugged. "Pretty well. He came in twice a week every week."

"I'm having a bit of trouble reconciling who I thought my father was to who he really was."

"Your father spoke of you often."

A slight blush stained her cheeks. "You mean you knew I was a photographer?"

"I did. John showed us your work on several occasions. You're verra good at what you do."

She took another long swallow of the dark ale. "You seem to know so much about me, and yet I don't even know your name."

"It's Laith."

"Laith," she repeated, letting it fall slowly from her lips almost like a caress.

He was instantly, painfully hard.

"An unusual name."

"It's a family name."

Her brows rose. "Do you have family around here?"

"No' for a long time."

"I'm sorry." She turned her glass around. "Can I ask you something?"

He gave a nod. "Of course."

"This pub borders Dreagan. What do you know of them?"

Laith was completely taken aback by her question. He thought she might ask something about her father, but never about Dreagan. "They distill the best whisky around, and they're good to the people."

"And my father knew them?"

"He did. John knew everyone."

She worried her bottom lip with her teeth. "It's odd, isn't it? To think you know someone, only to learn everything you believed was wrong. Scotland isn't my home. Hasn't been for twenty years. I don't want to stay here."

"You doona find it beautiful?"

Iona smiled. "I took plenty of pictures today to prove that I do, but I don't have time to take care of land."

"You inherited your father's land," he said, putting enough inflection in his tone so that she might believe he just guessed it.

"I did. I want to sell it, but it appears that I can't."

The door to the pub opened and Sammi walked in, her powder blue eyes crinkled from her smile and her sandy-colored hair pulled back in a ponytail. "Hey, Laith."

"Hey, Sammi," he called.

She came around the bar and put her purse beneath it, and then flashed a smile to Iona. "Hello there. You must be who everyone is talking about."

"That's me," Iona said ruefully with a lift of the ale.

Sammi stuck out her hand. "I'm Sammi. I work with Laith."

"Nice to meet you," Iona said as they shook hands.

"Same to you. We should have a dr—" Sammi began, but was cut off when the door opened again.

Laith had kept his connection to Dreagan from Iona so far, but with Tristan and Ryder strolling in, he wasn't sure how long that would last.

"Hang on," Sammi said and rushed around the bar to Tristan who grabbed her against him for a quick kiss.

Iona watched the scene before she turned her head to Laith. "Who is that?"

"That's Tristan, Sammi's husband, who just happens to be a part of Dreagan."

Iona watched the pair carefully. "They seem to really care for each other."

"They genuinely do," he said, unable to keep from frowning at her choice of words.

She turned back to him. "I'm usually on my own. I sometimes forget that I say things out loud that I should keep to myself."

"Doona worry about that here." He spotted Sammi bringing over Ryder and Tristan so nodded in their direction. "You're about to meet more people."

Iona sat straight and swiveled on the stool to face the three.

"Iona," Sammi said. "This is my husband, Tristan, and our friend Ryder."

Iona wore a friendly smile as she greeted them. "Hello."

Tristan bowed his head, but Ryder took her hand and

gave her a charming smile. Laith didn't like the way she blushed in return.

"I was just telling Iona that she and I needed to get a drink sometime." She turned back to Iona. "I used to be on my own, and then I met Tristan. Now, I can't seem to have enough friends."

"You got me, love. Is that no' enough?" Tristan asked Sammi with a wink.

Sammi pulled on his long brown hair. "You know it is."

Tristan yanked her against him. "When do you get off work?"

"No' until closing," Laith said with a chuckle. "You'll have to wait to have some alone time with your wife."

Ryder sat on the stool next to Iona. "Have you been to Dreagan yet?"

"No," she said and glanced at Laith. "I did meet Constantine however."

Laith tossed aside his towel. "At the funeral."

"We tried to speak to you," Ryder said, "But Con asked us no' to overwhelm you."

Iona frowned. "I'm sorry. There were so many people there and I don't remember many of them."

"No one blames you," Sammi said. She put a comforting hand on Iona's arm. "It's probably better that only Con approached you instead of a slew of men from Dreagan."

Laith watched Iona fidget under her embarrassment before she asked, "So what do each of you do at Dreagan?"

"Many things," Tristan answered.

Ryder raised a blond brow. "We doona just make whisky, lass. We run thousands of sheep and cattle."

"I had no idea," Iona said.

"Most of that land Dreagan is using for conservation," Tristan added. "The forests, the mountains, and such are all protected natural habitats."

Her smile faded as she stared into his eyes. "That's

nice to hear. I've run into plenty of people who could care less about conserving nature."

"No' everyone is a bad person," Laith said. Though there were more of them out there than she could guess.

Her coffee-colored eyes softened as they looked at him. "No, they aren't."